Kill Orders

Lijena was in a restful mood. The food and peaceful conversation Yorioma had given her gave her power to resist the inner demon that drove her relentlessly.

Suddenly, the inner voice began to speak again: "You must ride westward!"

"I must ride to the west," Lijena repeated, life-lessly.

"Resist him. Resist the demon!" Yorioma screamed.

"Kill the bitch. Do it now!" the demon whispered to Lijena.

Lijena was powerless. She moved toward Yorioma, hands reaching for her throat . . .

2
SWORDS·OF·RAEMLLYN

A YOKE OF MAGIC

ROBERT E. VARDEMAN
AND GEO. W. PROCTOR

ACE FANTASY BOOKS
NEW YORK

A YOKE OF MAGIC

An Ace Fantasy Book/published by arrangement with
the authors

PRINTING HISTORY
Ace Original/July 1985

ISBN: 0-441-94840-5

Ace Fantasy Books are published by The Berkley Publishing Group,
200 Madison Avenue, New York, New York 10016.
PRINTED IN THE UNITED STATES OF AMERICA

To Don Ivan Punchatz, a mage who weaves his spells
with brush and canvas

—Geo. W. Proctor

For Dr. James M. Young, diplomat, author, friend

—Robert E. Vardeman

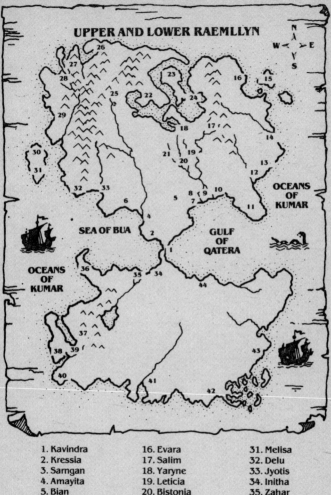

UPPER AND LOWER RAEMLLYN

1. Kavindra	16. Evara	31. Melisa
2. Kressia	17. Salim	32. Delu
3. Sarngan	18. Yaryne	33. Jyotis
4. Amayita	19. Leticia	34. Initha
5. Bian	20. Bistonia	35. Zahar
6. Cahri	21. Ham	36. Elkid
7. Chavali	22. Nawat	37. Uhjayib
8. Degoolah	23. Vatusia	38. Fayinah
9. Garoda	24. Rakell	39. Pahl
10. Jyn	25. Solana	40. Rattreh
11. Meakham	26. Faldin	41. Ohnuhn
12. Parm	27. Weysh	42. Gatinah
13. Qatim	28. Salnal	43. Ahvayuh
14. Orji	29. Yow	44. Nayati
15. Iluska	30. Litonya	

A YOKE
OF MAGIC

chapter

1

EIRENE'S TEMPLES POUNDED, and her heart lodged itself in the dryness of her throat. Her jade-hued eyes, saucer-wide with fear, darted about in panic like those of a doe cornered by a pack of direwolves as the guards, two on each side, led her into the great circular chamber.

Columns of the purest white marble, flecked with intricate patterns of gold, lofted around her, upward for three stories, to support a dome of crystal that opened to the blue, cloudless sky like some Cyclopean eye. Eirene's bare footfalls were mere whispers on the floor of Norggstone tiles. The inner light of that rare stone from Upper Raemllyn's northern province offered her no warmth, no comfort.

The Hall of Voices, a memory flickered in her panic-ridden brain. Once, when Bedrich the Fair had sat upon the Velvet Throne, she had entered the palace of the High King and stood within this chamber of light. Here Bedrich held audience with the masses each week, hearing their petitions, judging cases others of royal blood would have left to minor magistrates.

The glimmering of times past faded. Bedrich no longer sat on the Velvet Throne; Zarek Yannis the usurper now ruled here in Kavindra—in all Raemllyn's Upper and Lower realms. The Hall of Voices was no more. When this chamber was spoken of at all, always in low whispers with cautious glimpses over each shoulder, it was called the Hall of Screams. For it was into this hall in the High King's palace, where Bedrich once opened his arms to his people, that Zarek Yannis brought those who dissatisfied him to face the skills of the royal torturers!

Gaze rising to the series of balconies that circled the great chamber, Eirene found her tormentor. There in robes of deep purple and gold, with that toad of a mage Payat'-Morve at his side, Zarek Yannis peered down into his hall of terror like the demon Nyuria tending his pit of flames in Peyneeha.

"Bring her to me."

A feminine voice drew Eirene's gaze back to the floor of the Hall of Screams as the guards shoved her toward the right. There at the center of the chamber beside an altarlike slab of gray stone stood a young, raven-tressed woman in robes of black. The delicate beauty of her face was betrayed by the ice contained in her jet eyes and the cruel set of her thin lips.

"Strip Felrad's bitch and place her on the block," the woman in black ordered in a tone devoid of emotion.

A piteous cry pushed from Eirene's throat as the guards' hands snaked out, grasped the prison-gray sheath she wore, and ripped it from her body. In the next instant the guards were at her, lifting her into the air.

"Noooo! Please!" Eirene's voice could no longer contain her horror. Nor could her eyes withhold their flood of tears. "Mercy, please! I know nothing! *I know nothing!*"

She twisted, fought the viselike hands that lowered her atop the cold, unyielding stone. All to no avail!

The guards held her writhing body spread-eagle on the torturer's block while the woman in black lifted a hand, fanned its long, slender fingers, and made a pass over the supple nakedness of her victim.

Another startled cry escaped Eirene's lips. The stone—the very stone itself—opened! Manacles, living iron, grew from the rock to bind themselves about the girl's wrists and ankles. Eirene threw herself against the iron, again and again, fighting the metal like an animal caught in the jaws of a trap. There was no escape; the iron held, solidly rooted in stone.

The woman in black waved the guards back and walked to Eirene's side. Her hand shot out, fingers entangling in the fiery redness of the struggling girl's hair and jerking Eirene's head back.

"You know me not. But you *will* be one of Felrad's bitches who will never forget the name of Valora, apprentice to High Mage Payat'Morve."

Eirene's body went limp. Death, not ice, dwelled in Valora's jet eyes. Relish played at the corners of her mouth, a hint of an amused smile.

"I will ask my questions once—once only. Deny me the answers and"—Valora's smile—"the Death God Qar's own demons shall rent them from your soul! This I promise you."

"Please. I know nothing..." Eirene's voice faded as those eyes of death caught and held her.

"My first question: where are Prince Felrad and his forces?"

Eirene's voice returned in racking sobs. "I swear, I know nothing of Felrad. I have not shared the Prince's bed since Bedrich was mur—"

"My second and final question"— Valora ignored her—"where and when will Felrad next attack my Lord Yannis?"

"Nothing! I know nothing of Felrad or of his forces," Eirene pleaded. "Please, believe me. Felrad knows not that I even live!"

"Stupid slut!" Valora released her hold on the girl's flaming hair. Anticipation gleamed in her coal-black eyes. "You will tell me—eventually."

Arms lifting, her black robes spreading like the wings of some dark bird of prey, Valora's hands and fingers wove the air. Her voice, the sound of boulders grating, chanted low and rhythmic in a tongue alien to her victim's ears.

Again Eirene threw the weight of her supple body against the manacles binding her to the stone; the cold iron that bit into her flesh remained solidly embedded in the block. "I know nothing! Don't you understand? I am nothing to Felrad—nothing! I was but a . . . No! By the gods, no!"

The air shimmered above Eirene, a whirlpool of swirling currents that grew with each spinning revolution. With it came the smell of brimstone afire and the stench of seared flesh.

"No! No! No!" Eirene babbled now, her mind unable to accept, yet unable to deny, the misshapen thing that crawled out of that maelstrom and reached a clawed paw downward toward her vulnerably exposed breast.

"The pain grows too intense, my lord. Soon she will say anything . . . anything she thinks you wish to hear just to escape the agony."

No hint of satisfaction touched Payat'Morve's bloated face as he stared from the high balcony to the chamber below. Idly, to hide the excitement he drank from the scene, the sorcerer stroked the series of corpulent chins dangling beneath his face.

"An hour is enough for today. Bring her back on the morrow and the next day, and the next if need be. I promise to wear down her will and break her."

"You grow old and tired, Payat." Zarek Yannis' cold gaze remained fixed on the spectacle being enacted below.

Neither chain of iron nor strap of leather held the girl Eirene to the stone. Yet, in spite of her tortured writhings and spasmodic lurchings, her wrists and ankles remained against the rock as though tautly bound there. Her screams echoed through the domed hall, reverberated and folded onto themselves, although no man or woman touched her flesh.

"In the old days you were the first to suggest torture. How else did you attain such a mastery of the art?" A thin eyebrow arched high above a watery blue eye when Yannis glanced to his sorcerer for a brief instant before his attention returned to Eirene.

"This one may require more subtle techniques—torture, when, where, and how much to apply, is an art." Payat'-Morve's tone was devoid of enthusiasm.

His fingers worked on the dewlaps of his chins with nervous energy. All the usurper of the Velvet Throne said was true. Before they had joined forces, before Yannis had even a faint hope of attaining the ultimate rule of all Raemllyn by wresting the throne from Bedrich the Fair, torture had been a game of the most exquisite interest to Payat'-Morve. He had delighted in poring over his grimoires seeking out the proper spells to produce the maximum of pain with the minimum of physical damage.

Although he could not deny the excitement that the screams and the tortured knotting of muscle beneath the silken suppleness of Eirene's naked flesh awoke within him, he refused to allow immediate desires to rule him. In time his hungers would be fully sated by a thousand young women—and men—as beautiful as the red-headed wench below. But for now there were more important matters to attend.

Payat'Morve stared at the helpless girl on the block, wondering how much longer his and Zarek Yannis' destinies would be entwined. He had progressed while Yannis still sought the same goals and insisted on employing the same methods. Tried and true, Yannis said. Payat'Morve thought them puerile.

The time rapidly approached when the mage would no longer require Yannis. Still, Payat'Morve mused, the usurper presented possibilities for further advancement not found in others. Ones that should be fully explored before discarding the man.

Payat'Morve turned his inner vision toward Yannis, looking past the weathered, brown, leathery skin stretched drumtight over angular bones, the watery blue eyes now dancing with polar amusement at the sight of torture, the sinewy hands gripping the railing with maniac intensity—he looked past this and into the man's soul and saw the true darkness. The pit of depravity did not make Payat'Morve flinch. He had seen worse, much worse.

But how much longer could he use this vessel of power before Yannis turned on him? The mage suppressed the desire to shake his head, fearing the usurper king might take note. Still, his jowls were set aquiver.

Such questions provided the true spice for life. Walking the knife's edge, unable to jump left or right, or retreat, feeling the soles of his feet flay and bleed from the blade. *Ah! I play a dangerous game with Zarek Yannis—but one so deliciously flavored!*

"She knows of Felrad's plans." Yannis leaned forward and balanced his elbows on the marble balustrade. "Why else would he keep one such as she in his retinue?"

"She is comely, my lord. Perhaps Felrad used her only for his pleasure." Payat'Morve's gaze shifted to Valora for a moment, and he imagined his raven-haired apprentice atop the torturer's block.

His groin tightened. She would appreciate the exquisite pleasures of the pain he could provide; he could see it in her eyes as she so artfully wove agony through the fiber of Eirene's body, mind, and soul.

Yannis snorted. "Felrad's a eunuch. Look at how he plots, look at his tentativeness when he attacks. No, she is the key to his new assault on the Velvet Throne. You will turn that key and unlock the secrets she carries."

"As my lord commands," Payat'Morve said, bowing slightly. He averted his eyes to prevent Yannis from seeing the contempt seething there. Both knew this girl held no information. Yannis sought only pleasure from her suffering.

Or was it more? Doubt loomed, shadowing Payat'-Morve's confidence. Was this a test of his loyalty? Refuse to torture the girl and die! Zarek Yannis was his, of that he had no doubt, but Raemllyn's High King was like a direwolf on a leash, capable of turning and ripping out the throat of the man who held that leash.

Rumors abounded of wizards seeking to align themselves with the usurper. Even the name Lorennion had been mentioned. Had Yannis found another, one more powerful?

Payat'Morve edged the disquieting possibility away. In

all the realm there was none more powerful than himself, save Lorennion who had shunned the usurper and hidden himself in Raemllyn's wilds.

"Have your apprentice show me the demons employed." Yannis' fingers played along the length of a thin moustache that dangled well below the corners of his mouth.

"Lord, allow me." Payat'Morve's right hand gestured, fingers fanning wide for an instant.

Below, the air about the torturer's block churned, shimmered as though attempting to develop a life of its own. For a brief moment, Zarek Yannis's face twitched in panic as he glimpsed the three quavering images. Then his eyes narrowed and his head cocked from side to side, craning to better view the creatures his mage had summoned.

"What are they? It's like they stand behind walls of rippling water and smoke. Can't you make it clearer?"

"They are demons, my lord, of that I assure you. What you view is neither here nor in their own realm, but Between, that limbo of nothingness that separates the planes of existence. Perhaps this will help." Payat'Morve gestured again.

The quavering air steadied, but the smoke remained. It was enough. The mage detected a flicker of fear in Yannis' watery blue eyes.

"The one that sits at the head of the block"—the wizard's head tilted to an amorphous mass of oozing ocher flesh twice the size of a man, with a thousand glowing eyes each opened wide—"that is Wy-Ucod, who men name Terror. Above Felrad's bitch floats Az-garuk, called Fear."

Az-garuk's face was that of an Uhjayib gorilla; saliva and foam dripped from his curled, twisted lips and ran down yellowed fangs the length of dirks. The demon's body, too, was bestial, segmented like that of some blue-black spider. But no Raemllyn spider sported Az-garuk's ten arms, nor the hands with their recurved claws that ripped toward Eirene's breast.

"And the one behind your apprentice?" Yannis' voice was low and touched with awe as he stared to the misty figure who stood towering above Valora—a figure that changed with each passing heartbeat. First a fire-breathed dragon, then a rotting corpse, next a tricorn bull. Merely to stare upon its constantly shifting visages set the mind reeling.

"The most powerful of the three, my lord." Payat'-Morve's dewlapped jowls quaked as he spoke. "'Tis Yu-Vatruk, to whom we have given the name Nightmare. Yu-Vatruk is the focal point through which Terror and Fear enter the girl's mind and play upon the fibers of her raw nerves as a minstrel plucks the strings of a lute."

"Would that they were truly here rather than Between." The sentence came as a whisper from Yannis' tight lips.

If they were here, I would stand as ruler of all Raemllyn and you would be on the block! Payat'Morve thought. No mage could summon the great demons to this plane; that power had been lost ten thousand generations ago when Kwerin Bloodhawk and the wizard Edan had defeated the dark mage Nnamdi and shattered the sorcerous bonds that enslaved the world of humankind.

Until Payat'Morve held but a portion of that ancient power in his grasp, he would have to contend with his role of Zarek Yannis' lackey. But that day did not lie far in the future. Yannis had sources, and those sources would eventually provide the information he needed to lead him to the wizard Lorennion and his vast wealth of arcane knowledge.

Abruptly the great Hall of Voices lay silent. Payat'-Morve's attention shifted back to the block. Eirene lay still atop the stone; around her the three demons shimmered into nothingness.

"Valora?" the mage called below.

"The slut has passed out. Shall I revive her and begin anew?" Anticipation filled the woman's voice.

"Never mind. She'll not speak." This from Yannis, obviously tiring of his afternoon's diversion. "Guards! Throw a bucket of water on her to bring her from her sleep. Then do with her as you please. She is of no more value to me."

As Valora turned and walked from the chamber, one of the guards hastened from the room; the others stripped away their armor and battle masks. Moments later the first guard returned carrying a bucket of water, and Eirene was revived.

She hardly screamed as the four took her one after another.

"After your demons, my men bore me." Zarek Yannis turned, waving Payat'Morve to follow him to his quarters.

As always, the mage felt an ominous presence in the usurper's rooms of opulent luxury. Yannis had employed other sorcerers before Payat eliminated them, but their *presence* remained in the rooms—magicks of unknown and unknowable effect lingered. Here Zarek Yannis was truly invincible, even to Payat'Morve or the likes of Lorennion.

"You have done well, Payat." Zarek Yannis plopped on a velvet couch and snapped his fingers for a serving wench to bring wine. "How may I reward you?"

"But, lord, you obtained no information from the girl. My tortures were too feeble and ineffectual," Payat'Morve answered cautiously.

"She knew nothing. You cannot draw blood from a rock. You did well. Name your reward." Yannis drank from a golden goblet.

Payat knew the man had been amused, and this was the reason for the offer. He hesitated, however, in naming that which he wanted most. It could provide Yannis with a lever to use against him later. Yet there was a time for caution and a time for boldness.

"I would have command of a score of your hell riders."

"The Faceless Ones?" Yannis arched an eyebrow. "Why do you desire their company?"

Zarek Yannis played with him. The Faceless Ones were the demons once commanded by conquerors of ancient times and only recently awakened by Yannis with magicks Payat did not pretend to understand nor fathom. They were powerful adversaries, the Faceless Ones, and when his plans fell together they would be under his control. Until then, Payat'Morve had to play the sycophant, begging for crumbs tossed him by this arrogant man.

"They ride the length and breadth of Raemllyn. I would have them seek out the leaves of the *ntonio* plant needed for my conjurations."

"Fascinating. I thought the *ntonio* and its powers of necromancy but a myth." A thin smile played in Yannis' lips.

Payat'Morve felt the bite of the blade he trod. Did Yannis

suspect his true plans for the Faceless Ones? "Many ancient tomes mention the *ntonio*. With its leaves I could raise an army of the dead to serve my lord."

"An army of the walking dead . . ." Yannis' voice faded as though he pondered the possibilities of such a gruesome force. "You may have three of the Faceless Ones for a fortnight. And, Payat'Morve, keep me apprised of your researches. An army of the dead would have its uses."

"My lord is most generous. And he shall know the moment the *ntonio* is located."

"Now, I must be alone to think." Zarek Yannis' eyes rolled to the serving girl, who smiled in answer to such royal attention. "Felrad amasses an army. I must consider where and how to counter. If I've further need of you, I'll send a guard to your chambers."

"And I shall be ready to assist, my lord."

"Go on your way, Payat. I know you have other things to do." Zarek Yannis waved the wizard away, his attention returning to the serving girl.

"As my lord commands." Payat'Morve bowed deeply and waddled from the chamber, glad to be free. He would have to act quickly to dispatch the three Faceless Ones on their mission or Yannis might change his mind, as was his wont. The Faceless Ones were his only hope of finding Lorennion and the Blood Fountain quickly.

With its secret, the mage's thoughts rushed, *I shall be the ruler of all Raemllyn. No more to take orders from a petty tyrant, no more to fear fools like Lorennion. Total power will be mine!*

Payat'Morve entered his own quarters, checked the ward spells, and saw that Yannis had again clumsily attempted to breach the protection. Zarek Yannis fancied himself a sorcerer because he had somehow succeeded in resurrecting the Faceless Ones; his true powers were infinitesimal.

The sorcerer clapped his hands. Moments later the black-robed Valora entered and bowed deeply, saying, "How may I be of assistance, master?"

"My time draws near. Yannis, the fool, has consented to my request. Three of the Faceless Ones are mine to command." Payat paced in small circles at the center of his chamber, his pudgy fingers laced over his ample belly as he thought. "And I want you to bring the three to me."

"Aye, master! May the gods smile and deliver all that you have deserved but have been deprived of." Valora grinned widely, bowed deeply again, and started to depart when Payat'Morve called to her: "One moment. I am not to be disturbed by anyone. Is that clear, Valora? No one, not even Zarek Yannis."

The woman's eyes betrayed a flicker of interest; then her face fell into the impassive mask Payat'Morve had worked so hard to instill in her. One day Valora would learn all he could teach and become a master mage. Until then, Payat know he had her loyalty.

Until that day, he mused. All the more reason for sending forth the Faceless Ones and learning Lorennion's secrets. Valora would prove an over-able opponent—or an ally on the Velvet Throne.

"Is there more, my master?"

"Only that your control of the demons in the chamber was inadequate. Practice control of multiples and report back to me tomorrow evening."

"I will work on this, my master." The raven-tressed apprentice mage hid black onyx eyes with both hands and backed from the room, as was proper when leaving the presence of one of the premier mages of the kingdom.

"And, Valora, continue to ply the captain of the guard with your favors," Payat'Morve said. "Soon we shall have need of him."

As she left, Payat'Morve bellied up to his worktable and swept aside the litter atop it. Burned into the wood were intricate patterns, curlicues of arcane hieroglyphics, mnemonics for the summoning he must now perform.

The chant began, low, almost inaudible. Lips moving, bolder calling now, Payat'Morve built the power of the spell, wove new bindings, made the summoning more potent.

Wind whipped through the windowless room, catching up loose papers and sending them roaring in tight vortices. Payat ignored this manifestation. The chants grew louder, more insistent. He would not be denied, he would not be overwhelmed by the supernatural forces he summoned.

One vortex took shape, whirling, twisting, billowing out and surging inward and upward until the form of a miniature tornado raged by the room's windows.

"Minima," said Payat'Morve. "You have come."

"You summoned, worm. What is your desire?"

Payat bit back the retort forming on his lips. It was not the goddess who came at his summons, but a mere wind sprite, who Minima used as her eyes, ears, and voice. It would serve no purpose to antagonize either sprite or goddess. Let Minima take her feeble enjoyment by insulting him, as long as she provided his needs.

"Great Goddess of the Winds, I require a boon."

"Worm, you always ask but never give. I require obeisance!"

Payat'Morve clumsily dropped to his knees and began the invocations. He prayed and debased himself before the manifestation of this earth-bound deity. Winds whipped through the chamber, pulling at his robes and thin, sandy hair, coolly erasing the sweat beading on his brow.

"What is it you ask of me?" the howling voice of the Goddess of the Winds demanded.

The prayers have sated her need for worship. So few now begged her favor that any attention is surely flattering, echoed the mage's thoughts steeped in contempt.

"Minima, I ask for so little." Payat'Morve outlined what he desired.

The tornado spun faster and faster, a high-pitched wail coming from its heart. "So it shall be, worm!"

Then there was nothing.

Payat'Morve heaved himself off tired knees and sank into a heavily padded chair, fingers resting on his belly. The pieces of the puzzle of power fell together nicely. Soon, very soon, Zarek Yannis would be eliminated and a true ruler installed in his place.

The sorcerer was very proud of his accomplishments this day. His thoughts turned to Valora, wondering if she lay with the guard captain. Perhaps he could summon her afterward to his own bed. Yes, that would be suitable reward for all he had done this day. Payat'Morve chuckled, then began laughing aloud.

chapter
2

—KILL! KILL HIM! NOW!

The voice screamed within Lijena's skull, dominating her, stealing away her will. She had no choice; the demon had to be obeyed! She would murder this man whose bed she shared, whose body was united with hers. Her arm wrenched high, dirk tightly clutched in her fist.

The dagger fell, pale light from Raemllyn's two moons glinting along its slender blade as it plunged toward the heaving chest of an unsuspecting Davin Anane.

An awkward twist, an unnatural jerk in Lijena's rhythmic undulation, brought a sleepy flutter to the Jyotian thief's eyes—eyes that went round when they glimpsed the deadly point arcing downward. Davin's hands abandoned the silken warmth of Lijena's flesh and snaked out—too late to stop the deadly descent.

The dagger *did* stop—a scant fraction of an inch from his vulnerably exposed chest.

The point trembled, shook, strained to drive down and pierce his triphammering heart. Try as she did, driven as

14

she was by the howling demon commanding her, Lijena could not break the two hands firmly encircling her wrist: slender, cool hands that belonged to Selene.

Davin blinked up at his savior in confused relief.

"I should let her kill you!" Selene spat, allowing her grip on Lijena's wrist to slip enough to let Davin know the dancer could still do just that. Dark eyes danced with anger as she glared down at Davin. "How dare you choose her over me!"

"Selene, my love, I know how this must look, but it isn't what you . . ."

Davin's words faded, and the demon once more raged in Lijena's brain.

—Bitch! You have failed! Ere I am through with this frail form, you will serve me again . . . and again.

The voice and the horrid laughter that followed echoed in Lijena's head, then abruptly dissipated.

Her body went flaccid. The hands wrenching at her arms jerked them high, sending the dagger flying from limp fingers into the night's blackness. The hands jerked and shoved, and she tumbled to her side, rolling on the cold ground.

"Then magic is aplay!" Davin glanced up at his Huata friend Tymon, Selene's father.

The leader of the nomadic band nodded slowly, his face contorted into a frown, and pointed to Lijena's unconscious form. "Look at her. She is under some enchantment. That much is clear, but its nature? I cannot say."

"Is it necessarily from the box? Might not Masur-Kell have tracked us down?" Davin asked, trying to ignore the dread that climbed his spine like the drumming of icy fingers.

Davin Anane pushed a worried hand through his thick shock of black hair. Since his friend and traveling companion Goran One-Eye had been imprisoned for cheating at the gaming tables by Velden, Emperor of Thieves in the city-state Bistonia, Davin's world had turned topsy-turvy. To save Goran's life, Velden had given the Jyotian thief a geas—to rescue his niece Lijena from the hands of Tadzi, lord of the thieves' guild in neighboring Harn.

This Davin did, only to discover, when he had delivered

the beautiful, blonde-tressed Lijena back to Bistonia, that she was not Velden's niece, but the daughter of the thief emperor's most hated enemy Chesmu Farleigh. He had rescued his friend, but had unwittingly betrayed an innocent woman—nor had there been a way to free her from the maze of Bistonia's sewers where Velden reigned in his underground kingdom. With heavy heart and guilt gnawing at his gut, Davin had ridden from Bistonia to the walled city Leticia and joined Tymon's band of Huata.

Davin's gaze shifted to the flame-haired, hulking giant of a man who stood near the window of Selene's wagon. From all outward appearance, Goran, the empty socket that once held his left eye covered by a scarlet patch, was a man, a towering, muscular man to be certain, but a man. He was not; Goran was a Challing, a creature nine parts spirit for every one part physical—a changeling bound to his gargantuan form by the sorcerer Roan-Jafar, whose throat Goran had slit for summoning Goran from his own realm into this world men called Raemllyn.

Bound by duty and friendship for the Challing, Davin had gone with Goran to the sorcerer Masur-Kell here in Leticia to obtain magical potions to free Goran from his bondage to human form. While Masur-Kell had been unable to completely free Goran, he had given him a potion to alleviate some of the more restraining aspects of the bondage and return in part, although in random fashion, the Challing's magical abilities.

It was in Masur-Kell's home that Davin had once again seen Lijena as the young woman was sold to the sorcerer by the master slaver, Nelek Kahl. Davin had failed Lijena once, but not again. This very night he and Goran had crept back into the sorcerer's home, wrestled a demon, and fought the wizard himself to free Lijena from her captivity.

During the rescue, a small gold box had been taken as booty for their trouble—and they found only more trouble after Lijena opened the box and inhaled some of the chalky white powder contained within.*

*Swords of Raemllyn, Book One, *To Demons Bound*.

"It was the box. Would a wizard bother with a coma when he could reduce us all to ash with a single pass of his hand? No, this sprang from the box." Tymon's lips pursed and he turned back to Lijena.

"I can go——" Davin started.

Davin was silenced by a quick gesture from the Huata leader. The sounds of approaching horses came from outside the wagon. And above the *clop-a-clop*, the clank of armor and shield.

"Soldiers! We've delayed our departure too long," said Tymon and motioned to Davin and Goran. "It is time for you two to become Huata."

"But Lijena..." Davin protested.

"She'll be all right for a while. Selene, get Davin something more colorful. Goran's scarlets are bright enough, even for a Huata. The guards will never know the difference." Tymon pushed past Davin and went outside to greet the approaching soldiers.

Davin Anane watched anxiously as the Huata camp subtly changed. The few illicit activities that had been in progress moments ago vanished, replaced by innocuous ones. Tymon hurried to meet the officer leading the band of soldiers. Before he could speak, the captain snapped, "There have been complaints. You are stealing from the townspeople."

Tymon proved his acting ability. His bushy, gray-shot eyebrows arched up in surprise, and he extended his hands, palms up, in an imploring manner. "Captain, we are but honest performers struggling to survive. We give lively entertainment for the few coppers we collect. Witness. Why should we cheat anyone when all our people possess such superb talents?"

Tymon clapped his hands and jugglers performed. Sleight of hand tricks distracted a pair of the soldiers, and another wandered after a Huata who seemed to produce gold coins from thin air. The captain, however, gave no indication he found the displays to be the least bit amusing—or distracting.

"What's he do?" the captain demanded, pointing at Goran.

"Perform for the good man," ordered Tymon, unable to cloak his nervousness.

To everyone's surprise but Davin's, the red-bearded, barrel-chested Goran took a quick step, performed a cart-wheel, a flip, and then a handstand. Such agility in a man so large was remarkable. Then, Goran was not a man, but a Challing.

"And this one?" the captain pressed, jabbing a finger at Davin.

Before the Jyotian could reply, Salene jingled and jangled out of her wagon. She wore a full dancer's costume, replete with bells and silken veils that hid little and suggested much.

Davin and the others were quickly forgotten when Selene danced. The soldiers' full attention focused on her undu-lating hips and sensually rippling belly. By the time Tymon had forced a few cups of strong wine onto the captain, Selene had finished her dance and perched on the man's knee, her arm around his neck and her lips brushing his ear.

"Well, uh, things appear in order. We received word of, uh, hmmm, word of thieves in the group who assaulted the wizard Masur-Kell last eve. Hmmmm, that's nice." The man could barely keep his wits about him with Selene so seductively nuzzling his neck.

"But that cannot be!" protested Tymon, with just enough indignation to make it ring true.

"No, no, couldn't be," said the captain. He laughed at some indecent suggestion Selene whispered in his ear. "But we really must follow our orders. Men! Search the camp."

Davin silently released an overly held breath and relaxed. The soldiers making their lackluster searches would find nothing. The Huata were past masters at concealing what contraband they smuggled.

Lijena moaned and stirred. The voice called her from a restful dream.

—Rise. The time has come to leave. Let no one stop you.

She did as commanded without question. For when the voice spoke, her mind was no longer hers, but served that compelling demonic voice.

She took one step toward the wagon's exit and halted. A Letician soldier opened the door and stood staring in.

—Let no one stop you!

Coldly, emotionlessly, Lijena whipped her sword from its sheath and lashed out.

The guard's cry of alarm died in a wet gurgle as his throat opened from ear to ear. He stumbled back, then fell, a thick river of blood fountaining from severed arteries.

Davin had seen the soldier working his way toward Selene's wagon and moved to intercept him. He also saw the glinting tip of a blade flash from the wagon and trace across the man's throat.

"A trick!" Davin called out. "A trick for our guests! Let me do a trick!"

The diversion might have worked if the soldier had not died so messily. As it was, Davin only drew unwanted attention. The other guards—and their captain—turned and saw their comrade wallowing in a pool of his own blood.

Swords hissed from scabbards as the guards rushed for the wagon at the captain's command. Davin reacted rather than thought. His own longsword came flashing from its sheath. His wrist and forearm flicked. The foremost of the guards cried out and fell face down in the mud, his right hamstring neatly severed.

At the rear of the charging troop, he saw Goran leap to the back of a helmeted soldier, grasp the man's neck in those massive Challing hands, and wrench. There was a loud crack like that of dry wood snapping, and then there were only four guards with whom to contend.

To the left the Letician captain threw Selene from his lap and freed his sword, fully intent on skewering the lovely bosom he had snuggled but an instant before.

Davin ducked beneath a wild slash by one of the soldiers, received a nasty nick on his forearm from another's dagger, and managed to thrust just as the captain's arm descended. Flesh raked along the sharp sword edge.

"Aieee!" bellowed the officer, shoving Selene away and turning to face a real adversary.

Davin wanted no protracted battle. He swung his sword around, got a two-handed grip on it, and brought it straight down with every ounce of power he could muster. Blood sprayed in a shower. The captain spun and tried to run. He got four paces before he toppled onto his face, dead.

Davin pivoted ready to face a new attack. What he received was an armful of very warm and wiggling Selene. He offered no resistance to the mouth that covered his— one eye revealed that Goran and the Huata men had dispatched the remaining guards.

"He was going to kill . . . you saved me, Davin!" Selene managed between her grateful kisses.

"The least I could do." Davin grinned down at her.

Abruptly she shoved him away. "But that doesn't make up for what—what you were doing with that Bistonian, blue-nosed bitch! Nothing will ever erase the pain of finding . . ."

The sound of hooves echoed from behind the wagons.

"More soldiers!" someone cried.

"No!" Davin shook his head and said, "One horse only, and it's moving away from . . . Lijena!"

"Aye, my friend, that's her riding like the wind," said Goran. The red-haired giant lifted the tip of a bloody sword and pointed with it. "She's going northeast."

Davin glanced at his friend. "But Harn is to the west."

"And Bistonia is to the southwest," finished Goran. "Wherever she rides, it is not to her family."

"Good riddance," spat Selene. "I saw what happened. She cut down the soldier the instant he opened the wagon door. She panicked."

"Panic?" asked Davin. "She was in a coma when we left her. It's Masur-Kell's damnable magicks! They possess her."

"Let her go," Goran said. "She has been nothing but trouble. The skinny ones are always trouble."

"It might not be that easy," spoke Tymon as he moved to his daughter's side. "Whatever drives her is of magical birth. Davin, I think you have to find and stop her. You must."

"What is this, old man? A premonition?" demanded Goran. "The world ends unless we find her? Is that it?"

"Just common sense," Tymon replied. "Your destinies

are tied together. They have been ever since Davin kidnapped her from her uncle and traded her for you, Goran
One-Eye."

Goran glanced at the expression on his friend's face,
snorted, and silently went to saddle their horses.

"She rides like all the demons of Peyneeha are at her
heels," Goran complained as he slid from the saddle and
led his mount toward a narrow stream.

"Her horse will drop from under her. We'll have her
then!" Davin answered with a reassuring smile as his horse
drank.

In truth, he worried. They had rested their mounts several
times during the day—had to stop; Lijena did not. The gray
she rode should have been dead from exhaustion hours ago.
No ordinary horse was bred for such endurance.

Then, Lijena was not astride an ordinary mount; Davin
recalled the sleek, dappled gray mare she called Orria. The
horse had come from Lord Tadzi's own stable and had
probably cost the price of a hundred common horses. For
a high enough price, a man could buy a steed with bloodlines
that traced back to Lukiahn, the father of all horses.

"I'll drop before that mare. She's a desert mount, bred
to travel the dunes all day without rest or water," grumbled
Goran while he lowered himself belly to the ground and
noisily slurped from the stream.

Davin squatted beside the water, cupped his hands, and
scooped a drink from the clear current. The best he could
determine, the stream was a tributary to the River Faor,
which meant Lijena no longer rode northeast, but directly
north. An easterly course would have taken them across the
Faor hours ago. North, however, was not west—she still
fled away from Bistonia and Harn. *What lies to the north?
What draws her away from home and family?*

"Davin, what do you make of this?"

Goran's voice intruded on his thoughts. The Challing
stood pointing to a patch of dead grass beside the stream.
The Jyotian moved beside the withered spot. The grass was
ashen rather than winter fallow.

"I've never seen its like before. Notice the burn marks, almost as if a horse wearing a still-hot shoe seared the ground as it passed." Davin sucked at his teeth and scratched his head in puzzlement.

"Aye, I noted the black marks, but the rest of the grass isn't burned, just dead." Goran cautiously edged around the patch to avoid touching the withered grass.

"Some lack of the soil?" Davin glanced around and found a trail of the burnt hoof prints leading northeast.

"Lijena's trace is over here." Goran tilted his head toward deep impressions of shod hooves. "She's changed directions again . . . riding northeasterly now."

"Can this be something following her?"

"Some *things!* At least three. Behind her but ahead of us." Goran stroked his matted beard and slowly nodded. "My reading is that the grass is newly dead, no more than an hour or two at the outside. Lijena can't be much farther than that ahead . . ."

Davin didn't wait for his friend to finish, but swung back into the saddle, ignoring the protesting soreness of thighs and backside. Tymon's earlier warning about the magicks Zarek Yannis unleashed on Raemllyn wedged into his mind and would not leave. *It can't be! But what other steeds could fire the ground with their hooves?*

"Let's ride. We waste precious time!" Davin urged the Challing back into the saddle, then spurred his mount after Lijena.

Davin coldly eyed the blue-gray of the twilight sky. The Tear of Evening winked just above a stand of *morda* trees they camped beside, and the Jester rose, barely visible in the south.

The last heir to the House of Anane cursed beneath his breath as he gnawed a bite from a strip of jerked venison and chewed. A whole day they had ridden, and still they had not caught a glimpse of Lijena. And they had lost the trail of the fiery hooves!

Davin stepped across a stream barely wider than his foot and walked to where Goran piled kindling for a fire.

"Damnation! It makes no sense! Goran, did my eyes

deceive me, or were the last of those tracks smoldering?"

"Smoke came from grass turned to charcoal," Goran assured him. "Then the tracks just vanished . . . as though the mounts had leaped into the air and taken flight."

"Horses don't fly!" There was a sharp edge to his voice that Goran didn't deserve. *Or do these mounts have wings?* Davin tried to recall the old legends, but remembered no mention of fiery steeds with wings.

Davin plopped heavily to the ground and winced. They had ridden hard, and his posterior throbbed in testimony to the distance they had covered. "If it rains tonight, we'll lose—"

"Shh! Listen!" Goran hushed him.

Davin heard the hollow sound of pounding hooves. He jerked around. They came from the north, beyond the *morda* stand. He turned back to the Challing, who nodded, stood, and drew his blade. Davin followed suit, and then moved into the trees and up the rise on which they grew.

Only Goran's quick hand restrained Davin from rushing forward when he saw Lijena crouching by a campfire in the small valley below.

"But Goran, she's—" Davin bit off the words when he saw that she was not alone.

The other riders—the other three—had also overtaken Lijena.

"They're not just a tale to scare the younglings," said Goran.

"The Faceless Ones!"

The three riders reined in and held their snorting mounts just beyond the ring of pale light cast by Lijena's campfire. Their horses pawed the earth, searing the ground wherever they touched; their hooves were afire!

"She greets them," Goran said in a whisper.

Lijena walked toward the three. As she neared, the foremost of the demon riders grasped a longsword forged from crystalline flame. It blazed brilliantly as it slid from a dark scabbard, tiny tongues of fire leaping and dancing along its entire length. The Faceless One slashed at the air in front of Lijena, but she did not flinch.

The other two drew their swords of crystal fire, then

fanned out in a semicircle before the woman.

"We've got to help her. She can't fight them." Davin started forward.

"Stay," said Goran, wrenching his friend back by the belt of his breeches. "What can we do against *their* kind?"

The Challing was right. In the light cast by those hell-fired swords, Davin saw the heavy cowls pulled forward about their heads. No matter which way they turned, their faces—if they had any at all—remained cloaked in shadow. But the hands gripping those flaming blades were skeletal!

Lijena's head lifted to the unholy riders, and she spoke.

The Faceless Ones' horses snorted flame and reared, burning hooves pawing at Lijena. She did not move.

"What are they saying?" demanded Goran. "I can almost make out what they say. Almost."

Davin only shook his head. A trick of the wind caused only a snippet to come up the hill to where the pair crouched, watching.

The Faceless One in the center pointed his sword at Lijena and cried, abject fear in the steel-edged voice, "The Blood Fountain!"

Then the rider wheeled his horse and rode hard into the night, his passage marked only by the smoldering hoof prints of his steed. A heartbeat later, the other two howled like pain-wracked jackals, turned, and fled.

Davin's hand shook as he sheathed his sword. What could possibly make three of the Faceless Ones flee? What did the fearless fear?

Lijena? But why?

"Zarek Yannis truly has loosed them on the world again," said Goran, sinking to the ground. "This usurper king plays a deadly game."

Goran stated the obvious. With the evil of the Faceless Ones again unleashed, powers beyond understanding stalked Raemllyn.

And Lijena had frightened off three of them.

"The Blood Fountain," Davin mused. "What can that mean?"

"I know not," Goran replied. "But there is one who might!"

Davin nodded and glanced back to the campfire below. Lijena was gone!

"There. There she is!" Goran cried, pointing.

Atop a rise, Davin saw the silhouette of a woman low against the neck of a straining horse.

"We follow," he said in a choked voice. "We must."

For the first time, Davin Anane truly knew what Tymon had meant when the Huata spoke of interwoven destinies.

The clash of the metal against metal echoed through the valley, reaching their ears long before Davin and Goran caught sight of Lijena. They exchanged glances; such sounds meant only one thing—battle!

Spurring weary horses onward, the two freebooters pushed their mounts to the limits of their endurance. Davin felt his bay stumble, then regain its balance. For an instant he tensed, ready to leap from the saddle should the horse drop from under him. In the next heartbeat, the horse was forgotten.

There a quarter of a mile ahead, Lijena stood with her back against the gnarled bole of a *morda* tree with longsword drawn. The tip of that silvery blade danced menacing circles in the air before six men who steadily advanced on the frosty blonde with their own swords leveled to deliver death.

"Brigands!" Goran called above the pound of hooves. "She cannot stand against . . . By Nyuria's singed arse!" The Challing's voice roared in amazement as Lijena's longsword struck.

With a reckless abandon and disregard for her own life that left the six with mouths agape in surprise, the daughter of Bistonia pivoted, flung herself at the man advancing on her far right, and thrust, sword straight and steady. The brigand's eyes went wide in disbelief as Lijena's blade found its target, skewering from chest to spine.

Nor did she pause to watch the man crumple lifelessly to the ground. Wrenching the longsword free, Lijena spun and slashed. A man dressed in buckskin jerkin and breeches who rushed in to take advantage of the young woman's exposed back screamed as Lijena's blade raked across his throat. In the next instant he had joined his dead companion on his journey to the realm of Black Qar, God of Death.

"She fights like a demon!" Goran bellowed. An odd expression crossed his face when he realized the truth in what he'd said. Then he laughed loudly, pulled forth his blade, and spurred his mount forward with Davin but half a length behind.

By the time the pair reached Lijena, she had turned herself to the methodical slaughter of the remaining four.

Davin could think of no word more fitting than slaughter. Lijena's petite, harmless appearance was a deadly deception; she had fought with the fury and tenacity of a dozen men— or one demon!

Goran struck first. Leaning down from the saddle, he swung his sword in a whistling arc at the nearest of the four. There was a thud as steel met flesh, then a hand parted from wrist flew through the air in a spray of crimson.

Goran's victim's scream of agony brought Davin's own target wheeling about to face Lijena's unexpected rescuers. The brigand ducked, losing a feathered cap, rather than his head, to Davin's descending sword.

Instead of reining the bay around to meet the cutthroat, Davin agilely twisted and jumped from the saddle, landing in a crouch with sword raised and ready.

With battle cry tearing from chest and throat, he straightened, his blade lunging true for the man's throat. The highwayman slumped soundlessly to the ground, dead.

Davin's head twisted from side to side and found Goran had made quick work of the remaining swordsmen. He smiled and relaxed—and almost perished.

Lijena rushed him, blade high and aimed for a spot midway between his eyes. Reacting instinctively, he parried and let her sword pass harmlessly to his right. Dropping his blade and opening his arms, he caught her, spun her around, and tossed her to the ground.

The fall would have driven the air from the lungs of an ordinary woman—or man. But Lijena was no mere woman; a demon had been bound to her body by Masur-Kell's powder. With Davin's full weight atop, she struggled and twisted like a lion trapped in a hunter's net, all the while spitting curses into the face of her would-be rescuer.

Thumb pressing into the soft flesh of her wrist, Davin sought and found the nerve plexus just beneath the heel of her hand. She growled and bucked as he tapped that pain center, but her hand flew wide, loosing its grip on the hilt of her sword. Then he had her arms above her head pinned to the ground.

"Lijena!" he screamed into her anger-contorted face, not knowing if he spoke to a woman or demon, although both desired his life. "Damn you! Lijena, listen!"

A convulsive surge racked her body, and then she was still, eyes closed, and her breast rose and fell in the gentle rhythm of sleep. Davin stared down at her quiet form in disbelief.

"Is the wench dead?" the Challing asked, with an almost hopeful tone. He had made no attempt to disguise his disgust for Davin's role as Lijena's protector.

"She's in a coma. 'Tis the same deep sleep she fell into back at Tymon's camp. I think the demon drove her too far and her body rebelled." Davin rose and drew a deep, steadying breath.

"She's better off this way. Less trouble for us." Goran grunted and looked around at the carnage they had wreaked. "Let's be away from this place. It will soon smell of death and be abuzz with flies. Nasty little creatures flies. We can make camp amid those pines atop that hill."

"Perhaps she'll be better if she can rest." Davin nodded and bent to lift Lijena's flaccid form from the ground, then followed Goran toward the rise.

"Perhaps," Davin whispered hopefully, though doubting his own words, "the demon has left for good."

chapter
3

LIJENA BOLTED UPRIGHT. One moment she floated in the inky black of nothingness, and in the next heartbeat she was awake with eyes wide and confused. She hugged the warmth of the sleeping furs to her.

Where? Her frightened eyes darted about the forest that loomed high and dark about her. *How?* Cottony haze clogged her mind. She didn't remember this wood or coming here.

Da...Davin, a name floated in her mind as her gaze alighted on two men sitting cross-legged on the ground to her right. *Davin Anane and...and Goran One-Eye.* She recalled the peculiar, muscular giant with his clothes and eye patch of blinding scarlet who now chuckled as his teeth tore into a fist-sized piece of grease-dripping meat. *They rode in as the...*

The brigands! Lijena shivered and tugged the furs closer to her trembling body. An image of the six highwaymen bent on sending her soul to the Death God's realm of Pey-neeha filled her mind's eye.

And there was the terrifying memory of the bloodlust that had seized her, controlled her body and thought, launching her against the six in a berserker's rage without regard for life or limb. Even now she could not accept that she had been the fierce warrior who had easily slain three of her attackers.

A sword was alien to her, a man's thing; she had never held one until . . . She shook her head in frustration. Misty veils shrouded her brain, refusing to be pushed aside. She couldn't remember when she had gained possession of a sword—or where it had come from!

". . . tell you it's the truth. Qar take me if it isn't!" Goran's rumbling voice intruded into Lijena's thoughts.

"Qar will take you." Davin Anane laughed and tossed a well-chewed bone into the night's shadows. "There's no way you can convince me you took on an entire Amazon company singlehanded."

"I did! 'Twas a matter of Challing pride!" Goran said in earnest. "It took me all night long, but I did. Forty-two of them there were. On the brink of exhaustion the next day, I had a captain and two lieutenants feeding me. I was so weak I hadn't the strength to lift a poached egg to my mouth!"

"Now I know it's a lie." Davin raised his hand to waylay his friend's protests and continued, "You hate poached eggs. Not even the most comely of women could force-feed you one."

"Perhaps it was a rasher of bacon." Goran shrugged. "After such a night am I expected to remember minor details?"

Davin's head moved from side to side, and his eyes rolled to the left in disbelief. His reply to Goran's outrageous tale of Challing prowess was forgotten when he saw Lijena sitting upright and staring at him.

"Good eve. I thought you might sleep straight through till the morrow." A smile uplifted the corners of the young thief's mouth. "Come join us. It's not much, but we had scant time for a proper hunt."

A rootless disquiet wove through Lijena. She wanted to

find her sword and horse and flee, yet these men had rescued her. Still she felt as if *they* were her enemies, especially the swarthy, raven-haired one, Davin Anane, who gazed at her with—love in his eyes? *Can that be?*

The smell of roasting meat and her watering mouth edged away the bewildering vagueness of her memories. Clutching the furs about her, she rose and walked to the campfire and settled on the ground between Davin and Goran.

"It smells delicious." She watched Goran reach out, tear what appeared to be a leg from the spitted meat sizzling above the flames, and place it in her hands. "I can't remember when I last ate. I think that I could..." A lump solid and unmoving lodged in her throat. "I...can't... can't remember..."

The weight of those words and the gauzy patches of memory evasively flitting across her mind were too much to bear. Tears of frustration welled from her eyes to trickle down her cheeks.

"She's crying," said Goran in obvious amazement. "The rabbit's not that badly done. Davin cooked it himself."

Davin shot his friend a silencing glance as he wrapped an arm about Lijena's shoulders. Drawing her to him, he held her tightly until the racking sobs subsided and her head lifted.

"I don't remember." Her voice was a weak, confused quaver. "I don't know where I am or how I got here. Why am I...how can it—"

"Shhh. Give yourself time. It will come back to you." Davin reassured her and nodded to the leg of rabbit in her hands. "Eat. You're weak and need to regain your strength. The demon has driven you without mercy for two days. Your brain is confused, befuddled by the shock of such a creature dwelling within. Or perhaps the demon itself hides memory from you. A mind robbed of its past would be easier to dominate and control."

"Demon? What are you talking about?" Her gemlike eyes of aquamarine flashed.

"Next she'll be telling us she doesn't remember her own name!" Goran's disbelief drew a harsh frown from his Jyotian friend. The Challing muttered a curse under his breath, but did not press further.

"Eat, then talk. I don't want you starving to death on us." Davin lifted the rabbit to her lips, refusing any question until she finished the leg and then another. When she had washed down her meal with a healthy swig from a wineskin, he finally asked. "What do you remember?"

"Riding out with my Uncle Tadzi's guard . . . from his estate in Harn. After that, everything is a jumble." Lijena lifted an eyebrow when she noticed Davin grimace at the mention of Tadzi. "Do you know my uncle?"

"Uh, we've never met, but the head of the Harnish Thieves Guild would certainly like to meet me, I am sure."

"Why is that?" Lijena's brow furrowed, not in question, but as she fought aside the foglike veils and remembered.

Goran cut in before Davin could answer. "My friend has a bad character flaw. He insists on helping others."

Davin's head jerked around, and he glared at the Challing. "I saved your worthless hide! If I'd had a gram of sense I'd left you to rot in Bistonia's sewers!"

"What?" Lijena's disquiet returned, not because she was lost by the men's byplay, but because she had edged aside another layer of cottony mists and new, jagged slivers of memory slid into her consciousness.

"Goran had been captured by Velden . . ."

Her head reeled under the impact of Davin's words! Memories flooded her head. *Velden!* She had slain Velden with her own hands! She shuddered as she remembered Davin kidnapping her from her uncle in Harn and then selling her into Velden's hands.

"He traded you for me is what he did. Velden would have tortured me to death. Yehseen knows he gave it a good try while he had me!" The Challing snorted, and the single eye of his skull flamed alive with a fire of fevered intensity.

Davin saw the witch-fire and recognized the latent magicks locked within his friend angrily boiling to the surface. The young thief hurried on, hoping Goran could contain the magical powers that had, until recently, been totally beyond his control.

"Leaving you in the hands of scum like Velden was my shame—it gnawed at me." Davin's gaze, imploring now, returned to Lijena. "Velden played me like a pawn. There was nothing else I could do to save Goran."

"Amrik Tohon sold me into slavery," she said in a haunted whisper as more of the razor-edged fragments fell into their horrible places. "Amrik, my lover, sold me into the hands of a slaver."

She spun and slapped Davin's comforting hand from her shoulder. "Bastard! You fatherless whoreson!"

Lijena's rage flared. This thief from Jyotis was younger than the slaver Nelek Kahl and wore no moustache, but other than that the two might have been one and the same. Perhaps they were brothers. They shared a disregard for human life. Davin had just admitted he had kidnapped her from her uncle's care and traded her to the self-styled emperor of Bistonian thieves. That she escaped from Velden was mere chance.

But Amrik giving her over to a slaver! That cut to her very soul. And Lijena remembered more, much, much more. The journey to Leticia in Nelek Kahl's coach, the bartering of her body to the sorcerer Masur-Kell for his dark purposes.

Lijena's nails dug into the palms of her hands, leaving tiny crescents of blood, as she sought to hide her reaction to her memories from Davin and Goran. They were not to be trusted. They had initiated the chain of events that had stolen her away from her family and led to Amrik's treacherous betrayal.

Davin Anane, Jun—Velden's captain of the guard—, Amrik Tohon, Nelek Kahl, Masur-Kell: the names of those she had vowed to repay in full for the humiliation and degradation they had heaped upon her echoed within her head.

"We saw you enter Leticia with the slaver Kahl. There was no choice but to rescue you from the sorcerer—to make amends, in part, for all the sorrow I had unwittingly caused you," Davin continued.

"Some rescue!" Goran snorted with disgust. "We break into a sorcerer's quarters, and what do we have to show for it? You and an accursed golden box! Better had we left you in Masur-Kell's chains of gold."

"How dare you?" Lijena flared, a fire ablaze in her own eyes that had nothing to do with magicks. "You have no idea what Masur-Kell does to his slaves. He—he is cruel beyond your knowing of that word!"

"Goran's right on one point. That golden box should never have been taken." Davin suppressed the urge to once more grasp Lijena's shoulder in reassurance. In truth, life would have been easier had they left this daughter of Bistonia with the wizard. But that was something the last son of the House of Anane had never considered. One glance at Lijena and he understood. No other woman in all of Raemllyn had ever awakened the strange mixture of desire and ... and ... he wasn't certain of the other feeling tangled inside him.

Lijena sat straight at the mention of the box. The intricately wrought golden box! The murky mists bewildering her mind parted, dissipated. She pictured it as clearly as if it were in her hands this very instant. She had been hidden inside the Huata wagon and had opened the box's lid. A vagrant breeze caught a white powder inside and whipped it in a small vortex around her face. A quick inhalation and she had turned—odd.

The sharpness of her mind's eye blurred. The powder had produced a sharp, cold sensation in her nostrils, and then—all else vanished as if it had never occurred.

"We have followed you since you killed a Letician soldier and fled the Huata camp. I felt responsible for the demon possessing you," Davin said.

"Demon?" Lijena's head jerked around. "Again you speak of a demon!"

Davin studied her, but Lijena's expressionless mask betrayed no hint of emotion. Coolly her gaze returned to the embers of the fire without a hint of her inner thoughts or the hatred that seethed in her breast.

"The powder was but one of Masur-Kell's magicks," Goran said. "It bound a demon to your body and mind."

Half-remembered events flitted like ghostly images in

Lijena's head. No matter that Davin and Goran had rescued her from the sadistic mage. The demon they'd stolen along with the golden box had been released and now dwelled within her—if Davin were to be believed!

"To a demon bound," she whispered as she rolled the possibility around in her head.

"Not all has been suffering." Davin smiled. "There was at least one moment of happiness . . . of pleasure."

"What happiness?" Lijena's brow knitted.

"You don't remember? The two of us . . . in the Huata camp?"

"What? The two of us? What are you trying to say?" Lijena's eyes narrowed as she stared at the young thief.

Goran guffawed loudly, a broad grin splitting his face. "Some lover! She doesn't remember a single instant of your ecstatic coupling!'

"Is he saying we were lovers?" Lijena's entire body went cold with shock.

"We were," Davin said softly, slowly. "Yet, you have no memory of our bliss. 'Tis the demon! It erases parts of your mind for its own ends."

"There *is* no demon," Lijena said, but realized that only a demon could force her to lie with one such as he.

"There is a demon," Davin replied firmly. "The form is unusual, but it is the only explanation for all that we have witnessed."

"And you do not remember speaking with the Faceless Ones?" Goran asked.

"The Faceless Ones? Of course not. They are myth. Legend and nothing more," What was this ruse? Even if the Faceless Ones had existed, they had been put to rout centuries before when civil war wracked all of Raemllyn.

To think she had actually had commerce with these demons . . . This was the first outright lie that was too outrageous for belief! If Davin Anane wanted to convince her of this supposed demonic presence within her breast, he and his one-eyed friend would have done better to think of a less outré accusation.

"We saw you with a trio of the Faceless Ones," said

Davin. "They stopped and spoke to you for a few moments, then mounted and rode like Yehseen himself whipped them."

Lijena snorted derisively.

"It is true. They spoke with you, you said something that sent them running like curs."

"These do not sound like the Faceless Ones of legend. They were demons capable of fighting off odds of a hundred human warriors to one of their rank. They sniff spoor better than any hound and require no food or drink. And you're saying *I* chased off a trio of them with a single word?"

"Not a single word," Davin said.

"We overheard one of the hell riders cry out 'Blood Fountain.' Does that mean anything to you?" Goran asked.

Lijena shook her head. It meant nothing at all, other than being another fabrication on the part of these two rogues.

She tried to discard all she heard as lies, but her mind kept returning to something Davin had said—the part about their being lovers. Snatches of memory returned and told her this might actually have occurred, and, if so, the demonic possession from Masur-Kell's powder might also be true. There *was* no other way she would ever consort with the likes of Davin Anane—a man she had vowed to kill!

"I think the Faceless Ones fled because of the demon possessing you," said Davin with a sincerity that would have convinced her if she hadn't already known what a rogue and liar the man was.

"I further think," he continued, "that Goran and I can help rid you of the demon."

Lijena started to reject the offer, but something—some *thing*—stirred deep within her breast. The slithering, slippery feel of *it* rose, weaving dark netlike tendrils to ensnarl and control her mind. When she spoke it was its *presence* that supplied the words.

"I . . . do need help. I do feel it within, now and again. It frightens me terribly. You will help me rid myself of this demon? You won't abandon me to it?" Her words and tone were a plea.

Davin blinked at the sudden change in her attitude. Lijena had been openly skeptical of all he'd said. Not that he blamed her. The tale was difficult even for him to believe, and he had witnessed! Now she solicited his aid without so much as a small argument.

Lijena inwardly recoiled at the words that slipped from her tongue. They were not hers, but she could not stay them. The "voice" within her skull—she heard it clearly now—commanded, and she obeyed without knowing why.

"What shall we do next?" she asked.

"Get some sleep. Tomorrow the world will be clearer. We have all been through much and fatigue muddles our brains."

"Speak for yourself, Davin," cut in Goran. "It seems your wit is always muddled."

"Sleep, Lijena," urged Davin. "In the morning we will decide how best to solve this dilemma and drive the demon from your body."

"On the morrow," Lijena said, her eyes filled with the trust of a young pup. Quietly she stretched out beside the dying fire and snuggled into the furs' warmth.

That was what Davin and Goran saw and heard. Within Lijena's head raged a battle as she struggled to overcome the "voice" dominating her will. A battle that ended abruptly as swirling darkness sucked her downward in the oblivion of sleep.

Goran and Davin stared at the sleeping woman, her blonde hair spread like a silvery scarf over the edge of the furs. Davin heaved a sigh and shook his head.

"I don't think she believed us, Goran."

"She believed you were responsible for kidnapping her," said the Challing. His eye glowed with pale light now, a light that danced and sparked and grew like the sun rising above the horizon.

"We can help her. What else is there for us at the moment?" asked Davin.

"Don't try to persuade me to help when you haven't convinced yourself," grumbled Goran. "I have problems of my own. What need we of her troubles? What of our quest for A'bre? Have you forgotten that?"

"Your powers grow ever since we robbed Masur-Kell."

Davin ignored his friend's mention of A'bre, that legendary city Masur-Kell had said held the secret to return Goran to his natural state. How could the Challing think of chasing myths when Lijena was bound to a demon? "Do you think the demon dust got up your nose, too?"

"Nothing of the sort. His potion works. That's all."

Davin saw the magical glowing in Goran's lone eye and wondered what form this outburst might take. Goran One-Eye was not human, although the Challing assumed human form. He had been ripped from another dimension and bound in his present body by the sorcerer Roan-Jafar, whose throat he had slit. Only when Goran found the power within himself—or locked in some mage's spell or within fabled A'bre—could he shed the chains of human existence and return to the place of his birthing.

"The potion is about used up. What then?"

Goran shrugged. To him it was a matter of no real importance. He had existed with the sporadic magical outbursts. If the potion helped control them, fine. If not, he was no worse off than before. His goal remained the same: freedom from this body and return to his own plane of existence.

Davin fell silent. The world crashed in upon him, demanding attention in too many directions. He owed Goran his life a dozen times over. Of course he would assist the Challing in whatever manner he could.

But there was also Lijena now . . .

Davin sucked in a deep breath. If only the Sitala, those five deities who ruled fate, hadn't been so cruel in throwing the pair of them together. He leaned back in his own sleeping furs, remembering the feel of her body moving alongside his, the subtle touches, the stimulating movements, the hot breath in his ear, the tidal waves of desire that crashed within his loins as their lovemaking built and built.

He rolled onto his side and looked at the sleeping woman. For her he felt more than simple lust. He'd had his share of women; with Lijena new emotions surfaced, more potent ones than physical desire. If only they had met in a more conventional fashion. He knew she still blamed him for delivering her into Velden's hands, to the slaver Nelek Kahl, to the abuse and degradation of Masur-Kell.

Shame and guilt knotted Davin's gut. Now the gods presented him with a chance to amend all the wrong. If he aided her in escaping the demon's bondage, she would have to believe in him. *Have to!*

So it was that Davin Anane drifted into sleep, but his dreams were not of a man lifted by hope. He saw Lijena commanding legions of the Faceless Ones, laughing as she sent them forth to rape and destroy Raemllyn. The youth called out in his restless sleep, but no one save Lijena answered—by pointing a finger at him, directing the fiery hooves of the Faceless Ones' steeds after his fleeing form.

"Only a hundred bists? What are you trying to pull? You promised a hundred silver eagles and a hundred gold bists," the captain of Zarek Yannis' dungeon guard spat. "I can still take the wench back to her cell!"

The man in the black robes and cowl did not argue the soldier's abrupt increase in price for the girl Eirene. Instead, he withdrew a leather pouch from his waist and dropped it into the captain's open palm. "Place her in the wagon, Captain. And be certain your soldiers remove the corpse that awaits there."

"Aye, to be certain! There must be a body to sate the High King's hounds," the captain answered, motioning for his two companions to make the exchange. "The one you brought is young and red-headed?"

"And once lovely," the hooded man said. "She died last night from a jealous lover's blade. Treat her body as you have been ordered to treat Eirene, and Zarek Yannis will never notice the difference."

"It's my life I'm betting on that," the captain said with a grunt, then turned and followed his men back into Yannis' palace.

The man in the cowl climbed on the driver's board of the two-wheeled wagon and clucked a swaybacked mare into a lazy walk. Only when Kavindra's towering edifices hid him from the palace did he push back his hood and grin broadly.

It goes smoothly, Nelek Kahl thought. *In an hour the girl and I will be safely aboard the* Singing Dolphin *with sails set for the northern waters of the Oceans of Kumar.*

The slaver glanced back at Eirene's unconscious body. Before the scene that began this night was fully played, she would serve him well!

chapter

4

DAVIN ANANE LIFTED A HAND, signaling a halt. He turned toward his companion who crept through the forest fifteen strides to his right. Placing a finger on his lips, Davin nodded to a clump of thick, autumn-brown feathergrass twenty feet ahead.

Goran One-Eye froze at the Jyotian's signal, returned the nod, and stared at the dry shock of weeds. The high grass rustled for a moment, then lay still. A smile played lightly at the corners of the flaming-haired giant's mouth as he nodded again to indicate he saw Davin's target. When the Challing moved, it was with cautious deliberation, hefting one massive booted foot at a time and carefully placing it on the forest floor away from dry branch or twig, waiting, watching, ready to act.

"Now!" cried Davin Anane.

Both men hurled their crude spears, mere saplings stripped of leaf and limb. The knife-carved points struck true. Two rabbits, skewered through by the primitive shafts, jumped and lurched and fell, a hideous shriek escaping from one as it died.

40

"How is it they shriek so?" The small hairs on the back of Davin's neck bristled at the thought of preternatural forces aplay. "When did you last hear two rabbits sitting beside a watering hole chittering away? Mayhaps this wood holds some enchantment that gives its denizens voices?"

"Your imagination is fed by your unreasoning suspicion of all magicks, my friend." Goran laughed and pointed down at the brown hare Davin's spear had claimed. "'Twas just the air rushing from its lungs. Your cast punctured its chest cavity."

Davin quietly bore his chagrin. He did have a distrust of those things controlled by spells and chants—a distrust that had doubled during their recent encounters with the mage Masur-Kell, Lijena's bloodlusting demon, and the unholy Faceless Ones.

"I don't think these two will be sufficient. My appetite is hearty enough for a dozen men, and these are scrawny specimens." Goran held aloft his gray-furred victim, appraising its bulk and finding it sorely wanting.

"So find another. This one will be ample for Lijena and me."

Goran turned and peered at Davin, his one good eye narrowing. "You do have it bad for her, don't you?"

"I feel responsible for all that's happened to her, nothing else." Davin stiffened. What did a creature from another plane of existence know of honor? "If I hadn't kidnapped her to ransom your worthless hide, no misfortune would have befallen her."

"Oh? What of this lover of hers ... Amrik Toenail, or whatever? Did he not sell her into slavery? That was his betrayal, not yours!" Goran's bushy eyebrows arched.

"What of Velden? And Masur-Kell's demonic powder?" Davin stared at his friend with the realization that the Challing truly did not understand the feelings knotting his gut.

"If one accepted your logic, Davin, all that has happened these past weeks was caused because of playing cards. Had I not gambled at the Brass Cock in Bistonia none of these misadventures would have happened. Am I to forsake the gaming tables for the duration of my imprisonment on this chunk of clay you human beings call a world? Nay! What happens, happens. That is all."

With a shake of his massive head, Goran stalked off in search of another morsel for his morning repast. Leaning against the trunk of a long-needled pine, Davin waited impatiently for the Challing's return. As much as he hated to admit it, there was more than a hint of truth in what Goran had said.

But did he love Lijena? Davin admitted the frosty-tressed beauty awoke more than desire within him, but were the befuddling emotions he felt when Lijena was near love?

"Look at this one!" crowed Goran as he pushed through a tangle of underbrush.

He dangled a plump, fuzzy, orange-and-white-striped, catlike animal of indeterminate species by its tail. Davin wasn't certain what the creature with fangs the size of a man's forefinger protruding over its lower lip was, much less how to fix it. But that was the Challing's problem, as was its eating.

They walked in silence back to camp. As Davin's mouth opened to hail Lijena, a coldness settled in the pit of his stomach, and his greeting died in his throat. The rabbit he carried slipped from his fingers and fell to the ground as the young adventurer stared in disbelief.

"May Nyuria take her!" growled Goran. "She's made off with the horses. All the horses! I warned you about skinny ones! More trouble than they're worth."

Davin sank to the ground, plopping heavily on his backside. His curses began as mumbles, then built until his voice roared over Goran's angry bellows.

"Why did she have to take all *three?*" moaned Goran with head in hands as he dropped to the ground beside his friend. "Why not just one horse? We're stranded here in the middle of nowhere without transportation. Lost! Here we shall grow old and die!"

"First, we are not lost," said Davin, which wasn't a total lie. While he had never been this far into Raemllyn's northern provinces and was uncertain exactly where they were, he was quite capable of guiding them back the way they had come. He heaved himself to his feet. "Second, we have one means of transport remaining to us. If we start now, we might be able to overtake her."

"Afoot?" scoffed Goran as he glanced up.

"Aye, on foot." Davin nodded, motioning the Challing to his feet. "It won't be the first time for either of us."

"Nay, I couldn't take a single step. My strength has fled me," Goran shook his head.

Davin stared down at his companion with concern. "Are the magicks ajumble within you this morn?"

"Magicks, Nyuria's arse! I'm starving." Goran pointed to rewards of their morning hunt. "Let us eat, then go after her."

What his friend said made sense. Davin was positive his belly rubbed against his backbone. After a meal devoid of real taste, the two packed what belongings Lijena had left behind and started after her—on foot.

Lijena hugged low to the neck of the desert-bred Orria. With fingers entwined in the mare's blue-gray mane, she clutched to retain her seat in the saddle as dizziness assailed her, setting her head aspin like a cyclone.

Nor did the dappled gray aid in helping its rider preserve her precarious balance. Walleyed and nostrils flared, the mare kicked and bucked in an attempt to unseat the alien presence she instinctively sensed sat astride her sleek back.

It was the same "presence" that now recognized the danger it presented to the body it inhabited, a body it still had many uses for. Withdrawing from total control of Lijena's mind, the demon spoke:

—Quiet the animal.

Lijena's aquamarine eyes blinked thrice, as though she awoke from a deep sleep. Her tight hand gently stroked Orria's broad neck until the horse stood passively. Then Lijena sat straight in the saddle, her gaze moving over a plain of lazily rolling hills.

Where? She wiped a hand across the face. The cottony fog remained, blurring her thoughts. *Where am I? How did I get here?*

Everything had been crystal clear when she stole away from the camp this morning. Davin and Goran had odd ideas about ridding her of a nonexistent demon, which in no way coincided with her own plans of riding to Bistonia and rejoining her father. Chesmu Farleigh had surely returned to their home from his journey to Kavindra, Raemllyn's capital city. And just as surely he must think his only daughter dead, stolen away from his brother by kidnappers and foully murdered.

How easy it had been to take the horses; she recalled Davin and Goran leaving her alone in camp. And she remembered taking the three horses and reining southwesterly for Bistonia. Then?

She couldn't remember beyond . . . Lijena's blood flowed like ice as a half-remembered something flittered in her mind. Her head jerked around, searching.

The other two horses? The ice dropped several degrees in temperature. She shivered, not wishing to remember. *Where are the horses?*

A vivid image thrust itself before her mind's eye. She saw herself leaping from the back of Goran's mount onto Davin's bay as the first horse stumbled, then dropped to the ground.

I rode it to death! She clamped her eyes closed, trying to blot out a vision of the horrible last shudder that passed through the horse's lather-covered body.

And Davin's bay? She cringed as she realized the Jyotian's mount had also been ridden until its heart had burst from the strain of her unrelenting ride. *Two horses! I've ridden two horses to their deaths this day—without knowing it!*

Her hand returned to Orria's dappled neck, stroking now to comfort herself rather than the mare. Had she not awakened from the memory-erasing fit that possessed her mind, she might have killed a third horse.

What's happening to me? What malady has invaded my body, my mind? She bit her lower lip and held back the tears that blurred her eyes. Tears were of no use. Bistonia lay to the—she wasn't certain in what direction her home lay.

The sun rode high into the heavens on her right. But was

that east or west? She shook her head; she didn't know if it was morning or eve or the hours that had passed since she had fled Davin and Goran's camp.

West. She chose at random; until she identified the motion of the sun in the sky, she would rely on her guess. She also guessed that the plain she now stood on was north of Bistonia. *Which means south is behind me*.

She reined Orria about.

Pain lanced within Lijena's skull.

Orria took one step in the chosen direction, the agony pounded like a hammer on an anvil. Ten steps and Lijena clung to the neck of her desert-bred mount as the world whirled about her, trying to drag her from the saddle.

—North! Ride north!

Wide went her eyes, head jerking from side to side seeking the voice's owner. There was no one!

Orria's nostrils flared as the dappled-gray mare snorted and pawed the ground with her forehooves.

—There is much for you to do in the north. Do not fail me.

"No!" A piteous gasp escaped Lijena's lips. The voice came from within her own mind! *The demon! No! It can't be! It can't!*

—You *must* not fail me!

Lijena refused to accept the possibility her body and mind were now shared with some creature conjured from the dark realms. Her sickness now created voices in her head. She had to ride to the south, had to reach her home and safety.

The thought no more than formed, and blinding, white-hot pain seered through her skull. Her body jerked rigid, and she cried out.

—You *will* serve me! North, bitch! Or I shall fry this feeble brain of yours!

Immediately the agony subsided. And just as quickly, Lijena's legs rose to spur Orria southward.

Her booted heels never fell. Fire erupted within her head; glowing brands of pain sizzled through the tissue of her brain.

—North! Ride north now!

Again the fire flickered out, and once more she attempted

to direct Orria southward, only to suffer the unyielding pain
for a third time. And when the burning lessened, she stub-
bornly tried again and again and again.

When at last Lijena turned the horse's head to the north,
her body was drenched in sweat and her arms and legs felt
as though they were filled with jelly rather than the strength
of muscle and bone. Laughter echoed through the corridors
of her mind mocking her weakness.

—You will serve me! There is no other course for you.

Eyes flowing with tears, Lijena rode northward. Niggling
at the back of her mind was the thought that Davin Anane
was right! And she had left the only man who might aid
her stranded a dozen leagues to the south.

"Stop," Lijena pleaded, as her eyes rolled to shadowed
buildings on the eastern horizon. "I have to stop. The town
is so close."

—Ride.

Lijena struggled to pull back on the reins. She had ridden
Orria without mercy through the afternoon and feared the
mare would soon join Davin's and Goran's mounts in death.

Pain flared, and Lijena's hand went limp about the reins.

—Ride.

"An inn," she moaned. "I see an inn ahead. Can a few
hours be so vital? Let me rest. In a bed." A soft mattress
caressing her aching body would be the very heart of luxury.

—In time.

"Please. Food! I must have food. If I continue like this,
I'll pass out, robbed of my strength."

—I will not allow that.

Fire flared within Lijena's skull for an instant. When it
died, she rode onward past the inn, her head swiveling to
glimpse three patrons laugh and slap one another on the
shoulder in hearty camaraderie before entering. To eat. To
drink. Perhaps to take a room and sleep. To rest.

"My feet are blistered. A Challing was never meant to
walk, but to ride the currents of the air!" complained Goran
One-Eye as he plopped heavily on the bank of a small stream

and dunked his feet into the water.

His sigh or relief echoed through the small valley as the rippling coolness laved away the weariness left by the day-long hike.

"They're as much meant for walking as your arse is for sitting. And speaking of your well-padded hindquarters, get off them! There's two hours before sunset. We can make another league ere we camp." Davin Anane's gaze surveyed the rolling plain about them.

"What be the use? For two days we've followed the skinny wench and have yet to glimpse her—only our horses, which she killed." Goran slowly eased his feet from the stream.

"She doesn't know what she does. The demon controls her," said Davin, sucking at his cheeks. "And whatever it seeks is to the north."

"Demons tend to be simple-minded," Goran One-Eye said while he tugged his boots onto swollen feet. "If I'd known that, I might not have lost my eye."

"What?" Davin had been paying scant attention to his friend. "What about your eye?"

"The missing one, man! That's how I lost it. A demon stole it."

Davin's eyes rolled upward in disbelief. "I thought you lost it to a fire-haired wench who . . ."

"Nothing of the sort. I lost my eye to a demon who coveted it above all else in this foul world. He had only one of his own, set right here," The Challing gestured, stabbing the middle of his forehead with a strong, dirty-nailed finger. "With only the one, he lacked depth perception. He couldn't shoot arrows accurately, and his fighting, pah! His fighting abilities were awful. Couldn't judge distance at all."

"I didn't know that was a requirement for a demon."

"Davin, Davin," clucked Goran, "how can you be so ignorant? I thought you were the expert on demons. Aren't you after the one possessing the lass?"

"It wants more than her left eye."

"The same can be said of you. But that has nothing to

do with the demon who crept up on me while I slept." Goran shrugged. "He poked me in the ribs with a spear. In surprise, my eyes shot wide open. Fingers burning like the slopes of Mount Tenhine, he reached forth and grabbed and out popped my eye. The pain! I thought I would die on the spot."

"Too bad you didn't lose your tongue instead of your eye. It'd make the journey more peaceable."

"Peaceable, perhaps, but my single eye is still more observant than your pair. Look yonder." Goran pointed toward the east.

Davin squinted. Glints of metal and the unmistakable shapes of buildings rose on the horizon. *A town!*

He grinned, but caught himself before he sighed. It would not do to let the Challing know that he was also bone weary. He had pushed Goran mercilessly in hopes of catching Lijena. However, after the first day it had become obvious they needed horses if they were to match her pace, much less overtake her.

A town presented opportunities beyond horses. Hot food! Soft beds! And a flagon of ale would slide down the gullet nicely to wash away the dust of their two-day trek.

"I see the road, too," Goran said.

The "road" was little more than a dirt trail that wound through the rolling hills. However, Davin's attention focused on the metal glinting in the sunlight. "Spikes."

"Huh? Spikes? Of what use are steel spikes driven into the ground? Some type of defense?" asked the Challing.

"Unless I miss my guess, those are for impalement of convicted felons," Davin answered, his face wrinkling with disgust. "I doubt they would take kindly to the likes of you and me in yon hamlet. This is not a township to steal in lightly, even though our need is great."

"Doesn't worry me," said Goran. "We can be in and out before they can blink twice. What color horse do you want? I'll pick one out specially for you, my friend."

"The trail," Davin started. He stared toward the north. While Lijena's path had been singleminded, he feared the demon might shift direction. To lose her now after so many leagues was unthinkable. They had to keep to the trail, but they had to have horses if they were to overtake Bistonia's fair daughter.

He explained the dilemma to Goran. The Challing stroked fingers through his fierce red beard as he thought.

"There is only one solution," he said. "I like it not, but it is a solution."

"We split up? One of us continues on Lijena's trail and the other goes into the town?" Davin asked, although the answer was obvious.

"That is it. Who goes, who follows?"

All Davin had thought of in conjunction with the township—food, bed, and ale—had to be pushed aside.

"You go into the town, Goran," he said.

The Challing beamed with unrestrained pleasure.

"I'll keep on the trail," Davin continued. "Just be quick about getting those horses. I don't want to spend the rest of my life afoot."

"Some caution must be exercised," pointed out Goran. "Those steel spikes . . . you understand."

Davin Anane nodded and slapped Goran on the shoulder. "May fortune be with you. And may you be a better judge of horseflesh than you are of women."

"Fear naught, Davin," said the Challing. "I'll catch up with you long before Minima sends her winter winds." At this, the red-bearded giant went off, laughing heartily.

Davin hugged his doeskin jerkin to him as he turned northward. He had hoped that it was just his imagination that found a chilly bite in the air. In truth winter was long overdue in Raemllyn's upper realms.

chapter
5

THE RED-BEARDED CHALLING in human form glanced over a broad shoulder and watched his friend trudge up a grassy rise, then vanish down the opposite side. Goran smiled to himself. Although their adventures had forged strong bonds of friendship between them, the mortal occasionally proved to be a trial.

Goran One-Eye shook his shaggy head. Davin was much too serious—especially about the frosty-haired wench Lijena. She was only a woman, after all. Humans were, to the Challing, pretty much the same.

Though, he grinned with relish as warm memories floated through his thoughts, *that bar wench in Bistonia was a tad more than ordinary. And there was the other one. Dark-haired, I think . . . yes, definitely . . . at the Harn Spring Festival. I stole more than her father's silver. She will not soon forget me!*

Goran's lips pursed, and he whistled a sprightly, though off-key, tune as he strode toward the small town. *Ah, and there were others—will be even more!* he thought in antic-

ipation of the pleasures awaiting discovery in this unex-
plored township.

His lively melody ended as his whistle shot up two oc-
taves, then died in mid-note. Ahead of him five steel spikes
shafted from the ground. Rusty flecks marred the metallic,
mirrorlike surfaces. The Challing approached the silvery
shafts with eyes narrowed. Blood, not the effects of air and
weather on metal, were responsible for the splotches of red
that ran in a rivulet pattern down shallow depressions in
each of the spikes.

A blood gutter! Goran's lips pursed once more, but there
was no joy in his whistle now. He traced the ragged line of
red downward. Amid a sea of autumn-brown grass grew
patches of green at the base of each spike—grass with roots
that nurtured on the gory juices that had recently rained in
profusion from above.

Such it is with life, the Challing tried to be philosophical
in spite of the chill that suffused him. "One dies and another
prospers."

Turning from the gruesome reminders of the fate awaiting
in the town ahead for a thief with less than quick wit and
fingers, Goran walked on. He whistled once more to escape
the vision of those blood-stained spikes and the imagined
feel of steel skewering coldly through his bowels, along his
spine, and shafting out his screaming mouth.

Only when he passed the first of the thatch-roofed cot-
tages ringing the township did the Challing edge the spikes
to the back of his mind and turn his attention to his purpose
in leaving Davin Anane's side—horses—and perhaps a few
coins of silver and gold to give weight to their money
pouches.

Spying a round-shouldered man pulling a cart piled high
with fresh-cut hay, Goran doubled his pace until he walked
beside the man. "Pardon, good sir, but can you tell what
fair metropolis I have chanced upon?"

"Eh?" The man, a farmer by the look of his drab, weathered garb, lifted his head and turned a questioning face as
drab and weathered as his clothing toward the fire-haired
stranger, then looked back at his feet.

Goran carefully held his irritation in check as Davin had

instructed him to do on numerous occasions. Humans could be so vexingly stupid at times. He repeated his question, this time in simpler terms.

"You want to know what the town's called, is that it?" The man's head rose a second time, and he peered at the Challing through cataract-fogged eyes and shook his head as if the answer eluded him. The next sound he made was an explosive "Jurka."

"By the gods, bless ye," Goran said.

"'Twas the town's name, not a sneeze." The man wiped his running nose on the sleeve of his jacket, readjusted the weight of the cart's shafts, and plodded along without another glance at Goran.

Jurka. Goran rolled the feel of the name about in his head until he mastered the explosive pronunciation of both syllables, then strolled into a town that was far more pleasing to the eye than its name was to the ear.

Cobblestone, not packed clay, formed Jurka's streets, and there were even street-sweepers to keep debris piled tidily in the gutters. To be certain, the streets were narrow and cramped, but lining them on each side stood brightly painted and very prosperous-appearing shops, and homes of stout timber and fire-baked mud brick.

And in these streets was a steady throng of people who seemed happy enough with their lot in life. Merchants stood in doorways loudly boasting of the quality of their goods, men hurried about occupied with their various pursuits, children skipped and played, women smiled. More than one interested feminine eye lingered on the mountain of a man with hair and beard as red as the scarlets he wore: a fact that expanded Goran's barrellike chest to the point that wooden buttons threatened to rip free of their holes.

There were certain compensations to this human form that had bound him since he had been so cruelly ripped away from his home, the realm of Gohwohn. While some might have found his size fearfully large, more were the maids and matrons intrigued by the muscles that rippled beneath the cut of his garb and the fierce, ruggedly handsome face with its single, gold-flecked jade eye. Nor did

Goran's eye patch detract from that interest; it only served to enhance feminine fantasies.

And there was the stealing! In Gohwohn, a world of plenty, thievery was unheard of. However, here in Raemllyn where greed often seemed to be humankind's dominating motivation, stealing was an art, and Goran One-Eye was an exceptional artist!

Like an artist, it was the act, not the completed work, that brought the thrill. To be certain, gold and jewels did feed the human tastes he had developed for rich foods, gaming tables, colorful clothing, and beautiful women. Yet it was the actual act of the thief, the life-death tightrope he precariously trod that brought the pounding excitement that almost equaled the pleasure he found in dallying with Raemllyn's lusty daughters.

Yes, there were pleasures to be found on this world of clay, but Raemllyn was not Gohwohn, and to return to his own mystical realm was what drove Goran One-Eye, searching for a mage powerful enough to restore him to his natural form and send him back across the dimensions. *Masur-Kell said I was to seek A'bre, city of legends. And Davin promised...*

An appraising gaze from an approaching honey blonde with a wine jug hugged to her bosom edged away thoughts of Gohwohn and A'bre. A twinge of guilt shot through his breast when he imagined Davin in the wilds on foot, doggedly tracking Lijena, while his eye feasted on such beauty. In the next heartbeat the guilt and Davin evaporated in the young blonde's beaming smile.

"Pardon, my dear," he hailed the girl, who batted long eyelashes shyly. "I am a stranger in your fair Jurka. Could you direct me to a blacksmith?"

"The smithy?" The lovely flower of Jurka arched an eyebrow slightly. "I would have thought you a smithy yourself with such powerful-looking arms."

Goran couldn't resist flexing those tree-trunk-sized arms. The girl's lips formed a silent "oh," and her eyelashes batted in double time as powerful muscles rippled. Nor could Goran restrain a smile at her obviously pleased reaction to his human form. Challings in their natural state were much too amorphous for physical posturing.

"I have done such work, but I found it simple and mindless. I prefer more intricate pursuits now."

"I thought working with metals was very hard to learn." Her soft blue eyes still admired the bulge of his arms.

"Difficult?" Goran chuckled, thoroughly enjoying her interest. "For some perhaps, but not for Goran One-Eye."

Her gaze moved across his broad chest, which the Challing thoughtfully expanded until the buttons of his shirt threatened to pop. Then she perused him from the top of his tousled red head to the tips of his trail-worn boots. Goran's smile widened; he was but minutes in this hamlet, and already a Jurkian blossom was in his palm waiting to be plucked—and Davin Anane thought himself to be irresistible to the fairer sex!

"The smith has a stable on the east edge of our town." The honey-haired beauty turned and pointed to the direction from which she had come. Then her cornflower blue eyes rose to Goran again. "My name is Klora. I work at the Inn of Four Memories. Come by later and see me. Perhaps we can . . . discuss how difficult it is to learn the ways of working metals."

Klora shifted the weight of her wine jug to her left arm, then reached out with her right hand, hesitantly touching one of Goran's mighty biceps.

"It is real." Goran thanked the mage Roan-Jafar for binding him to such fine human form.

"I hope everything else is, too." Klora's tone and her dipping gaze left no doubt as to her meaning. She brushed deliberately against him as she passed, smiling and repeating, "The Inn of Four Memories."

Goran took in a deep breath, carefully tucked the inn's name away in his mind, and then released the breath in one explosive blast before proceeding eastward.

As he walked, his single eye took in all the details: an unlocked door, a window easily jimmied, a shop with far too much inventory in the window, the fat purses of even fatter merchants. The thought of the steel impalement spikes deterred him slightly, but there was no harm in merely daydreaming of what he could do if he were to ply his chosen trade.

After all, wasn't he half of the pair who had stolen the proceeds from the Harnish Spring Fair? Hadn't he deflowered one of the loveliest of ladies in the bargain—the Spring Queen herself?

Daring hardly describes it, he thought in smug self-satisfaction as the smell of burning coals drew him to the smith's forge.

"Have ye business, or do ye merely wish to pass the time of day?" A man almost as massively built as Goran himself lifted an eye from the glowing horseshoe he hammered on his anvil. "If it's the latter, I have little enough time as it is."

Although the man was dressed in coarse homespun shirt and breeches covered by a dirty leather apron, wore his brown hair in a tangled mat that appeared never to have been introduced to a comb, and sported a rough dark stubble on cheek and chin, Goran was not taken in by the untidy hayseed appearance. Something about the glint in the smith's eyes bespoke of a sharp mind residing within that crude skull.

"I'm in the market for a pair of fine steeds. Throughout Jurka, they sing praises of the horseflesh for sale within your stable, and of your fairness as a trader." Goran began by applying a thin layer of butter to the man's ego.

The blacksmith spat, spittle hissing angrily as it struck the white-hot coals. "That's what I think of fine and fancy talk. I'm the only trader in town."

Again Goran saw the sharpness in the smith's eye, heard the determination in his voice. This man was the type who would make sure that any competition did not linger long in Jurka—either by brain or brawn.

"Perhaps we can do business."

"If you've enough coins jingling in that purse of yours, we can." The man eyed Goran, then added, "I don't need help right now. So it's cash or nothing. No trading of a few days work for any of my beauties."

"I have ample coin, good sir. May I look over your stock so that I can come to a decision?"

The smith tossed the horseshoe back into the coals and motioned the Challing into the stable after him. In an instant, Goran memorized the layout of the flatboard barn. When he returned in the darkness, it would not do for him to stumble over a pitchfork or bump into a stall wall laden with tack.

The smith's price for each of the horses left Goran with no doubt that he would have to steal the horses, although he had never intended anything else. "Magnificent animals, good sir. I am buyer for a third party and am empowered to buy as many as ten of your animals."

The man spat, demonstrating that he was unimpressed.

"Is there a discount for, say, a dozen?"

"Nay—for any number."

"I see. My principal is a man of some reluctance to pay top coin, even for such fine steeds. He prides himself on obtaining the best for less than others might have it."

"Damn peculiar, if you ask me." The smith returned to his forge, pulled the horseshoe from the coals with long-handled tongs, and placed it atop an anvil.

"He is a peculiar man. Very rich, I might add, and good enough to me, but unwilling to allow me to purchase under those terms." Goran studied the man, realizing the smith had set his price and would not accept one copper less. "I will have to confer with him."

"Do that." The smith raised his hammer high and brought it down atop the glowing "U" of metal with a resounding crash. "And remind him, he'll be finding no finer horses for at least a hundred leagues—or any other horses for sale—than he'll be getting at the stable of Assel son of Assel."

"I shall inquire, good sir, and see if my principal is amenable to your price," Goran said and paused waiting for an answer that never came. "Good day to you. I shall return, oh, let us say tomorrow." Still the smith offered no answer.

As Goran turned and walked off, he thought, *By noon tomorrow, I'll be five leagues away with the pick of your noble string. Why pay an exorbitant amount for fine horses in the light of day when they can be had for nothing—after dark?*

Goran spent the remainder of the day peering into every niche and cranny in Jurka, and within an hour he intimately knew the details of the most prosperous businesses, the moneylenders, and most importantly of all, the routes taken by the wardens. Jurkian wardens patrolled more frequently than in other cities Goran was familiar with, but the officers were no more alert. An appropriately applied diversion would work as surely in Jurka as it did in Harn or Bistonia or Oraid.

Twilight darkened the streets, and Goran judged that it would be folly to attempt his theft until the town was settled in for the night. Men and women slept most soundly at four in the morning. It was at that time he would divert the wardens with his ruse and make his unchaperoned choosing from the stables.

Besides, he was in no rush. He had yet to cool his palate with the self-promised ale. And there was a matter of a honey-blonde maid with blue eyes who wished to discuss metal working and other matters with him. Stopping a by-passer, he received directions to the Inn of Four Memories.

Five minutes later Goran One-Eye pushed his way into the smoky inn and looked about. His eye alighted first on the supple, shapely form of Klora, who waved at him and smiled winningly; then his gaze moved to something he valued even more highly: the gaming table.

Dice spun and rolled on the felt pad, coins changed hands, and a new player tried for luck with the dice as the Challing approached the table ringed with a motley assortment of Jurka's citizenry.

"Be there room for another?" he asked, pushing his way through the spectators.

His pouch held the weight of five silver pieces, a lackluster stake that doubled by the time he stood at the table thanks to the unknown generosity of a caravan drover and Goran's light fingers. When the dice eventually found their

way to his hands, the Challing again doubled the silver
eagles in a single roll. Then he doubled it again with the
second tumble of those two cubes of ivory.

"The red-hair's got the luck on him," cried one of the
onlookers. A flurry of excitement passed through the room
as the inn patrons pressed close to watch.

There appeared some truth to the man's words. Goran
had always been drawn to the gaming tables, but the times
Jajhana had frowned on the Challing far outnumbered the
occasions she had graced him with her smile. But this evening she positively beamed her radiance down upon him.
By the grace of the Goddess of Chance and Fortune, within
ten throws of the dice he had accumulated a huge pile of
silver eagles, which were changed into gold bists.

"You *are* lucky!" Klora rubbed up against him like a
sensuous feline. Her words came as a throaty purr and were
answered by Goran's paw-sized hand stroking that fine mane
of hair dangling halfway down her back.

"With you beside me, luck will increase!" he laughed,
and pulled her close for a loud, smacking kiss. When they
parted, he ordered a round of drinks for all in the Inn of
Four Memories and still had a sizable pile of bists in front
of him.

"All or nothing," Klora urged. "You are lucky. You can
win. I know it!"

She shot a knowing glance toward the stickman running
the game. A small smile turned up the corners of her mouth.
The man nodded.

The dice were pulled in, then passed back. Goran lifted
the two cubes and started to roll, then he paused. His on-
again, off-again magical sense felt like a volcano erupting
within his skull. Yet he needed no preternatural insight to
tell him that the stickman had switched dice, and that it was
impossible for him to roll and win with these. He had been
around long enough to know—and to know that Klora had
given the signal.

Still, for Goran, this was the way of the world. He reveled
in this matching of wits. And tonight, there would be more
than a simple contest of wills.

"Klora, my lovely, kiss the dice for luck. Your sweet

lips can turn even lead into gold." He opened his palm and
held out the dice.

She stiffened slightly at his offhand mention of lead—
the way the dice felt in his hand, the painted spots had been
drilled and refilled with lead to affect the roll.

"For luck," the honey-haired beauty said. She leaned
forward and kissed the cubes.

Witch-fire flared brilliantly in Goran's eye as he rattled
the dice in his hand and slung them toward the green felt.
They danced and sang across the table, tumbled and tot-
tered—urged and directed by magicks the Challing summoned—before coming to a halt in the center of the table
for all to see.

"He rolled the Emperor's Eyes! He wins all!" roared one
of the onlookers.

Goran saw the trouble brewing with the stickman, who
was pointing an accusing finger at him. No stranger to such
claims as the man was likely to make, the Challing let out
a bull roar that drowned the man's claim that the red-haired
giant had used loaded dice, and all within the inn were
silenced.

"Friends! I cannot accept such a large amount of money
without sharing it with you. Drinks for everyone—for the
rest of the evening!"

"Knew he was a regular sort when I first laid eyes on
him," said one man. Another claimed, "Good friend of
mine." Still another cried, "A prince of a fellow. Not a
cheap bone in his huge body!"

The stickman scowled as a flurry of hands slapped the
Challing's broad back. Goran winked at the man, who was
now helpless to start anything in an inn suddenly filled with
the giant's new-found friends. Goran pulled four full pouches
of gold bists to him, tossed one to the stickman to cover
his wild buying spree, and still remained a wealthy man.

Wealthy enough to actually consider purchase of Assel's
horses. That consideration lasted all of five seconds. The
Challing had found little enough excitement of late. The
horse theft would add to his pleasure almost as much as
gambling—and winning—had.

Hours still remained until the time arrived for the theft.

His thick arm circled Klora's waist and pulled her close. She didn't resist.

"Does luck ride with me further this night?" he asked.

"Who can say?" Klora said coyly, but her eyes were lit with an intensity that matched Goran's. "I tire of this place. Too many people. Let us discuss the future of your . . . luck elsewhere."

"A more private location?" he said, enjoying the byplay. "Quieter? Such as your sleeping quarters?"

"Why," exclaimed Klora, as if the idea had never occurred to her, "you're as clever as you are lucky. I would never have thought of such a fine place as that!"

Arm in arm they left the inn; someone led a rousing cheer as Goran passed through the door. He turned and bowed deeply, then spun and melted into the night with Klora at his side. They walked a few blocks toward the edge of town until arriving in front of a small wooden structure.

"We must be quiet when we go in. The landlady is . . ."

"A light sleeper," Goran finished for her.

They both laughed, pretending to sneak inside, and made their way up creaking stairs to a nicely appointed bedroom.

"This is truly my lucky night," said Goran.

"And why do you say that?" Klora asked, reaching behind her back to unfasten her skirt and let it drop to the floor.

"Luck with the dice, and luck in finding a woman with such fine tastes."

"In what? My sense of color? My decorating abilities?"

"In men," said Goran, sweeping her into his arms and carrying her to the bed.

Goran's inner sense awoke him four hours after midnight. There was work to be done and fine horses awaiting the taking.

A broad grin spread across his face. The Challing's human senses tingled with excitement; his pulse raced. Though he grumbled and cursed his imprisoning form, there *were* compensations. By all the gods the inhabitants of Raemllyn worshipped, he loved nights such as these as much as he relished soaring on Gohwohn's winds!

Easing his arm from beneath Klora's head, he edged back the blankets and rolled from the bed. Quietly, he moved around the bed to the room's sole window. It was a tiny aperture paned with crudely blown, green-tinged glass. But it was glass rather than gut-covering.

Outside a soft yellow glow radiated from the small town, the flickering of torch flames and braziers hung along the streets. Light Jurka might be, but shadows abound to hide a willing thief, even one the size of Goran One-Eye.

The Challing's gaze returned to the small room and Klora's sleeping form. In truth, he was hard pressed to leave. The woman was beautiful, and oh, the pleasures they had shared in the passing of a few short hours. However, duty called.

Finding his discarded clothing on the floor, he swiftly dressed and carefully double-knotted his three gold bulging pouches to his belt. Klora might not appreciate his cavalier departure, but there was little he could do about it. By the time she roused for breakfast, he intended to be leagues to the north with the stolen horses.

Goran stepped to the door of the room and paused for a moment, looking back at the sleeping Klora. He blew her a kiss, smiled broadly, and started to leave.

Goran froze.

Outside in the corridor he heard muffled voices. Men's voices—and the whisper of steel blades escaping leather sheaths.

The memory of the glinting steel spikes outside Jurka flashed before his mind's eye, and with them an ice floe that spread up his spine. Goran tensed as the footsteps drew closer, stopping outside the door.

chapter
6

LIJENA'S LEADENED EYES CLOSED, lulled by the rhythmic, lazy strides of her mare Orria. The weariness of her body and mind melted together, guiding her toward the open arms of sleep. Gratefully she accepted the invitation of that caressing embrace, only too willing to lay aside her confusing jumble of thoughts if only for a few minutes.

Head nodding chin to chest, she sighed softly. She felt herself slump toward the neck of the dappled gray, caring little that the slow-motion fall would eventually tumble her from the saddle to the grassy prairie. All that mattered was that she slept, that she found stolen moments of rest.

—Ride!

Lijena's eyes flew wide, and she sat straight in the saddle as the screaming voice shattered the soothing fog of sleep. For the past hour the demonic voice had abandoned her head, allowing her to slow Orria's pace to a gentle walk, and lulling the mare's rider into believing that she would be granted the sleep and rest her body craved.

"I'm faint," she mumbled, no longer caring that she

babbled aloud to a voice no one but she heard like some half-wit. "My head . . . so light. Must rest . . . sleep."

Lijena's eyes closed again as her weary muscles went flaccid, and she once more slumped forward. Like jelly shifting in a bowl, her body leaned to the right, beginning to slide from the saddle.

—No! You will not fail me!

The roaring anger did nothing to prevent her from spilling onto the ground. Through the cottony clouds clogging her mind, Lijena heard Orria snort. She managed to tighten her fingers around braided reins, clutching, stopping the animal from shying away and wandering off into the night.

—Up! On your feet, bitch! Climb back into the saddle and ride!

"Tired. Can't go on," she murmured. The voice refused to leave her alone and let her sleep.

—There will be time for rest later.

"Rest?" Her voice quavered in disbelief. "You will let me rest?"

—Another league. You must ride another league, then there will be shelter.

"Tired." Lijena's head tossed from side to side, and she batted the disembodied voice away with her free hand.

She felt a movement within her—head? Body? The demonic force worked its subtle magicks. She could not resist the thought that edged out of the fog. *Only a league? I can ride a league . . . then rest.*

—Yes! Only a league more and there will be shelter, rest, and *food!*

"What?" Lijena sat and paused a moment before pushing to her feet.

—Food.

"I can eat? When? Where?"

—To the north. Ride northward.

Lijena's stomach rumbled hollow and empty, reminding her how famished she actually was. When had she last eaten? She remembered the rabbit Davin and Goran One-Eye had given her. But when had that been, yesterday? The day before? Longer?

The promised food guided her to Orria's side, where she managed to slip a foot into a stirrup and lift her hands to the saddle. However, she couldn't find the strength to drag her body back up into that seat of leather.

"Can't go on. Too tired." Fatigue slurred her words, and frustrated tears welled in her eyes as she leaned against the mare. "I can't do it."

—You will obey. You *will!*

The empty rumbling of Lijena's belly transformed into knifing pain. She cried out, clutching her stomach as shards of broken glass shredded her innards.

"Stop. Please, stop!" she pleaded as the slicing agony doubled her over.

—Ride or you'll die here, writhing as I wrench your entrails from your body!

The pain slackened enough for Lijena to stand upright and pull herself into the saddle. And when she spurred Orria northward in a loping gallop, the gut-twisting torment completely subsided. She rode through the darkness, sustained by the sole thought that but one league lay before her.

—The lights . . . look and see the lights.

Lijena's head lifted. Across the featureless sea of grass came the yellow glow of lights beaming from windows.

An inn! Her hope soared. The voice had not lied; there would be food and sleep.

—Ride toward the lights. There will be food.

Digging her heels into Orria's dappled flanks, Lijena drove the mare forward in a full run. Orria stumbled, nearly unseating her rider before she got her hooves under her again.

Somewhere within Lijena's mind dwelled the realization that she pushed the horse dangerously close to the limits of her endurance, but she didn't care. All that mattered was that the gray mare carried her to the inn and the promised food and sleep. Her heels lashed out again, and Orria strained forward.

—Good. A few more minutes and you will be at the caravansary.

Lijena paid no heed to the voice. Her full attention lay

on the two-story inn and its many glowing windows. The acrid odor of Orria's sweat turned to lather invaded her nostrils, and she heard the rasping sound of the mare sucking desperately for each breath. Still she drove her across the prairie until she at last drew back on the reins to halt before the caravansary's entrance.

Lijena released the reins and slid from the saddle. For a minute she stood, gaining control of legs that threatened to turn liquid on her, before stumbling toward the lighted windows and a single door.

Reaching the portal, she braced herself against the solid wood as her legs once again threatened to give way beneath her. From within came the sounds of clinking plates and mugs, soft laughter, and the buzz of dinnertime conversation.

—Food. Nothing more! Eat, then ride to the north!

Ignoring the demon's command, Lijena's hand sought and found the door's latch. Her fingers fumbled awkwardly for a moment before lifting it from its niche; then, shoulder against wood, she pushed inside.

All movement in the room ceased abruptly as heads and eyes turned toward her. Lijena saw mouths open and lips move, but she was unable to discern the words that passed from those mouths. She blinked and staggered forward.

"Food," she said weakly. "Anything. I need food."

"Get her a plate!" This from a woman dressed in a floor-length gown of rich, forest-green velvet, who rose from a table at the back of the caravansary and rushed toward Lijena. "Poor dear. What's happened to you?"

Lijena blinked at her; she comprehended her question, but found no answer in her brain. Through the befuddling haze of confusion, she managed a weak smile. The woman was beautiful, like a fairy from the tales told to children. Lijena reached out to her.

"Was it brigands? Some of them from down the road? The Woodrey boys again?" The woman took Lijena into her arms.

All Lijena could do was shake her head before she collapsed, falling into the darkness of unconsciousness.

*   *   *

As Raemllyn's sun settled low on the western horizon, Davin Anane found a soft-looking spot beneath the boughs of a large-boled pine, amid a wood growing for an acre to either side of a tributary stream that ran into the Kukis River to the south. An ironic smile touched his lips as he surveyed the site. The Kukis ran a few miles to the west of Harn where he had first glimpsed Lijena and begun this misadventure.

This fact had little bearing on his present position, which was unknown to him, as was the grassland he had crossed all day. The woods did give him some comfort as he dropped to his knees and gathered dried pine needles into a thick, crude mattress over which he spread his sleeping furs. The pine grew a quarter of a mile from the stream, thus placing him out of the path of night predators seeking the water. The thick boughs above also provided some protection should the dark cloud bank rolling in from the west bring rain with it.

Or snow, he thought with a shiver as he slipped between the furs and drew their warmth snuggly under his chin.

He sighed as the last traces of a golden-pink sunset were washed away by inky night. It had been a long day, longer than he had anticipated. He had hoped Goran would have been able to find horses in the small hamlet to the south and follow immediately. Instead, his weary feet had trod at least another seven leagues before he came upon this wood, and still there was no Challing with fresh mounts.

Davin shivered again, although not because of the increasing chill in the air. An image of those steel spikes outside the town and Goran being lowered onto a wickedly honed tip flashed in his mind.

Spike? By Nyuria's arse, it's probably some large-bosomed wench that's detained him! Nothing more. Davin tossed restlessly to a side, forcing the possibility of such a gory ending to his and Goran's friendship from his thoughts. Goran was an adept thief, almost as good as Davin himself. The Challing had quick fingers and a quicker mind and took chances only when the situation warranted.

He's too smart to risk his life for a pair of horses, Davin thought with a grimace, *but stupid enough to wager his hide on a roll of the dice!*

Hedonistic pursuits were of more than mild curiosity for the Challing—they were a passionate obsession. Davin lacked a clear mental image of Goran's native land, or the Challing's true physical form, but he suspected Gohwohn was less than the heaven Goran so often and so loudly proclaimed it to be. Why else did the one-eyed changeling in human form drink so deeply of Raemllyn's pleasures?

Davin sucked at his teeth and shook his head. His worries about his friend were wasted. Goran held an innate sense of survival, even with his proclivity for getting into seemingly impossible situations. He was quite capable of fending for himself.

But Lijena . . .

Davin rolled on to his back and lay with eyes wide, staring up at the bower formed by the limbs. The shadow play there formed startling outlines, silhouettes, faces—and the face he focused on was that of a blonde daughter of Bistonia.

Where does the demon drive you? he asked the night. *And for what purpose?*

Davin Anane closed his eyes; he had no answers to the myriad questions that surrounded Lijena Farleigh—and himself. Nor was there sense in even thinking about them until he had overtaken the young woman.

So it was he drifted into a sleep troubled with fluttering images of Goran and Lijena dancing across the surface of his mind. The disturbing dreams subtly changed, twisted into visions of nameless demons stalking him through Raemllyn realms. No matter where he turned, hid, ran, the demons found him, seeking to sink taloned claws into his chest. And behind them, with Bedrich the Fair's rotting head held high on a pike like some gruesome banner, came Zarek Yannis, urging his hell-spawned creature onward.

"Yannis!" The name came as a curse from Davin's lips as he awoke, heart hammering and sweat drenching his body.

Drawing a steadying breath, Davin rubbed a hand over his face. Yannis' leathery visage remained etched before his mind's eye. Why? The usurper of the Velvet Throne knew nothing of the fallen House of Anane and its sole heir. Nor did the thief Davin Anane pose a threat—although Davin prayed that one day Raemllyn's gods would allow him the pleasure of ending Yannis' life with a well-placed sword thrust.

Tymon would interpret the dream as guilt placed on my soul for the denial of my heritage. Davin tried to make light of the disturbing nightmare as he pushed himself up on elbows and glanced about the wood. *But then my Huata friend finds far too much meaning in dreams.*

A dry twig snapped.

Davin's head jerked to the left, listening; he heard nothing. It was that very nothing that brought the Jyotian thief scurrying from the sleeping furs. The night was too quiet. Something silenced the voices of nightbirds, and it was close by.

Leaving the furs doubled to imitate a body within, Davin worked his way on hands and knees away from the tree and crawled under a thornbush. The long spines nipped at his skin, but he remained silent. If he were wrong about unwanted guests, he'd have paid for his caution with a few bloody scratches. If he were right, his very life lay in the balance.

Straining hard to hear even the slightest of sounds, he sat beneath the bush and waited. He had convinced himself of possessing an overactive imagination when he heard the harsh hissing.

A heartbeat later the odor of burning turf wafted in his nostrils. Two seconds passed, and he heard the clank of weapons above the pounding of his own temples.

Zarek Yannis doesn't know I exist! Davin refused to accept the demonic images that floated in his mind as he peered out from under the low branches of the thornbush. Then there was no way to deny his fears. A hundred yards distant, he saw two coals burning in the night—these coals floated in the darkness at waist level and were not coals at all, but eyes—fiery orbs.

The Faceless Ones!

Another set of the hellfire-lit eyes appeared beside the first, then a third pair. Shadows amid the night's blackness, he could see their dark forms now. The Faceless Ones knelt on all fours and sniffed at the ground as a hunting hound might. They followed a trail with unerring skill and implacable determination.

Davin did not wait to determine what trail the demon spawn followed; he already knew—a trail that would lead them to his bundled sleeping furs, then to the bush concealing him. He backed from the thornbush and quickly checked himself for additional cuts. He bled slightly from two scratches on his right hand and three on the left.

"Yehseen's shriveled staff!" he cursed under his breath. Legend held that once the Faceless Ones had the scent of blood there was no escape for their victim.

Sucking away the droplets of crimson oozing from the scratches, Davin glanced back at the trio of Faceless Ones before sinking into the concealing shadows of the woods. In the darkness he dared not move too quickly for fear of stumbling and injuring himself, or worse, making enough noise to draw the demons' attention.

Thrusting aside the obvious question of who had set the Faceless Ones on his spoor and why, he attempted to focus on the immediate problem—how to get away from them? *There must be a way. There has to be!*

Some distance from his camp, he fell into a long-legged run. Fear tugged at his heart with each stride. To be caught by the hell riders meant death, but how did a mere mortal escape them?

The tales of their earlier incarnation described these hell creatures as warriors second to none in ability. Each Faceless One matched—out-matched—a hundred human weaponsmen. They needed no food or rest, had acute senses, superior strength, and were vulnerable only to magical attacks. If a hundred warriors had scant chance against a Faceless One, what hope did a lone thief from Jyotis hold?

A howl, like that of a baying hound, sounded behind Davin.

A glance over a shoulder revealed that his fleet race

through the woods had been for naught. The Faceless Ones
followed—no more than a hundred strides off his heels.

They ran on all fours, and their eyes burned with maniac
intensity from deep shadow. No hint of facial structure
showed from under the thick woolen hoods they wore pulled
forward. From beneath the hems of those robes trailed thick
tails with glinting scales that writhed in serpentine coils.

Davin blundered forward, caring little what direction he
ran as long as it took him away from these demons escaped
from Peyneeha's lower levels. Ahead he saw a low-hanging
branch above the path he ran along.

Leaping, Davin caught the limb and swung upward. As
agile as a monkey, he scaled the heights of the oak tree,
searching for a limb that would lead him into the branches
of a neighboring tree. He found none. Nor were there many
more limbs left to the oak. He glanced overhead. The top
of the tree ended six feet above him. The branches there
were ill-suited for supporting the weight of a man. He had
climbed his way into a dead end. He could do nothing but
cling to the trunk and pray to each and every god for de-
liverance.

Shuffling sounds came from below. Looking down, Davin
saw six burning eyes peering up, seeking their prey among
the autumn-barren branches.

"Let them continue on, Yehseen," he called on the father
of the gods.

His prayers went unanswered. One of the Faceless turned
and barked like a jackal. The other two chorused the yapping
as their skeletal hands grasped the gnarled trunk and began
to climb, like spiders that found handholds where none
existed.

Wood cracked, then splintered beneath Davin's booted
feet. His surprised cry echoed above the doglike barking of
the Faceless Ones as the branch supporting him gave way,
and he tumbled downward.

From branch to branch he careened through the night.
One instant he saw six glowing eyes glaring up at him; in
the next he slammed belly first into a limb and was tossed
topsy-turvy into the first of the Faceless Ones, dislodging
the creature from the trunk. Then another branch caught the

thief's side, and the night echoed hellish yowls as the first hell rider toppled into its companions, jarring them from the oak.

Davin didn't question which of Raemllyn's gods brought him thudding to the ground on his backside. That he still lived was all that mattered. Ignoring the protest of his bruised ribs, the Jyotian struggled to his feet and glanced around.

The three Faceless Ones already stood. In their hands blazed longswords of crystalline flame. Not on human flesh did those sizzling blades fall, but on the demons themselves—two of the hell riders attacked the third!

Without pause to consider the twist of fate the Sitala worked, Davin stumbled off deeper into the forest, taking advantage of whatever demonic madness had possessed the trio.

Water splashed under his boots.

Glancing down, he smiled. He stood ankle deep in the stream that fed the wood—and water could hide his scent!

Hope flaring anew, Davin ran with the current as it wound southward. It flowed, grew, tributaries joining it, adding confusing confluences. When the water widened and deepened, Davin swam. Using a breast stroke to avoid both noise and unwanted ripples, he swam as hard as he had run.

Tiring after only a few minutes, Davin knew the Faceless Ones would eventually catch him if he persisted in flight. He controlled his panic and thought for the first time all night. Avoidance had to serve him rather than flight, and fighting them was out of the question.

He had to confuse them, fool them, let them pass him by.

His exhaustion served him well now. Sighting a small stand of reeds, Davin silently paddled toward it. A quick jerk brought free a hollow stem. Not even taking the time to clean away the mud clinging to it, he stuck it in his mouth and dived for the bottom of the stream.

Remaining underwater proved more difficult than he had anticipated; his natural buoyancy kept forcing him to the surface. Davin finally wrapped his legs around the stems of other reeds and clung for dear life.

Peering up through the clear water, he saw burning eyes

staring down at him. He almost betrayed his position by
rising to the surface, mistakenly thinking he had been discovered. The eyes were those of a hell rider, but they moved
on, their prey lying undetected but mere inches beneath the
water's surface.

Time lost meaning for the Jyotian as he clung to the
reeds, sucking in foul-tasting air through the stem, feeling
the heat leeched from his body by the water's chill, fearing
return of the demons.

Even beneath the water, Davin heard the screams that
echoed throughout the forest: cries that came from no human
throat, of that he was sure. The Faceless Ones vented their
rage at losing their appointed victim. Then there was silence.

Davin waited beneath the water until the gold of dawn
streamed across the sky above. And then when he rose, he
felt a clutching fear that the Faceless Ones sat patiently
waiting for him to betray himself. No yapping barks of
descending demons met his ears, only the sweet songs of
forest birds greeting the new day.

Cold and wet, Davin Anane waded from the stream and
cautiously picked his way back to his sleeping furs. Bun-
dling himself tightly in their warmth, he fell asleep with
teeth achatter and cursing the strands the Sitala wove that
drew him to the attention of the Faceless Ones and the man
who controlled them.

chapter
7

GORAN ONE-EYE THREW HIS SHOULDER against the door as the shuffle of booted feet approached the portal to Klora's room. Simultaneously his island-sized paw shot out and found the doorlatch.

"Roan-Jafar's rotting corpse!" The Challing cursed the mage who had drawn him from Gohwohn's bliss into Raemllyn's troubled realms.

The latch was a wooden rod no larger in circumference than Goran's little finger. Two loops of leather on door and frame were all that held the dowel in place. Neither wood nor leather would long deter a man intent on entering, much less the small army that moved in the hallway.

"Wh-what's happening?" a sleepy voice murmured from behind the Challing.

"We'll soon have visitors that I fear bear us ill will," Goran whispered as he turned. "If Jajhana graces us with a smile, we'll be away from here ere our visitors come rudely barging in."

Klora, honey-hued hair in disarray and minus even a stitch of clothing, sat in bed rubbing sleep from her eyes.

A questioning frown knitted her lovely brow when she saw Goran, and her head cocked as the commotion outside mounted.

"Ansisian be hanged!" Klora's eyes went saucer-wide.

"No time to curse the God of Sleep. Move that lovely arse . . ." Goran's own single eye widened.

Klora's perplexed frown transformed into a twisted mask of anger. With a cry of rage tearing from snarled lips, she vaulted from the bed and launched herself head first at Goran's legs.

Displaying an alacrity that belied his mountainous bulk, the Challing lithely sidestepped her open-armed tackle.

"Dammit!" the woman shrieked as her naked form sprawled on the wooden floor, and her arms embraced empty air. "Break down the door! He's getting away! Damn all of you! Why didn't you come at the appointed hour?"

Goran shrugged; he should have realized that the owner of the Inn of Four Memories would not allow him to escape with three pouches abulge with gold. But then Klora was such a pleasant diversion, capable of befuddling the mind of the wisest of men.

"Farewell, my lovely." Goran One-Eye opened a palm beneath his red-bearded chin, pursed his lips, and blew that tempting diversion a kiss. "Give my regards to our children!"

Goran spun, took a stride, then leaped over the narrow bed. The heel of his right boot snagged the bed sheets, nearly tripping him as he stretched out an arm to throw open the room's sole window. It was the selfsame sheet that Klora grasped and wrenched when she pushed from the floor and threw herself back onto the bed as the Challing attempted to wiggle his ponderous bulk through the tiny opening.

The tug of cloth yanked Goran One-Eye's right leg from under him. He twisted and plopped heavily on his backside, kicking and swearing as he freed himself of the cumbersome sheet.

The sound of a well-placed boot against wood resounded through the small bedroom, followed by a dry snap as the thin dowel splintered in twain. The door flew open and four men with swords and daggers drawn stalked across the threshold. They weren't the army of weaponsmen Goran had imagined, but then it only took one blade to rob a man— or a Challing—of his life.

"He's still got the money!" Klora screamed as Goran attempted to stand. "Take him. *Now!*"

The four advanced, their mouths bearing confident smiles of victory. After all, they were four against one. And the man on the floor had yet to draw his blade, nor did he even have the proper number of eyes!

Acutely aware of his disadvantages, Goran held himself back until the foremost of his adversaries placed a boot on the discarded sheet. A bellowing roar tore from the Challing's throat as he grasped an edge of the sheet and yanked, using the same tactic Klora had employed to topple him.

And with equal success! The leading brigand cried out in surprise as he tumbled backwards, arms aflail. His companions scurried aside, giving the falling man wide berth to avoid being accidentally skewered by longsword or dirk.

The moment of confusion was all the Challing needed to shove his hulking body from the floor.

"Must I do everything myself?" Klora raged, her nakedness trembling in fury. She flung herself at the flaming-haired giant, fingernails raking like a cat's claws.

Had the circumstances been more intimate, Goran would have welcomed another playful romp with this alluring beauty. To be certain, he delighted in a lovers' wrestle as much as the next man, but not with his life hanging in the balance.

Ducking under Klora's lashing arms, the Challing caught her about her slender waist. In the batting of an eye, he hefted the woman and easily tossed her into the four swordsmen. Laughter rolled from the giant's chest and throat as all five went down into a writhing pile.

"Surely, my lovely, you don't expect such oafs to relieve me of my gold?" Goran was beginning to enjoy this.

One of the men wriggled from beneath Klora's squirming body, rose to his knees, and swung his sword at Goran's ankles. The giant lifted his foot and brought a heavy boot down on the blade's tip. A metallic twang reverberated within the room as tempered steel snapped in two.

Before the kneeling assailant grasped what had occurred, Goran's left foot lashed out, the toe of his boot catching the man under the chin. The weaponsman's head jerked back, accompanied by a sharp crack as his neck was snapped by the impact.

"Is the money worth your life, giant?" This from Klora who now stood with her three armed accomplices. "Pass over the pouches, and we'll let you live."

Goran snorted; the woman was transparent. The determined set of the weaponsmen's faces revealed that they had no intention of letting him live, not after he had taken a life. The Challing shrugged and shook his head in answer.

"Get him!" Klora waved her companions forward.

Right hand dropping to his sheathed blade, Goran One-Eye stepped forward to meet the attack. Or started to step forward. What he did was stumble, then fall, his feet once again entangled in that damnable sheet.

Rather than struggling against the linen, the Challing rolled to elude the singing swish of blades swung downward to abruptly end his life. Evade the deadly steel he did, only to discover himself in a most untenable position. His sword was pinned under his heavy body; his legs were wrapped mummy-tight in linen sheet.

"Die, swine!" Klora snarled as she snatched a sword from one of her unsavory companions, grasped it firmly in two hands, and swung it high above her head.

"Pig? You bed with pigs? I'd thought better of you." Goran grinned up at the woman whose blade would sever his head from body in another moment. His pulse raced wildly, his temples pounded, and his mouth was suddenly dry as the Great Desert of Nayati—but he felt no fear!

Klora hesitated. "His eye!"

Goran's single orb, aglow with the flaming green of witch-fire that boiled and churned, fixed upon her. From that eye erupted a shaft of light that struck her nakedness like a column of water, bathing her entire body.

"My flesh burns!" Klora screamed. Her sword forgotten,

it fell to the floor while her hands batted at the green glow enveloping her.

The brigand to her left abruptly lunged, his sword point directed straight for Goran's heart. The swordsman screamed even louder than Klora when sword and sword hand simply vanished.

"Amazing," muttered Goran, realizing Masur-Kell's potion once more worked within him, unleashing the magical potentials of his Challing-born form. But as was the case when Goran had faced the sorcerer's own demon guard, he had absolutely no control of those magicks.

The remaining two robbers, faces masks of terror-bred determination, struck in unison, swords leveled to impale the red-bearded giant's chest.

Goran cried out as his single eye exploded with heat and fire. Rays of brilliant green light lanced forth to strike the foremost directly in his face.

When the glaring green faded, the attacker was minus nose. There was no gaping, ragged hole of bloody and seared flesh. The man's smooth skin was simply without a nose, nor was there a trace that his face had ever sported a nose! The brigand dropped sword and dagger, clutched his noseless face, then ran from the bedroom bleating like a sheep.

The flaring witch-fire cost the last of Klora's playmates his ear—and a quarter of his head with it. The man never took another step, but sank down, instantly dead.

Kicking free of the ensnaring sheet, Goran One-Eye rose to glare at the sole remaining attacker, whose eyes shifted between the giant and the smooth stump of his right arm.

"Arrgghh!" the Challing roared, sending the man scurrying from the room after his noseless companion.

"A mage," Klora gasped, shrinking back into the corner of the bedroom. Her nakedness no longer flickered with a green aura. "Please . . . please don't harm me!"

Goran towered over her, his chest expanding as he sucked in a deep breath. For a moment he considered repaying the honey-tressed temptress in full for the hospitality she had shown him. Then he laughed and dug into one of his bist-laden pouches and tossed ten gold coins onto her rumpled bed.

"There, Klora, for an entertaining evening!" At such a price the Challing might have enjoyed the pleasures of Raemllyn's most skilled courtesans for a week. But tonight had brought Goran excitement beyond carnal lust.

Stepping over the two bodies sprawled on the floor, Goran hastened from the room and down the narrow staircase. He emerged on the night-shrouded street, looked left and right, and caught his breath. The night was younger than he had thought.

Fully a score of men armed with swords, dirks, and clubs filed down the street. As the head of the definitely angry-looking mob was the noseless thief, who pointed at the Challing in human form. A second later the men broke into a dead run heading directly for Goran.

The Challing grinned, focused his eye and thoughts on the charging horde, willing the witch-fire to flare anew and sunder various parts of their anatomies into nothingness. Goran's grin faded—nothing happened!

Without pause to curse the fickled comings and goings of his magicks, Goran did the only sensible thing left open to him. He ran.

Darting around the corner of the building, he ran down a dark alley, turned onto a torch-lit street, found another alley, and shot into it. Searching a third street, he almost ran full tilt into a pair of peace wardens on patrol. He slowed, sauntered by, getting only slightly curious glances from them, then rounded another corner and ran for his life.

Goran entered another alley and got halfway down the narrow path between two buildings when a dozen men stepped into the opposite end, blocking his exit. Skidding to a halt, the Challing wheeled and retraced his path at full speed.

On the street, he heard a low rumble of voices coming from the right; so he fled to the left, crossing the street, and found an alley a hundred strides ahead, which he ducked into. Only to come to a dead halt once more. Angry voices and then six men entered the opposite end of his chosen path. That same rumble of blood-lusting anger came from behind. He had boxed himself in!

Backing from the alley, Goran's eyes darted up and down the street. Men approached on both sides; there was no escape.

Leaning back against a wall, the Challing gasped as his breath suddenly came short and quick. His head swirled as though beset by the vertigo-inducing perfume of the black blossom of a night lily. His vision blurred as if a milky veil had been passed over his eye. In the next instant, it was as though he saw with a crystal-clear perception he had never known in this realm of men. Yet, there was something askew with his eye—a different perspective, as if he had stepped into a hole and become several feet shorter.

Goran shook his head to clear his mind on the abrupt sensory assault. The dizziness, the perplexing change of perspective were undoubtably merely side effects of Masur-Kell's potion and his reawakening magical abilities. But for now those abilities had fled him. It was cold steel that would serve him now. His hand dropped to his sword, readying himself for the battle, prepared to leave a dozen dead or dying ere he fell.

From three directions they converged on him, but not one man offered a threatening move. Goran received the shock of his life when the man whose nose he had removed came up to him, eyed him, and moved on without saying a word.

Thus a score of men passed him by, leering strangely in his direction, but none uttering a sound.

Goran stared after them in disbelief and confusion as they stalked down the street and disappeared into an alley-way. Releasing an overly held breath, he lifted a hand to wipe the beads of sweat from his forehead—and gasped.

His hand was no longer *his* hand! Where once had been a hairy fist huge enough to engulf an entire mug of ale, now slender, feminine fingers wiggled.

"A wench's hand!" he said aloud.

He pressed that unfamiliar hand to his . . . breasts! Two of them—firm and upthrusting they rode high upon his—*her?*—chest!

A giddiness assailed the Challing. Then a rush of fear

that gave way to pleased laughter. He had altered form! After five years of imprisonment, gone was the ponderous bulk of Goran One-Eye, replaced by the shapely curves of a woman. And a comely one if he was any judge.

Running a hand over the new body, the Challing relished the delightfully different sensations that suffused each cell of this strangely exciting human form. Staggering with the intoxicating power of his discovery, Goran made his way through the night-veiled street to Jurka's town square and the fountain flowing there. With slender hands on the brick trim, the Challing peered into the water.

"Bah! A skinny one!" a voice an octave higher than the one to which the changeling was accustomed came from the reflected red lips.

The water's mirrored image revealed a decidedly human, and decidedly feminine, form and face—that of Lijena Farleigh—complete with two aquamarine eyes!

Goran could readily see why none of Klora's brigands had suspected this delicate form to hide the giant they chased. Although his former body and this new one wore the same scarlet clothing, on this thin frame they were loose and flowing—aye, even baggy. The scarlet blouse and breeches appeared as transformed as was he.

The Challing grinned. Nor had his pursuers seen the heavy-laden pouches now hidden beneath the folds of the bright blouse that trailed well below his—her?—waist.

Eventually, he decided, one of the dim-witted brigands might make the connection between a bearded giant in scarlet and the lovely blonde in ill-fitting garments of the same hue. But for the moment, the Challing felt secure in the unexpected disguise.

Goran's eyes narrowed as he/she studied the reflected image carefully. He shook his head and sucked at his lips.

"This will never do! This Challing prefers women with more meat on their bones."

Goran stared into the water and concentrated, remembering in minute detail the features of that fair flower of Harn whose bed the Challing had shared during the Spring Fair. Then he awaited the transformation to a more eye-pleasing shape.

Lijena's image remained.

Perhaps the potion limits the shapes I can assume?

Focusing on the form the changeling had worn for five years, Goran willed the return of barrel-chest and thick, muscle-rippling arms. Again there was no transformation. Lijena's breasts remained, as did her face, slender waist, and curved hips.

The sorcerer's potion is as weak as water! My changeling powers still elude me! I've merely exchanged a he for a she! Goran pulled the scarlet eye patch from an unfamiliar brow and stuffed it into a pocket. With two good eyes, the Challing had little use for it now. *A male's body for a female's body . . . 'twill take time to accustom myself to that!*

Goran grinned. The Challing had been too long in Raemllyn, locked within the body that men called Goran One-Eye for far too many years. He—Goran had come to think of himself as male—was neither a human male nor a female, but a Challing capable of becoming either, or both at the same time if so desired, or any of the three other sexes in his native Gohwohn. At least he would have been if he possessed his full powers.

Goran isn't even my name, but one given me by Roan-Jafar! the Challing thought, carefully avoiding even mentally pronouncing his true name. To do so would be tempting fate. There were those who could read thoughts, and to learn the true name of a Challing was to enslave the mystical creature, binding him to another's will. *Not that I'm not already thrice bound to this miserable world!*

"Ah, Davin, if you could only see me now," Goran said aloud. "What a pleasure you would take in this . . ."

Goran had intended to say *jest,* but it was the word *pleasure* that rolled over in the changeling's mind. Goran now-of-two-eyes smiled.

Equipped with a female's body, a whole new world of sensual experimentation lay open to the Challing. As Goran One-Eye *he* had deeply savored the pleasures of one half of the human race. Now *she* could fully explore the sensations belonging to that other half.

Gadi, Gemina, Geela, Gressa. The she-Challing who had been a he for five years explored possible names as she

stood straight and admired her reflection. This new body
might have been too thin for Goran One-Eye's tastes, but
she was no longer that burly giant. There was a certain grace
to this new form, a suppleness that she found pleasing. And
it was a body she already knew human males found desirable.

Glylina! That shall be my new name! She laughed—a
new name for a new body! She posed as the frosty-haired
beauty stared up at her from the water. She would have to
get new clothing. The scarlet hue she wore was appealing,
but the man's shirt and breeches hung on her lithe body like
potato sacks. She could buy . . .

No! Just because the Challing was now female didn't
mean she had to change professions. Thievery still brought
a shiver of delicious excitement to the changeling. Of course,
Glylina would have to use her wits where Goran One-Eye
had too often relied on brute strength. *Davin will . . .*

For the first time she considered Davin and the horses
she had come to Jurka to steal. What would he think of the
Glylina-Goran transformation? Would he still help her find
A'bre and the way back to the realm of Gohwohn? How
would he react to a woman as a partner?

Glylina shifted her weight from one leg to another, admiring the subtle new way her human hips swayed suggestively from side to side. Long-fingered hands seductively
slid down her sides and over the womanly flare of her hips—
stopping when a clatter sounded from across the square.

"What you doing out so late?" came a string of slurred
words.

Glylina swung about and saw a man staggering toward
her, a wine jug clutched in one hand. The man's eyes were
bloodshot and his speech thick with the effects of one or
five too many cups of wine.

Glylina's aquamarine eyes glinted with impish witch-fire.
Let the horses wait! Let Davin wait! The Challing had been
granted a new body, and she was intent on exploring it—
fully!

"Good morn," Glylina called out. "Come. Join me. Here."
She patted the rim of the fountain, then daintily perched a

well-shaped posterior on that rim.

"Best sight I've seen since arriving in this miserable city," the man mumbled as he accepted the seat beside the Challing. He blinked hard, then took another deep drink from the wine bottle. He shook his head as he looked at Glylina and took still another drink.

"I disturb you so?" she asked, enjoying her new role immensely.

"You remind me of one I seek."

"Oh?"

"Looking for her for weeks. Someone said she was seen in this vicinity. With her kidnapper. Qar take him!" The man guzzled another swig.

"Kidnapper? My!" Glylina pushed aside a stray strand of blonde hair and batted her eyes. "Are you on some noble mission?"

"I'm no hero," the man grumbled. "She was stolen out from under my very eyes. My best friend Portrevnio was killed by the kidnapper. The bastard broke my own legs too!"

Portrevnio? Glylina was certain she had heard the name before. But where?

The man leaned close to confide, "Revenge is what drives me. And the money's not bad either. Her uncle offers ten thousand golden bists reward to the man who returns her to his palace."

The man peered drunkenly at Glylina again, then finished off the last of the wine before casting the bottle into the fountain. "But I can see now that you're not the one I seek. Lijena would never wear such . . . such clothing as this." He reached out and stroked her arm.

"Lijena?" Glylina's eyes narrowed. Her drunken companion wore the body armor of a personal guard and his weapons had seen long and hard use. *Portrevnio . . . Lijena . . . a kidnapped niece.* A shiver worked along the changeling's spine.

"Lijena—the one I seek. You look *so* much like her. It's uncanny." He lost his balance as he spoke, toppling back toward the fountain.

Glylina reached out and grabbed his collar. Goran's strength would have prevented the man's fall without effort. But the Challing's new form possessed only a fraction of the sinewy power of Glylina's counterpart. She had to spin around and plant both petite feet against the fountain rim to keep the man from tumbling in.

"Thanks. I'm called Cens." A hairy hand was thrust forward as the man sat straight.

Glylina accepted the proffered hand, and found herself pulled into Cens' embrace with wet lips meant for her mouth smacking loudly on her cheek.

She stiffened; she wanted to delve the carnal pleasures of womanhood, but not this way! She wasn't some soulless, unfeeling slab of meat to be used to relieve male lust at a man's convenience!

"Soft. You feel so soft." Cens nuzzled her neck. "When I collect Lord Tadzi's reward, we will live like royalty, my little wren."

Lord Tadzi! The pieces fell into place. Glylina's mind raced; Davin had killed a guard called Portrevnio when he had kidnapped Lijena. And he had broken the legs of another of Lord Tadzi's guards—a soldier named Cens!

"All I have to do is find that bastard Davin Anane and free Lijena," Cens mumbled.

"Who?" Glylina asked, fearing she had heard correctly.

From the corner of an eye she saw the noseless man and his armed companions searching for the elusive Goran One-Eye. She felt a sudden desire to be rid of Jurka and Cens. With her lack of control, she might slip back into the male Goran at any moment.

"Davin Anane, the kidnapper," Cens repeated. "Lord Tadzi has a good intelligence network in Harn. The man was seen robbing the Harnish Spring Fair. Him and some oversized gorilla."

"Gorilla!" Glylina exploded, then suppressed her rising anger at hearing her former self being described so.

"Huge man—barrel-chested. Not at all like yours." Cens parted the fabric of his alluring companion's blouse and slipped his hands within to cup her breasts. "Yours is so much nicer. A man could get lost here."

Cens leaned forward, his lips tasting the summery warmth of the creamy mounds his fingers now kneaded.

"Not here." Glylina eased away from his slobbering kisses. "Let's find a more private spot."

"At this hour where's more private?" Cens blinked at her.

He couldn't focus well enough to see the armed men parading back and forth seeking out Goran. The Challing knew that sooner or later they would come and question them—and she might revert to her original human form.

"Come on!" Glylina slipped a slender arm around Cens' waist and urged the man to his feet, guiding him eastward toward the stable.

"Where we going?" Cens mumbled, a hand finding its way back into Glylina's blouse to busy a nipple with thumb and forefinger.

"To play a little trick on a friend of mine." Gritting her teeth, she ignored his rude treatment of her body.

"Trick?"

"He runs the stable. He's always playing practical jokes on me. It's time I get even with him. I need the aid of such a strong one as yourself. Come, it will be fun. And then afterward there is fresh straw and we can..." Glylina allowed her words to trail off enticingly. It wasn't her fault if Cens got the wrong idea about what would happen "afterward."

Cens grinned with lecherous intent and did his best to walk straight and steady. Glylina almost laughed when he mumbled something about her, "looking so much like Lijena, that bitch," but kept the man moving rather than exploring further into this chance similarity.

"There," she said, holding Cens upright. "There is the stable. I have this all planned out. Stay here while I go behind the building. In a few minutes set fire to that muck pile." Glylina pointed to a mound of manure and straw near the north side of the stable. "You do have a tinderbox, don't you?"

"Aye. With fine Harnish flint." He produced a small box

from a pouch hung on his belt. "But a fire? Where is the jest in that?"

"The stench of all that burning dung will leave a smell he won't be rid of until the spring rains." Glylina did her best to assure Cens with the lightest of laughs. "He'll think it's hysterically funny. Trust me."

"And after?" Lechery was in the soldier's eyes again.

"Afterward, ah, trust me." Glylina batted her long eyelashes and quickly kissed his lips.

"Set fire to that?" Cens nodded to the manure pile.

"Go. Do it quickly. We mustn't be seen, or it will rob the jest of all its surprise."

"Right."

Cens blundered off and began working on the fire, while Glylina darted toward the south side of the stable, praying to Raemllyn's gods that the man didn't set his own wine-besotted clothing afire before igniting the manure.

Pausing beside the barn, she watched the sparks fly from Cens' Harnish flint, catching the straw. Within seconds flames roared upward, whipped by a night breeze that drove them toward the barn. She grinned; soon the fire would spread to the structure itself, but not before the Challing had claimed her prize.

Glylina wasted no time as she rushed into the barn through a side door and picked and saddled a pair of mounts for herself and Davin, then freed the remaining animals from the stalls and drove them out the open portal.

By the time she mounted a roan gelding and rode through the doorway with a bay for Davin on a rope shank, flames licked across the barn's roof and fire bells rang throughout Jurka. She glanced over her shoulder as she spurred into the night to see the dour blacksmith, Assel son of Assel, running down the street in a nightgown, shouting and pointing at the drunken, hapless Cens.

Glylina felt a momentary pang of remorse for Cens and hoped the man was far more glib when sober than when in his cups. One of Jurka's steel spines was no fit ending for any man, even one who sought the life of her friend Davin Anane.

Then Cens was completely forgotten as the wind caught her long blonde hair and set it astream behind her. She laughed as her still unfamiliar body easily matched the rhythm of the bounding roan.

Raemllyn could never be Gohwohn, but there were certain compensations for being bound to human form! And like Goran before her, Glylina would drink deeply of each and relish the new sensations they brought!

chapter
8

THE SOFT SOUND of a woman humming wove into Lijena's mind. Stirring, she smiled, rubbed her nose, and sleepily rolled over in the luxury of a down-mattressed bed. And she froze.

The bed ... the warm comforter tucked snugly beneath her chin ... Something was wrong, very wrong! Her eyes flew open, and she stared about in cold panic.

She *did* lie in a bed, warmed by a thick comforter. And that bed was within an immense room awash in bright sunlight that flooded through a series of six windows with draperies drawn. The room's construction was simple, white walls with dark-stained, bare-ceiling beams. But those walls were adorned with elegant tapestries and paintings depicting scenes from the lives of Raemllyn's gods.

The furniture, too, was simple. But that same elegance was displayed in rich velvets and silks used in the upholstery.

Where? Lijena drew a deep breath in an attempt to clear the remnants of sleep from her head. A coy, musky sweetness, the scent of perfume, wafted in her nostrils.

The daughter of Bistonia closed her eyes and smiled with contentment. Where or how she got here didn't matter as long as she wasn't astride a horse, riding as though all the demons of Peyneeha were at her heels. She felt marvelous! She had slept, and her stomach no longer growled and knotted with hunger.

The sound of a woman's gentle humming once again touched her ears. Rolling her head on a satin-covered pillow, Lijena peered to her left. Across the room a woman dressed in a white-aproned, forest-green dress sat at a small table busily crushing dried leaves between her palms and placing the resulting powder into a blue vial. A dozen vials of various hues lined the opposite end of the table.

"Winter approaches, and these herbs will help waylay chills and fevers," said the woman without looking up in a voice as soft and gentle as her humming. "Many who visit me during the coming months will have need of such remedies."

Dusting off her hands on her apron, the woman stuffed a cork in the blue vial and placed it beside its companions before rising and smiling at Lijena. "How are you this morning? You have had quite a ride, quite a night."

"What do you mean?" Apprehension sharpened the edge of Lijena's voice. How much did this woman know about her ride?

"Your dreams—nightmares. They wracked you all night long. You tossed and turned so that I decided it best to stay with you." She untied her apron and tossed it atop her chair, then crossed the room to place a cool palm on Lijena's brow. "I felt a touch of fever last night. But this morning, nothing. There's even a blush of the rose in your cheeks."

"You watched over me all night?" Lijena's forehead furrowed with uncertainty as she stared up at her beautiful benefactor. "Why?"

"And what else was I supposed to do?" The woman arched her eyebrows and ran a hand over her long, sleek, nut-brown hair. "What with you staggering into the caravansary last night in need of a friend. It was simply a matter of common decency, though there's nothing common about decency in these times."

"These times?" Lijena remained cautious. She vaguely remembered the woman rushing to aid her when she had entered the inn last night, but one incident was no foundation on which to build trust. Davin Anane and her own lover Amrik Tohon were harsh reminders to be wary of those offering betrayal disguised as comfort.

"There is an oppression upon the land that sweeps across Raemllyn from Kavindra. Common decency seems a minor thing to bemoan when greater things are lost to us each day. But I do so mourn its passing." The woman stared into space. Her expression was of one who saw not her surroundings but sought a world that lay in the past.

"Zarek Yannis." Lijena could not repress the shiver that came when she pronounced his name. "Do you have reason to fear the High King?"

"No more than any woman or man fears the usurper." The woman shook her head and smiled sadly. "No, no, my fears are common to all women who must fend for themselves in this world—keeping a roof over my head, food in my stomach, growing old alone, the beauty of youth fading. The caravansary and what few items I have in this room are the empire I have forged for myself."

"The inn is yours?" Lijena studied the woman. Her fear of aging seemed senseless; if she had seen her thirtieth year, it would have surprised the young woman. As to fading beauty, again the woman had no reason to fear.

"Oh, forgive my bad manners. I stand here telling you my life's history, and I've failed to introduce myself. I am Yorioma Faine, owner of the Golden Tricorn." The woman feigned embarrassment by placing a nervous hand on her breast. "And your name?"

"Lijena Farleigh. I . . . I ride to the north."

"Northward?" Yorioma's eyebrows arched again. "Whatever for? Travel much farther to the north and you'll ride right into the Bay of Pilisi. Or do you journey to Nawat on the other side of the bay?"

"There is . . ." Lijena stammered. How could she tell

Yorioma she was driven by a demon bound to her body? "I
. . . I . . . don't know."

Yorioma frowned, then smiled knowingly. "Ah, the secrets of youth. When I was years younger, I, too, often
made mysterious journeys. Although, to be honest, none of
the men who awaited me were worth it. The majority of
them aren't . . . But then I suspect for one so young, they
all must still seem fascinating."

"No, it's not like that." Tears welled in Lijena's eyes.
"I'm . . . within me . . . it drives me. I've ridden days without
rest, without food."

"Driven," said Yorioma, with such an abrupt sobriety to
her tone that Lijena's head jerked up.

"I don't know why I ride north. I . . . I just have to," the
sole daughter of the House of Farleigh tried to explain, but
words fled her mind.

"Shhh. Do not push yourself. Lie here and rest." The
gentleness returned to Yorioma's voice. "I'll go downstairs
and fetch you a breakfast tray."

—Tell her you're not hungry. Then dress and ride. Today
you race Minima's breath westward.

In spite of her empty stomach, Lijena obeyed the demon's
command. She shook her head and said, "Please don't bother.
I must dress and be on my way."

Lijena threw back the comforter and started to rise. Then
Yorioma's hands were on her bare shoulders, and the older
woman's brown eyes stared directly into Lijena's.

"You need a bath. Food and a bath. The hot water has
been drawn in the small room at the end of the hallway."
Yorioma spoke, each word crisp, clear, and firm, as though
she commanded a child. "Go and bathe. By the time you're
finished the meal will be waiting for you."

"I must ride," Lijena answered. "I travel west this day."

"Bath. Food."

Yorioma's words lashed like a whip across Lijena's demon-
ridden brain. The young woman's head reeled under the
verbal assault, then she steadied herself for the demon's
raging demands. The voice inside her skull was silent. She
blinked and stared at the inn's owner in confusion. It was

as though the woman's pronouncement had left the demon mute.

"There is a robe." Yorioma pointed to a chair near the door. "Take it and go bathe. Now."

Without even a thought of protest, Lijena did as Yorioma Faine commanded. When she returned from the steaming bath, the grime of her long ride washed from body and hair, Yorioma pointed to a tray of sliced meat and fruits on a table beside the bed. Lijena needed no more than a whiff of the food to convince herself that she was on the edge of starvation. She had wolfed down two slices of the meat and a small apple before she paused for a breath.

"You have a good appetite," said Yorioma with an amused smile, "especially hearty for one who denied any desire for food."

Lijena shrugged, unable to answer the caravansary's owner without revealing the horrible truth about the yoke of magic she bore.

"While you eat, I have business to attend. Stay here and wait for me. Stay."

Yorioma's words again carried that sting of a lash to them, which made Lijena sit upright and almost drop the *yalt*-fruit she held.

"I'll remain here." She glanced at the older woman and nodded.

"Good," Yorioma Faine said as she left Lijena alone with her tray of food.

Yorioma crossed the distance from the rear of the Golden Tricorn to the stable in brisk, businesslike strides. Stalls usually filled with guests' horses stood empty. Now that the day had dawned bright and clear, the merchant caravan that had spent the night in the inn had moved eastward. Only when the sun dipped would other travelers seek the caravansary's shelter.

Yorioma entered the barn, her attention drawn to a smallish man with a well-waxed moustache standing indolently by one of the stalls while his black mount dined from a feed bag. For a moment she considered demanding pay for the horse's oats, then pushed the thought aside. She had little time—and even less patience—for Sentan Briss.

"You have news for me?" Yorioma asked without preamble.

"You confuse our roles, my lady." Briss made no attempt to conceal a smirk as he tugged a straw from a pile of hay to his right and poked it into his thin-lipped mouth. "What news have you for my master? Nalek Kahl expects good news. Do not disappoint him."

Yorioma said nothing. As with each of Sentan Briss' visits to the Golden Tricorn, her mind was crowded with sundry ideas for eliminating this little toad without alerting the man he served. With Zarek Yannis becoming bolder by the day, perhaps she could slit Briss' throat and convince the slaver that Yannis' soldiers had done him in.

Perhaps one day I will be free of this worm who links me to my past. But not this day.

"The news," insisted Briss.

"I have the woman he seeks."

Sentan Briss smiled.

Yorioma felt dirty just looking at him. The man's smile managed to convey honest warmth and the feeling of something obscenely unclean at the same time. All that Briss did had the curious and unsettling mixture of crossed motives attached to it.

"Nelek Kahl will pay well for this."

"Why does Kahl seek her?" Yorioma asked, fearing to press too hard and arouse Briss' suspicion. "She is attractive, but there are others I have seen who are lovelier."

"You are lovelier, my dear." Briss smiled, letting his gaze suggestively trace over her body.

If he had reached out to touch her, Yorioma would have broken his hand. But the man seemed to know instinctively—and taunted her without moving a muscle. Once she could have demanded the man's head for the lecherous gleam that now lit his beady eyes.

"The other business with Kahl," said Yorioma. "It proceeds according to plan?"

"Of course, though my master finds Lijena Farleigh of

more pressing importance. The other can wait, for a time. When can you arrange for her transfer?"

"Why does he seek her? And with such generous rewards?"

Briss shrugged and worked the straw from one side of his mouth to the other. "A slaver can have any woman he wants. My master no doubt has developed an odd taste for her. Who can say?"

Yorioma had dealt with Nelek Kahl for the past four years—since she had fled Kavindra following Bedrich the Fair's defeat at the Battle of Kressia—and knew the man did not have an "odd taste" for any woman. His lusts were open and obvious. His business dealings were motivated by serpentine logic, not by his personal life. There was more to Lijena than Yorioma had yet discovered.

With any luck, she might be able to discover why Kahl desired the woman so. Such knowledge might be turned to her own advantage.

It *would* be turned into advantage, Yorioma assured herself. For a woman in her position, a member of Bedrich's royal family hiding here in the middle of nowhere, who feared the moment Yannis' informants would uncover her true identity, she had to turn anything and everything to her advantage.

"Tell your master that the girl will be here, waiting for him," Yorioma said. "He must come personally to retrieve her. No factors, no assistants, no messenger boys."

If Briss took offense at her insult, he did not show it. He spat the straw from his mouth, pulled the feed bag from his mount, and swung into the saddle.

"I will pass along this information. I am sure he will be here within a week."

"Where does he come from?" she had to ask.

"Bistonia . . . when I last saw him."

Yorioma hid her amazement. For Nelek Kahl to leave his den of safety was unheard of: a fact that only confirmed her suspicion that Lijena was no simple slave to the man. The young woman was a key to . . . Yorioma didn't know to what, but she was certain Lijena's value went beyond mere wealth.

"A week. That's all I can hold her," Yorioma said.

"You will hold her as long as necessary," Briss said, his voice cold.

"You know why that might be impossible. If you don't, Kahl does." Yorioma stood firm.

Briss' face twisted, but he said nothing, only clucked his mount forward through the stable's open doors.

Silently, Yorioma watched Sentan Briss ride southward while she shuffled around the few pieces she had of an incomplete puzzle. Briss had made no protest when she had demanded that Nelek Kahl himself come to the Golden Tricorn within the week. It meant that Briss lacked what little intelligence she had given him credit for, or else Lijena Farleigh was far more important than Yorioma had first suspected.

Important enough for Kahl to risk being caught conferring with a member of Bedrich's family! An offense that will cost us both our heads if we are found out. Yorioma pursed her lips thoughtfully. Zarek Yannis' slaughter of all those with royal blood in their veins, and of those who aided members of Bedrich's family—even a distant cousin such as Lady Katura Jayn, who now wore the name Yorioma Faine—was well known.

Yorioma's gaze lifted to the second story of her inn. If Nelek Kahl would indeed be here within a week, she had little time to unlock the secrets Lijena held. But it would be enough—had to be!

"Such an appetite!" Yorioma grinned widely. "You compliment my cook Grick too highly by sending back another clean plate. He's insufferable as it is after your enthusiasm for his breakfast. Just because he hasn't poisoned anyone in almost a week doesn't mean the man can cook."

"The food's excellent!" Lijena licked her fingers in a most unladylike fashion. "Tell Grick his efforts are gratefully appreciated. And, uh, could I have another helping of those honey cakes?"

Yorioma nodded and gestured to a maid silently waiting by the door to the room. When the maid had collected Lijena's plate and left, the Golden Tricorn's owner settled a chair beside the bed and studied her young ward.

Lijena stretched and laughed. "I feel wickedly lazy! I've done nothing but eat and sleep away the whole morning."

"After such a hard ride, your body needs rest." Yorioma smiled.

While Lijena had slept, Yorioma had focused her limited arcane powers on the young woman in the hope of discovering the secrets she held. What she had found was a demon-born barrier surrounding Lijena's mind. Yorioma was skilled, but her knowledge was lacking. The shield had been too strong for her to penetrate.

"But I haven't a single copper to pay for all you've provided." Lijena sat in the bed and stared at her benefactor, her gaze caught by a flicking motion of Yorioma's left hand.

"Nor do I expect a single copper for the little I've given you." Yorioma's hand moved more slowly now, weaving from side to side, holding the young woman's attention.

If Yorioma intended to discover the key Lijena held, Lijena had to face and conquer her inner demon, free her mind and body from the magicks binding them. By accident, Yorioma had provided Lijena with the basic requirements to begin that task—rest and food.

The demon maintained power over its host by employing simple exhaustion. As long as it relentlessly drove Lijena, depriving her body of all but the nourishment needed to maintain life and denying her brain sleep, she was in its total control. But sated and rested, all Lijena needed was a mentor to show her how to exert her own will, to drive the demon from body and mind. Yorioma was that self-appointed mentor.

If it were in her power.

No master mage capable of performing geases and spells was Yorioma Faine, nor even a full-fledged witch. Her skills were minor when compared with the powers of the sorcerers her family once employed. Yet over the years she had watched and read and learned. Enough to insinuate her will with the weaving of fingers and hand in such a way that Lijena was totally unaware of what was happening.

"I feel dizzy," Lijena complained.

Yorioma said nothing. Her full concentration funneled toward making the young woman do her bidding.

"The room spins so," Lijena murmured, her gaze still on Yorioma's left hand.

"Do you know a man called Nelek Kahl?" Yorioma began.

"Yes. He took me to the sorcerer Masur-Kell." Lijena had meant to say "sold me to," but something dark writhed within her mind, twisting thought and speech.

Yorioma contained her excitement. Kahl dealt with a mage! She had been right; this young woman's value had nothing to do with gold and silver. "And there you were instilled with . . ."

"A demon." The darkness directed Lijena to finish the caravansary owner's sentence.

"Where do you ride? Where does this demon drive you?" Yorioma asked softly.

—You must ride westward!

"I must ride to the west." Lijena's voice was suddenly dull as the demon rose to exert its will.

"Resist him. Resist the inner demon!" Yorioma recognized the intrusion of the creature that had been instilled within this young woman's body. "Listen to me. You are fed and rested. You are strong. Aid me. I want to aid you. Fight the demon and obey me."

—Kill her!

Lijena shivered at the dual orders battering at her senses. The demon exerted its full power on her.

—Kill the bitch! Do it now!

"Tell me why Nelek Kahl now seeks you." Yorioma summoned all her skills to coerce Lijena, but felt her control slipping away. Her powers were limited; what she sensed within Lijena might move mountains, create new worlds, send this one spinning into its sun. Lijena was the conduit for the powers being tossed about so casually by . . . who?

—Kill her!

Lijena edged aside the bedcover, stood, and moved toward Yorioma, like one sleepwalking. Her hands lifted, and her fingers clenched, then relaxed. In seconds those hands

would find Yorioma's slender, swanlike throat and crush all
life from it.

"Sit!" Yorioma commanded.

—You must ride to the west. I have given you the rest
and food you wanted. Now kill her, then ride. Do as I
command or feel the pain!

To emphasize its power, the inner voice reawoke the
abdominal pains it had created the night before. Lijena
clutched her belly, crying out as agony knifed through her
gut.

—Kill!

Only when Lijena directed all her attention toward killing
Yorioma did the pain abate enough for her to move. Her
arms rose once more, hands wide to encircle Yorioma's
throat.

Yorioma stood, body tense, face white with strain. The
woman knew she battled beyond her power, yet she dare
not slacken her attack one iota.

—Kill the bitch!

"I obey," said Lijena, her voice devoid of emotion.

Sweat beaded Yorioma's brow as she fought a losing
battle for control of Lijena's mind. Lijena advanced, hands
outstretched. Yorioma stood her ground, muttering a spell
of sleep—to no avail. Lijena stepped closer.

"Do not force me to call upon the gods!" she pleaded
with Lijena—Lijena's demon. "You cannot stand against
them!"

Lijena's fingertips brushed Yorioma's neck.

Yorioma twisted and ducked to avoid that strangling embrace. Simultaneously, her right foot lashed out, slamming
into the side of Lijena's left knee, sending the young blonde
crashing to the floor.

"Ansisian!" Yorioma called on the God of Sleep, then
began a chant she had learned so long ago—at such a great
price.

Her fingers drew patterns in the air. Yorioma's voice rose
and fell as she summoned the power of the God Ansisian.
And there was the pain. It began as a dull throb at the center
of her skull and hammered outward. Yorioma steeled herself

against the agonizing pounding, forcing firmness into her voice though tears streamed down her cheeks.

Lijena pushed herself from the floor and again advanced, death promised by her clutching fingers. With a surge of demonic power, she lunged forward for the kill.

No longer a simple hammering, the pain contained within Yorioma's brain transformed into a thousand spinning shards of razor-honed steel that sliced into the very fabric of sanity. This was the price of Ansisian's aid to mere mortals—pain, ever-increasing agony. If she could but endure the white-hot slivers that shredded her grip on reality for but a few seconds longer!

Lijena froze in midstride.

The chant now a high-pitched wail that shrieked from her lips, Yorioma continued to weave the spell, forcing each word through the barrage of pain tearing at her brain, up her throat, over her tongue and out her lips. Lijena's face turned from pasty white to brilliant red as the strain within her mounted, as the demon struggled against the powers Yorioma summoned.

"Kill you!" Lijena screamed over the innkeeper's strident wail. "Kill you and ride west!"

Abruptly Lijena went limp and sank into a pile in the middle of the bedroom floor. Just as abruptly, Yorioma's chant died. The woman staggered back on legs weak and watery until she found a wall to support her trembling body. She closed her eyes and through clenched teeth offered a prayer of thanksgiving to the God of Sleep.

That prayer was answered. Gradually the pinwheeling razors dissolved and the pounding hammer returned. For now that was the best she could hope for. Hours would pass before the hammer within her skull would at last stop its terrible assault on her brain. But then she had been prepared for this when she had called on Ansisian. For all magicks there was always a price.

Slowly opening her eyes, she drew a hand across her sweat-glistening face. Lijena remained on the floor, the gentle rise and fall of her breast the only sign that life remained in her body. The hint of a smile touch Yorioma's lips as she stood straight and drew in several deep, steadying breaths.

Certain strength had returned to her legs, Yorioma crossed to the fallen woman, knelt, and took Lijena in her arms like a mother cradling an injured child. Rocking to and fro as she held the unconscious woman to her breast, Yorioma began a soft crooning meant only to soothe.

"There, there, my little one," she said. "Everything will be all right. Fight that demon within. Fight it and I will help you." Tears still flowed down Yorioma's cheeks. "I know you can fight it because I have done the same. Oh yes, I know what agony you feel."

Yorioma Faine began crying openly, clutching Lijena's limp body to hers—crying for this innocent child caught in the grasp of a power beyond her understanding—crying for herself.

chapter
9

DAVIN ANANE'S CHATTERING TEETH mutilated a curse that derided Goran's ancestors from their inception in a maggot-swarming muck pool to his mother's ability to service ten lovers—at one time. Hugging damp sleeping furs about his lean, muscular body, Davin rubbed at the chilling moisture on his arms and chest. The effort did little except to raise another layer of gooseflesh on his bare body.

Tentatively he tested the end of a log with an extended big toe, found the heat bearable, and poked the log farther into the sputtering campfire. A shower of cherry-red sparks shot upward as the wet wood struck the flames. Davin caught his breath and held back the barrage of curses that formed on his tongue as the fire flickered low.

"Burn," he urged, fearing he had completely smothered the blaze that had taken him an hour to start.

A breeze from the north that sought to transform the beads of water on his naked legs into ice whipped across the glowing embers. New tongues of yellow flame licked upward, sizzled against the log, and finally ate into the

wood. Inch by inch the blaze rose higher, radiating a new
wave of heat through the Jyotian thief who crouched shivering and miserable by the small fire.

"The gods have not totally abandoned me," Davin muttered as he opened the furs and let the warmth bask over
his chest.

His eyes lifted to the slate-gray sky overhead. The boiling
black clouds that had emptied an ocean of water atop his
head had passed. Although there was no indication the sun
would burn through the overcast, at least the sky no longer
threatened another drenching deluge.

"I should have been born a merman. Gills would have
served me better than lungs this past night and day." He
reached out and ran a hand over his clothing, which hung
draped from three sticks shoved into the soft ground. It
would soon be dry enough to wear, though Davin did not
relish the thought of donning doeskin jerkin and breeches
that now felt as stiff as uncured cowhide.

"I live—waterlogged to be sure—but I live." He shuddered.

The reaction came not from cold but from the memory
of the three demon riders he had eluded last night—and his
helplessness before their swords of crystalline fire. Davin
Anane had faced and won myriad battles in his young life.
He feared crossing steel with no man on the face of Raemllyn.
But the Faceless Ones?

How did a man battle demons with the strength of a
hundred and hope to emerge victorious? He shivered again,
unashamed of the terrifying chill flowing about his heart.
*What has Zarek Yannis unleashed upon this world? Is there
none powerful enough to face and destroy him and his
minions?*

Prince Felrad, the murdered Bedrich's true heir, pushed
into Davin's mind. Tymon had said the prince amassed an
army in the northern provinces.

Rumor also placed the prince and his meager forces in
the four corners of Raemllyn—all at the same moment.
Similar rumors declared that Felrad's head now adorned a
pike in Yannis' throne room, or that the prince rotted in the
usurper's dungeons.

And if Felrad does live? He is no more than a man.
Davin shook his head. In the all but forgotten past Kwerin
Bloodhawk and the mage Edan had defeated the dark wizard
Nnamdi and his legions of Faceless Ones. That had been
in another age, a time of giants and heroes when magicks
still ruled Raemllyn. No such heroes now strode across the
land.

Davin's gaze shifted back to the blaze and the flames,
which reminded him of those grotesque orbs of fire that
burned within the Faceless Ones' cowls. Could any man of
flesh and blood hope to stand against such demons?

No mere man or woman can . . .

Davin's thoughts stumbled. *Lijena!* She had stood and
faced three of the Faceless Ones and sent them screaming
into the night. How? Why? And the Blood Fountain the hell
riders had mentioned, what did that mean?

The rustle of grass to his right drew the last son of the
House of Anane from his dark ponderings. There staring at
him out of the shin-high prairie grass was a plump, fuzzy,
orange-and-white-striped, catlike creature with round eyes
as orange as its fur. The animal curled back its lips to expose
curving yellow fangs and emitted a sound that was somewhere between the yap of a small dog and the spitting hiss
of a large feline.

Then it was gone, scurrying back into the cover of the
thick grass.

Davin blinked; Goran One-Eye had killed a similar creature the morning Lijena had made off with their horses. Yet
in all his travels Davin had never seen or heard of such an
animal.

The pounding of hooves jerked his head about. Hand
dropping to his sword on the ground beside him, he yanked
the sleeping fur around his waist and tied the corners so
that he wouldn't stand naked before whoever was riding so
hard toward his position.

Cautiously, breath shallowing, Davin rose. He had eluded
the faceless hell riders once. Doing it twice hardly seemed
possible, especially here in the middle of this open grassland.

He sighed in nervous relief when he saw Lijena astraddle

a roan horse with a saddled bay in lead. The frosty-haired young woman raised an arm and waved.

"Ho, Davin," came her greeting. "See what I've brought!"

"Lijena!" He called out in unrestrained joy. She should have been days ahead of him, yet she now rode to rescue him from his seemingly endless trek. "Lijena, how? And Masur-Kell's demon?"

"Demon?" her oddly pitched question answered as she drew the roan to a halt beside the thief. "I've never been possessed of a demon! Though I'm liable to be possessed of the croup unless I warm myself by that fire. I was caught in a downpour a league back."

"The same that drenched me." Davin grinned and displayed his makeshift fur breechclout. He then held up his arms to help her from the saddle. "Come sit by the fire and dry yourself."

Lijena slid from the roan's back into his arms, pressing close enough for him to feel the intimate contours of the supple body beneath the soaked, baggy clothes of scarlet she wore. For an instant, her aquamarine eyes lifted, adance with an impish light. Then she wiggled past him and squatted on her heels by the campfire, rubbing her arms.

Both the roan and bay dropped their heads to the thick grass and began to chomp loudly. Assured the horses were content to graze rather than run off, Davin turned back to the campfire, still unable to believe Lijena had returned for him.

"What of your mare Orria? Did you ride her into the ground as you did Goran's and my mount?" He tilted his head toward the roan as he joined her by the blaze.

Lijena shrugged and rubbed at her arms. "Do you have any dry clothing? I'm chilled to the bone."

Davin reached out and tested his own clothing again. He felt spots of dampness here and there, but those would dry on his body just as well as they would dangling from the sticks.

"Let me dress, then you can have my furs while you dry your clothing."

Lijena's head slowly turned to him, and a coy hint of a

smile upturned the corners of her mouth. "Are you suggesting that I disrobe . . . here, before your eyes?"

"I'll avert my eyes." Davin's brow knitted. Lijena's tone lacked the indignation he had grown to expect from the woman. "You may do the same as I dress, if my nakedness offends your sensibilities."

"I see no need for you to dress." Lijena's long cool fingers reached out and rested on Davin's bare thigh, then taunted their way upward. "We are both chilled. Could we not warm each other . . . as man and woman?"

Davin grew more confused with each passing moment. Did the demon still possess her, urging her to sample the pleasures of the flesh? "When last we were together . . ."

"When last we were together," Lijena whispered, her exploring hand working inward, "there was not ample time."

Davin's eyes narrowed suspiciously; he eased her teasing fingers away. "Lijena, is it the demon's voice I hear? I want to believe this is you . . . but I am hard-pressed. You appeared out of nowhere astride a roan gelding rather than your Orria. And your clothes? These are sizes too large and are more suited to Goran's taste than . . ."

She leaned to him, quieting his questions as her mouth pressed to his and her fingers once again slipped up the interior of his thigh.

Davin's resolve melted. He had desired other women, lusted for them. Lijena awoke more than desire; why else would he follow her across half of Upper Raemllyn? His arms encircled her slender waist and drew her to him.

And in the next instant he thrust Lijena away as her flesh turned clammy, hardened, flowed.

Staring in horror, Davin watched the blonde's svelte frame ripple as though it had suddenly gone liquid. Ivory arms and legs swelled, taking on a ruddy hue. Frosty tresses as fine as silk from the Isle of Pthedm shriveled, coursed, and bled red.

The flowing flesh solidified, transformed into a muscle-hard hulk, and stretched the wet scarlet fabric to the point of ripping. Lijena—*her* body—was no more, replaced by—*his* body!

"Goran!" Davin shouted, then sputtered incoherently as he stared at the fiery-bearded, one-eyed giant and slowly moved his head from side to side in disbelief.

"Aye, it does appear I've returned." The Challing's paw-sized hands patted his chest and legs, then felt of his arms, making certain all the parts were in the proper places. He drew his scarlet eye patch from a pocket and covered the dark socket of his left eye.

"Goran . . . why . . . how could you do such a thing to me?" Davin sputtered on.

"Me?" Goran stared at his friend with an expression of total innocence. "'Twas not me! Nay, it was *Glylina*, a shameless wench. Lusty as a mink in rut, that one. Would that I could find such a woman on this miserable ball of clay!"

Davin found his senses and his tongue and his rage! At the top of his lungs he berated his friend until he finally gasped for breath.

"Such creative cursing. I am proud of you, boy. I knew you'd one day master the language." Goran laughed heartily as Davin sputtered again. "It is a pity I lack control over this wondrous ability. Another few minutes and I might have discovered secrets unknown to man."

"You slimy, *pletha*-loving son of a demon! How could you do such a thing to me?" Davin's wrath left him tongue-tied once again.

Goran shrugged. "One form is as good as another to me. I discovered that I had the knack for assuming female form when you abandoned me in that miserable little hamlet of Jurka. It pleased me to keep it. And why shouldn't I learn what it is like making love *as* a woman rather than *to* one? You weren't averse as long as you thought I was your precious Lijena. Where lies the real difference now?"

Davin stared at the bulging biceps, the thick chest, the hairy ears and bushy beard. "Do that to me again and I'll cut out your tongue and stuff it up your arse!"

"Had you first discovered me—how long ago? more than a year?—in female form, my friend, you would not harbor such absurd prejudices now." Goran shook his head. "I, as

Glylina, was simply being true to my nature—my Challing nature. For I am neither male nor female, nor even human, but a Challing."

Reason punched through Davin's anger, which only galled him all the more, for there was more than a seed of truth in what his changeling friend said. If he had come upon Goran in a female guise even half as comely as that of Lijena's, he would never have been able to think of him—her—it—in any other fashion.

But he hadn't. The first he'd seen of Goran had been as the burly, hulking male form, and Davin was forever locked into thinking of Goran One-Eye as "he."

"Come, Davin, cheer up. You might have enjoyed it almost as much as I would have. Curse this inability to control my form!" Goran stood, laughed, and slapped his friend on the back.

Davin's anger faded somewhat, but he didn't feel entirely secure in doing more than returning a sickly grin. "Goran, if you ever try to deceive me in this way again, I'll personally feed you to the wolves one small bite at a time."

"My control," lamented the Challing, "is faulty, but I see how it disturbs you. I will never knowingly gull you—unless circumstances so warrant. Now dress and let's be on our way. These grasslands offer little shelter should the sky decide to open again."

Unless circumstances so warrant. Davin rolled the phrase over in his mind, recognizing how little the Challing had limited himself with that wording. He also realized that it was the strongest commitment that he was likely to get from the red-haired giant.

While the Jyotian thief discarded his fur breechclout and dressed, Goran retrieved the roan and bay and led them back to the campfire.

"You did keep to Lijena's trail, didn't you?" Goran asked, then added hopefully, "Or perhaps the rains have washed the spoor away?"

"Her trail lies there." Davin pointed to a path of trampled grass that lead northward. "She's at least two days ahead of us now. Probably three. She gives her mount little rest."

Goran grunted as he handed Davin the bay's reins, then swung into the roan's saddle, glumly sitting there watching Davin bury the small campfire with dirt before mounting the bay.

"Goran," Davin asked as he mounted and nudged the horses northward, "a question. If you can adopt any shape you desire..."

"When the magicks are upon me," Goran cut in.

Davin acknowledged this and went on, saying, "Why can't you restore your lost eye?"

"I thought I had told you of the reason why the eye will never again appear like this one." Goran placed a callused thumb under his good eye and drew down the lower lid until bright pink showed.

"I don't remember..." Davin began, then stopped, silently cursing himself for so easily providing his friend the opportunity to add yet another tale to the mystery surrounding his missing eye.

"As you are undoubtedly aware, I lost my eye when, in this very form, I was forced to wrestle crocodiles in the war pits of the Suzeraine of Droos."

"Droos? Where's that?" Davin mumbled, not wishing to encourage the Challing.

Goran paid the Jyotian no heed. He had begun his story and would finish it, no matter how skeptical Davin became over trivial details.

"They had me by the short hairs, the Suzeraine's guards did. I'd been caught trying to filch her crown jewels. Alas, I made the mistake of attempting the theft while she wore them. How was I to know she was such a light sleeper?"

"Should have drugged her. I should be drugged," Davin lamented.

"Drugs wouldn't have worked. She had an official taster. Ah, that saucy wench had a taste to her, she did! But the Suzeraine was a suspicious bitch, always on her guard, and ordered Allina not only to sample her food but to lie in her bed to make certain there were neither poisons on the silk sheets nor odious creatures placed therein."

"Your eye," prompted Davin. "Why not restore it?"

"This is a complex tale of magicks and arcane lore," said Goran, as if explaining to a dim-witted child. "Allina was in the bed while the Suzeraine slept most uncomfortably in a nearby chair. How was I to know?"

"Yes, how," Davin answered dryly.

"The room was dark, and I took my pleasure in the bed, thinking this the best way of insuring the Suzeraine would sleep soundly."

"But it was Allina."

"Exactly. By the time I was finishing, the Suzeraine awoke and summoned her guards. Both Allina and I were seized for treason and crimes against the realm. Of the girl I know naught what happened, but I was foully cast into the war pits where I fought a variety of opponents, both human and other."

Goran shook his head as if in sad remembrance. "Those were evil times for me, friend Davin. Every day I battled and every day I grew weaker. They fed me swill. I took to devouring the creatures I slew, ripping raw haunches off their still quivering bodies and gorging myself until the guards stopped me. The taste of the warm blood still lingers. At times, I fall into slumber dreaming of it trickling down my chin, staining my beard."

"Thus is explained your lack of table manners," Davin commented and was ignored.

"I prevailed through my great strength and even greater cunning. I remember it as clearly as if it were yesterday. They cast me into the war pit, but instead of sandy floor, it had been flooded. Crocodiles swam maggot-thick in that water. I fought. The froth, the battle, the blood! One by one I killed the beasts until only a single crocodile remained—the grandfather of all fanged lizards! Terrible!"

"We agree on that."

"Then," said Goran, his voice lowering to a dramatic level, "it happened." The Challing's voice sank to a conspiratorial whisper and continued. "The huge water reptile opened its mighty jaws and snapped at me. One six-inch-long fang caught me on the side of the head—drove through and into my eye! Blinded!"

Goran dramatically lifted his eye patch and displayed the sunken pit. The patch fell back into place.

"Blind in one eye—that eye is lost forever! But I fought as I have never fought before or since. Anger lent strength to my already great sinews. I erupted in a frenzy of activity and caught the crocodile's small foreleg. I ripped it off and beat the beast to death with it!"

"A neat trick in deep water." Davin grimaced.

"I was *furious!*"

"But your eye. Why can't you restore it, if you can change your shape into," Davin swallowed hard, "that of Lijena when she has two perfectly fine orbs?"

"It has to do with where the fang entered my eye. In this form it is permanently damaged. No amount of restoration will return my vision." Goran hesitated, then added, "At least, I don't believe it will."

Davin drew a deep breath and turned to his friend. "I have my own tale to tell, though it's not as fanciful as your own. Last night I faced Zarek Yannis' hell riders."

"Oh?" Goran lifted one bushy eyebrow in open disbelief.

"True. Three of them—no doubt the three we saw conversing with Lijena—found my trail." Davin recounted the details of the encounter and his eventual escape beneath the water. "I lost them by cleverness."

"Drowning yourself was a very clever way of eluding them." Goran sucked at his teeth. "And you doubt I battled for my life in the death pits of the Suzeraine of Dalos."

"I thought it was the *war* pits of the Suzeraine of *Droos?*" Davin replied without protest to Goran's doubting of his encounter with the Faceless Ones.

In truth, Goran probably believed his account of the attack, but the changeling would never admit it—not when he had such a ripe opportunity for needling a friend. *And if he doesn't believe me,* Davin thought, *can I find fault? I find it hard to believe myself!*

"Droos, Dalos, they have much the same ring to a Challing's ear," Goran shrugged, then shouted, "Davin, look!"

The Jyotian's hand dropped to his sword hilt, ready to wrench steel from sheath. Then he relaxed when he saw the

Challing holding out one meaty paw, examining it as if he'd never seen his own hand before.

"Isn't this a wondrous feat?" Goran asked. The brawny hand shifted and flowed, altering form and becoming thinner, whiter, more slender and feminine.

The transformation began at the fingertips and worked up the knuckles and palm to the wrist and up the arm, where it stopped just short of the elbow. Sweat beaded on Goran's forehead, as if he battled tremendously strong foes.

"The change. I can't make it go past my forearm. But it is quite the trick, isn't it? That potion of Masur-Kell's allowed me to regain some small measure of my former magical skills."

The Challing sounded self-satisfied, and Davin had to agree that it was a talent that might prove useful in the future if properly applied—and not used as a prank.

Davin cast a sidelong glance at his friend and had to smile. Goran's face contorted with the strain of attempting still another transformation. This time the Challing lifted his eye patch. He shook his head and even reached up to the empty socket, then pulled his finger away quickly to hide the motion. Apparently his powers did not extend to restoring his lost vision. In disgust he dropped the patch back into place, then glanced at Davin to see if his fellow adventurer had noticed.

Davin rode on, eyes ahead on Lijena's trail. Perhaps one day Goran's power would grow strong enough to conjure up a second eyeball—but not this day. Which was perhaps just as well; there was nothing for the Challing to see except league upon league of featureless prairie that stretched about them like a sea of grass.

chapter
10

"WE'LL HAVE TO STOP SOON," Goran grumbled, his one eye peering at the sky overhead disdainfully. A low growl rumbled in his throat. "Bah! It's getting darker."

"That's what happens when the sun goes down. 'Tis a daily occurrence, in case you've not noticed ere now." Davin leaned low in the saddle and squinted at the ground below to assure himself they still followed Lijena's northward trail.

"There should be at least an hour 'fore sunset. The darkness has nothing to do with the sun's setting. It's these damnable clouds." The Challing ignored his companion's sarcasm and cocked his head from side to side. "It'll rain soon. Either we find shelter or we'll be drenched—as drenched as you were after you went sleepwalking and tumbled into that stream in the wood."

"I told you I fled the Faceless Ones." Davin gritted his teeth. Goran refused to believe the hell riders had sought him that night two days past.

Righting himself, the surviving son of the House of Anane glanced up, following the changeling's lead. Ominous clouds of boiling black blanketed the sky from horizon to horizon. Davin cursed under his breath. Lijena's spoor was hard enough to follow as it was. The last thing he needed was a storm to erase all trace of where her horse passed.

"We *should* seek shelter, Davin," Goran repeated. "When these clouds open up it'll . . ."

"If it rains, it rains! There's nothing either of us can do about it. Nor will we be finding any shelter in this desolate grassland. Do you see a tree or even a bush?" Davin made no attempt to lessen the edge to his voice. As though it were not enough to contend with the demon possessing Lijena and hell riders brought forth from Raemllyn's ancient past, the elements now conspired against him.

"And there's a stillness to the air I don't fancy," Goran continued, paying little heed to the Jyotian's sharp tongue. "There's not even a hint of a breeze to stir the grass. Have you noticed it grows more difficult to breathe with—"

A peal of thunder drowned the Challing's words. To the west, closer than Davin liked, jagged legs of lightning danced from the clouds' dark bellies and walked across the prairie. Thunder crashed a heartbeat after.

"The gods argue," Goran muttered glumly. "Yehseen hurls his fiery insults at Black Qar for stealing his favorite concubine. And Qar? Who knows what evil the Black One conjures? Perhaps Death will wrestle its father from his lofty throne this eve."

A heavy raindrop splattered onto Davin's forehead, and lightning danced again, this time to the north. Another drop of water feeling as large as a kelii's egg smacked into the back of the thief's hand.

"There might be fires if Yehseen's anger doesn't subside." Goran stood in his stirrups and glanced about them.

Eye-searing bolts leaped to and fro among the clouds on all sides now. Then the rain came—a torrential wall of water fell from the sky as the clouds released their heavy burden. And with the downpour, the winds, howling and whipping.

"There goes the trail!" Goran shouted over Minima's furious roar. "What now?"

Davin stiffened; did he detect a hint of relief in his friend's

voice? Did Goran expect him to abandon Lijena because of
a storm!

Turning to the massive Challing, Davin called out, "We
ride north, you ugly lout! We ride north!"

Leaning into the lashing wind and rain, Davin Anane
urged his bay forward with heels to flanks.

Davin blinked and wiped a hand across his eyes. The
effort was ineffectual; rain blurred his vision the instant his
fingers dropped. Nor could he locate the flash of light he
thought he had seen. All that remained was the darkness
and the constant rain.

"Davin, we must stop for the night," Goran called to
him. "If not for ourselves, then for the horses.

"Soon," was all that the Jyotian thief answered.

In truth, he knew that the Challing was right. The horses
did need rest. Free of saddles and forelegs tethered, all they
had to do was duck their heads to the wind and sleep.

However, there would be no rest for their riders this night.
Although the fury of the breaking storm had passed, the
rain still fell in buckets. The best Davin and Goran would
be able to do without proper shelter would be to squat on
the muddy ground with sleeping furs over their heads and
feel miserable.

Davin peered into the inky darkness ahead. Did he fool
himself with false hope? Lijena's days-old trail had been
hard enough to follow before the storm. Now it was totally
lost. What chance was there in ever finding the demon-
ridden woman again? Especially here in these northern lands,
which neither Goran nor himself knew.

*Perhaps Goran is right. What word or sign has Lijena
ever given to indicate she needs or even wants our help ...
my help?* Davin bit at his lower lip in frustration. In fact,
the young blonde had done everything possible to discourage
him, including attempting to run him through with sword
and dirk.

It's not Lijena, but the demon that seeks my life, Davin
told himself. *But why? Is there some link between—What?*

He swiped at his face once again and stared ahead. By

all the gods, he swore he had seen a light blinking. Now it was gone.

"Goran, tell what you see ahead of us."

"Leagues of water-logged riding with the fool of fools for a companion," the Challing replied. "What am I supposed to see?"

"I thought I saw a light . . . twice now," Davin answered. "Perhaps someone camps ahead."

"Someone camped ahead? Your eyes play tricks on you. Who would roam this grassland? Brigands? Ha! Slim pickings for highwaymen in this god-forsaken land! Or perhaps its the burning orbs of Yannis' Faceless Ones that you see ablinking at you out of the night. You'll not find a stream to fall into here. Not that it matters. How could either of us be more wet than we are now?"

Davin shivered in spite of himself. He had not considered the hell riders. His right hand eased to the hilt of his longsword.

"Lights!" Goran snorted. "Next you'll be telling me its the legendary spires of A'bre you see rising . . . Nyuria's arse!" Then the Challing sputtered, "There *are* lights ahead! There, see? Three of them!"

"Three? Nay, five! No, four!" Davin shouted back at his friend. There were three lights now, then six, and they moved, although none were in pairs. "Lanterns, Goran, they're lanterns. There *is* a camp ahead."

"Friends or foes?" Goran said with sudden caution.

"You noted the lack of rewards for highwaymen in this prairie," Davin replied. "'Tis probably a caravan."

"Aye, or mayhaps soldiers bivouacked in the storm."

"Yannis' troops?" Davin caught his friend's meaning. "There's but one way to find out—we ride in slowly, and hope we can see them before they see us."

Goran simply grunted as his heels nudged the roan into an easy trot. Davin did likewise while his gaze remained on the moving lanterns ahead.

"Whoever they are, they make no effort to hide their presence," Goran said. "I can see a score of lights now."

As did Davin; many of the yellow glows remained stationary as though coming from windows of . . .

"Huata! Davin, 'tis a band of Huata." Goran One-Eye flashed a broad grin at his human companion. "Luck is upon us!"

The Challing was right. No others traveled in such square-constructed wagons as those Davin now discerned except Raemllyn's nomadic Huata.

"Luck?" Davin smiled at his friend. "I thought the Huata disgusted you—tricksters and thieves? That it was a Huata who robbed you of your left eye?"

"Davin, how could you say such? The Huata are but simple entertainers who roam the length and breadth of this world bringing joy to all they come upon. The Huata are like a family to me," Goran protested.

"And leaving all with lighter purses," Davin answered. Not that he minded. Huata mentors had instructed the Jyotian in the finer points of his chosen profession—that of a thief!

"Lovely Jajhana finally smiles," Goran said. "That bitch goddess has frowned o'erlong at us. Now we can sleep warm—and perhaps with something soft and wiggly and willing."

"You're staying in your male form?" asked Davin.

"It suits me for the nonce not to become Glylina," said Goran, preferring that reply to the truth, which was that he lacked the control of his magicks to change form at will.

With their approach cloaked in darkness and the constant drumming of rain, the two practically stood beside a Huata guard before they were noticed. The man who huddled bundled in a slicker nearly dropped the lantern he held when Davin said, "Good eve, sir."

"We are a peaceful band of travelers," the startled man sputtered the Huata's usual disclaimer. "We mean no harm. Send away your soldiers and allow us to pass through this land unmolested."

"Varaza?" Davin squinted and leaned toward the man.

The man lifted his lantern high. "Davin? Davin Anane? By Yehseen's shaft, it is! Aye, and Goran One-Eye with ye!" the Huata cried in true pleasure. Then he turned and called out to the five circled wagons, "Hide the women! No, hide the silver, *then* hide the women! We have thieves for guests this night!"

In his next breath, the Huata leader summoned two men to care for Davin and Goran's horses. He turned back to his two old friends as they dismounted. "I know not what brings you this far north, but there's food and warmth in my wagon."

Goran slapped the smaller man's back. "I'll take a triple serving of both!"

"And perhaps a gallon or two of mulled wine to chase away the inner chill, if I remember your thirst correctly," Varaza answered as he led the pair to his wagon and waved an arm up toward its door.

Davin climbed the three steps, opened the door, then froze when he saw the Huata had another guest waiting within.

Goran shoved him into the wagon, grumbling, "Isn't it enough to force me to tramp through the rain? Now you force me to stand in it!"

But Goran, too, fell silent when his eye alighted on Varaza's guest.

"Davin, my brother!" A man dressed in silk blouse, black satin breeches, and boots that rose to cover his calves, pushed from a pile of cushions to thrust out an open hand toward the thief.

Davin ignored the proffered hand, although his gaze never left the man's face. "Varaza, since when is Huata hospitality extended to butchers?"

"Davin, Davin, the years have left you unchanged. How long has it been, five years? Six? Seven?" The man smiled and shook his head when Davin offered no answer. "Come and sit beside me. Enjoy a cup of this delicious wine. Stolen, I suspect, from the best of cellars. Am I right, Varaza?"

"Lord Berenicis, it is our custom to offer shelter to any requiring it. I had not known there was animosity between you and my good friend Davin Anane. I would have..."

"Animosity?" Berenicis laughed and brushed aside a strand of sandy hair that fell into his eyes. "We bear each other no ill, do we, Davin? Are we not both fugitives? You from Jyotis and I from Zarek Yannis?"

"There is a difference, Berenicis." Davin controlled the seething hatred that built within his breast. "I was never given the name 'Blackheart' by Jyotis' citizenry. You ruled our homeland with a bloody hand. I had hoped Yannis had taken your head when his armies marched through Jyotis."

"*My* homeland, brother, not yours. My land. You were not born to rule Jyotis as was I. Had you been, you might have an understanding of how such titles as 'Blackheart' are given to persons in positions of responsibility by the ignorant peasants they serve." Berenicis sank back onto the cushions and sipped at his goblet of wine while studying Davin through cold, gray eyes. "As to my head, Yannis offers a thousand gold bists to the man who brings it to him on a pike."

"The usurper has placed a price on the heads of all those with Bedrich's blood in their veins," Varaza said, handing Davin and Goran cloths with which to dry themselves and then waving an arm toward the cushions scattered about on the floor.

Davin sat as far from Berenicis as possible within the cramped confines of the Huata wagon. He noted nervous uneasiness in Varaza's dark eyes, as though the Huata leader fully recognized the potential danger abrew here.

"And what of the taxes you used to break the backs of your subjects? Is that the way *responsible persons* serve Jyotis?" Davin made no attempt to disguise his contempt.

Had he met Berenicis outside, the man who was single-handedly responsible for the destruction of the House of Anane would now lie dead in the mud. Here within Varaza's wagon Lord Berenicis the Blackheart was protected by Huata hospitality as were Goran and Davin himself.

"Gold and silver are needed to raise an army to protect Jyotis from Zarek Yannis." Berenicis glanced at the thief over the top of his goblet. "Perhaps if I had been as hard as you imagined, my army would have been large enough to have withstood the usurper's forces, and Jyotis would still be a free state."

"Wine, Davin? Goran?" Varaza poured two goblets of wine like a man floating oil on stormy waters.

The Challing downed his glass and held it out for more. Davin's went untouched.

"I have never seen such foul weather," Berenicis said in a conversational tone, "not since Bedrich died at the Battle of Kressia. The skies opened then, and the gods wept for weeks. You would have thought Yannis had sense enough to take those heavenly tears as an ill omen. Instead he claimed the gods spat on Bedrich's memory."

"Speak not of Bedrich," snapped Davin.

"I am merely attempting to pass the time," Berenicis answered coolly. "You are remarkably sensitive on a number of issues, aren't you? The weather is no fit topic; mere mention of our late High King Bedrich sends you into a paroxysm of anger. Should we discuss lawbreaking?"

"Those charges against me were trumped up. You sought my head for reasons having nothing to do with theft of the High Chamberlain's jewel case."

Berenicis made a vague gesture with his hand and smiled, as if this were past and now meant nothing. "The jewels were incidental, the guards you so foully killed were closer to being members of the family than mere soldiers."

"Then this is why you fled Jyotis," spoke up Goran, working on his fourth goblet of mulled wine. "I see it clearly now. This is the swine who ruled Jyotis and falsely accused you of murder. You fled, he was deposed by Yannis, and . . ."

Goran stopped in mid-sentence when he noticed Berenicis' cold, gray eyes turn to him. If the Death God Qar had eyes, they were the same hue as this Jyotian lord's, and contained the same lack of human emotion. Goran chose to finish the remainder of his wine rather than continue speaking.

"Your traveling companion is what I'd expect from one such as you, Davin," said Berenicis. "Rude, brutish, uneducated, but he does appear to have a strong sword arm. You are, no doubt, the brains of this thieving duo, and he is the brawn. Does it work well for you?"

"At least we do our own thieving and don't rely on squads

of soldiers to take it from poor peasants."

"Ah, then you rob from the rich because they are the only ones with gold." Berenicis laughed. "I *knew* you were the brains. That oaf would probably be out robbing blind men and beggars without you, Davin."

Goran's face turned as red as his beard. He started to rise, but Varaza's hand cautioned him to do nothing. The Huata were brigands and thieves on their own, but they observed strict rules of honor when it came to the treatment of their guests. Violence between those sharing their wagons was strictly forbidden. And it was death to any man, or woman, who violated that custom.

"It is a pity you did not find a more charming companion. He would have been a great help in interceding with Bedrich on your behalf."

Davin fought to keep his calm. Berenicis attempted to anger him. Nothing had changed between the two. Davin had sought Bedrich's aid, and the High King had turned away from him, for which Davin had never forgiven the man. But the point was moot. Zarek Yannis had usurped the throne from Bedrich and left Bedrich's body impaled for crows to eat. Berenicis' heavy-handed rule had nothing to do with Bedrich's murder. The Blackheart had aggressively plundered his own kingdom even while High King Bedrich ruled.

"Food," said Varaza. "You must eat. Try some of this." He indicated a covered tray on a small table. "My youngest daughter prepared it for Berenicis, but there is enough for all."

Varaza looked skeptically at Goran, as though estimating the flaming-haired giant's appetite, then shrugged it off.

Berenicis did not touch the food, nor did Davin. After questioning glances at both men, Goran proceeded to methodically clean the tray.

"Really, Davin, my long lost brother," said Berenicis with a hint of a sneer in his voice. "Jyotis has not been the same without you."

"I am sure it hasn't been the same since you were driven from the kingdom."

"Petty, very petty. I expect more from you. Times have changed for the both of us; we should bury old hates. We are both Jyotian, after all. That must count for something, if you choose to deny any other bond between us."

"The country of our birth is *all* we have in common," Davin answered firmly.

Berenicis shook his head, then laughed. "You go too far in that. But perhaps there is fresh ground on which we can meet. Since leaving Jyotis, I have sought whatever aid I could to depose Yannis."

"You seek the Velvet Throne for your own," accused Davin. Simply being so near Berenicis awoke memories he had carefully locked away in the dark recesses of his mind. Only the knowledge of how seriously the Huata took their hospitality prevented him from drawing his dagger and opening Berenicis' throat from ear to ear.

The dashing, some might even say handsome, Berenicis lounged back with all the grace of a young lion as he returned Davin's gaze. It seemed incredible that one such as he could have legitimately earned the appellation of Blackheart, yet Davin knew full well that such was the case. He had run afoul of the former ruler too many times. And now Berenicis had the temerity to claim a kinship—or at least a meeting of purpose.

"It seems farfetched that we might share the same goals," Davin said and took a swallow from his goblet. It burned his stomach. Or was the fire merely his own bile?

Berenicis shook his head and smiled almost sadly. "The old memories are still strong in you. In myself, also, I'm afraid. But we *can* be allies, *should* be allies in these troubled times. I have never sought the Velvet Throne for my own. Regaining Jyotis' freedom is all I desire."

"With you ruling again, no doubt," Goran muttered.

Varaza hastily refilled the Challing's mug to keep him occupied.

Davin held his tongue, but frowned skeptically. Berenicis had never openly sought the Velvet Throne; however, it was well-known that he coveted the High King's seat in Kavindra.

Noticing his fellow Jyotian's expression, Berenicis chuckled. He shook his head and reached down and pulled forth a sword wrapped in oiled leather.

"I seek to reunite this blade with its sheath—for Prince Felrad," he said.

"Felrad?" It was Davin's turn to shake his head. "I have heard the prince died more than a year ago—killed by Yannis' forces in Sarngan."

"Felrad lives. He was sorely wounded, true, but he survived and is now stronger than ever."

"Where is his base?" asked Goran. "It has been some time since Prince Felrad held court."

"That is both his strength and weakness," admitted Berenicis. "He moves constantly, always a step ahead of Yannis' troops. But as he moves through Raemllyn, he recruits, lets people see that he lives, and stirs new hope for a better future."

"And what concern is Felrad to me—or you?" Davin tried to sound unconcerned in spite of his racing heart. *Felrad lives!*

Berenicis cradled the sword in his arms like a baby. "A future under the rule of Zarek Yannis should be of concern to everyone—even *thieves*. Felrad is acknowledged heir to the throne: our only hope for a united force that will rise against the usurper. I work to restore the crown to that heir."

"And he has promised you Jyotis?" Davin stated more than he questioned.

"My dear brother, am I not Jyotis' rightful ruler? Yet to depose Yannis I would accept far less in way of reward."

Davin said nothing. Berenicis always played the deep game, manipulating courtly intrigues and pitting one faction against another for his personal gain. If he supported Felrad, it was because he saw the prince as an easier target than Yannis: use Felrad's wide public support, and then, after he assumed the Velvet Throne, assassinate him. Altruism had no meaning to Lord Berenicis the Blackheart.

"Felrad camps some leagues to the south. I know naught of his plans. He moves daily, and I find him only through the Huata, who provide a marvelous communications network." Berenicis inclined his head slightly in Varaza's direction. "Prince Felrad has entrusted this marvelous weapon to my care. Here, examine it."

Berenicis passed the oiled leather package to Davin, who hesitantly accepted it, fearing it trapped.

As he unwrapped it, however, he found no clever trap. The blued-steel sword within possessed a well-honed edge, balanced beautifully in his hand, and felt as if it had been designed for him and him alone.

"A good sword, but nothing special that I see."

"Examine it more closely," urged Berenicis. The expression on his handsome face caused Davin to minutely study the hilt, the pommel, the shank.

On the blade he found faint runes, cuneiform writings worn down from years of polishing. Davin puzzled through the first few of the runes, not having the need to read such since his days in Jyotis. When he translated the third, he did his best to mask his surprised reaction.

Berenicis laughed openly at him.

"Yes, Davin, this is the Sword of Kwerin, Bloodhawk, Raemllyn's first High King. Swung by true heroes through the centuries, this blade has resulted in more victories than any other device in our history—including conjurations of the Faceless Ones."

"How did you come by this?" Davin's surprise sent his heart pounding. Kwerin Bloodhawk had ordered this sword forged by his master sorcerer Edan. Legends told of Kwerin meeting entire legions and vanquishing them singlehandedly, using this blade.

Davin hefted the blade again and shook his head in wonder. Myth. It had to be myth. This was nothing more than a finely wrought sword. Of magicks he felt none.

"Felrad discovered it."

"Why give it to you?"

"I am merely the temporary keeper. I seek its complement, its sheath. When fully sheathed, the blade is renewed and glows with magicks. Felrad has reason to believe that the old stories of Kwerin defeating hundreds—thousands!—singlehandedly, using this blade, are fact."

"Where is the sheath?" asked Goran. "Felrad must know that you will never return the blade to him once you unite the pair."

"Ah, but you are wrong, hairy one. Felrad believes the opposite—and it is truth. Once the blade and sheath are joined, I *will* return them to Felrad. With him lies my destiny. Or so it is spoken."

Berenicis glanced toward Varaza, who solemnly nodded. Davin wondered if the Huata had a larger stake in this than was apparent, and on whose side did they toil?

"It is said," Davin replied, "that this blade can slice through any substance, even the hardest armor or densest stone. You would give up such?"

"I am not the monster your mind conjures, Davin. My allegiances are firmly sided with Felrad. He trusts me, and he is not wrong in doing so." Berenicis leaned forward, hands on knees and face earnest. "Help me—help Felrad! Varaza and his band and I journey to the northwest, to find Lorennion."

"Lorennion?" cut in Goran. "This name is familiar. What place is this?"

"Who," explained Berenicis. "Lorennion is a master sorcerer rumored to hold the sheath. I have been given the mission of taking it from him. For Felrad."

"Lorennion," mused Davin. "The name, now that you have mentioned it, prods old memories. He stays distant from the routes of man. Hides in the forests or mountains. To the northwest?"

"To Agda's foreboding mountains and forests," said Berenicis. "'Tis a wild, virgin land. Little is known about it. But I go there for Felrad—my prince."

Goran and Davin exchanged glances. Berenicis Blackheart emphasized his devotion and loyalty overmuch, a sure sign he lied through his perfect white teeth.

"Felrad becomes a force to be reckoned with," said Berenicis, "and with this sword in his hand, not even Zarek Yannis and his pet wizard Payat'Morve can stand before him long. Help us, Davin. You are clever, and your strong arm can be a boon to this mission."

"It pleases me Felrad still lives and opposes Yannis. I have no love for that tyrant. But you make your request at a poor time. I have other duties pledged, other missions to perform."

"More important than saving all of Raemllyn from Yannis?" prodded Berenicis. He took the Sword of Kwerin from Davin and gently wrapped it in the oiled leather, as if he handled something alive. "What mission could be more urgent? Or would bring you so far north?"

"I do not spy for Yannis, if that's what you're implying," snapped Davin.

"Davin! Never would I even tender a moment's thought on such an awful thing."

Davin glared at Berenicis. The hatred between them still lived and writhed like a poisonous snake. The surface of that blood feud had been hidden cleverly enough, but the maggoty underbelly of the animosity remained—and would until one of them lay dead awaiting Black Qar's guidance to Peyneeha.

"The quest I have undertaken does not conflict with yours. Rest easy on that score," Davin said.

"The Huata have room for you and your hairy friend. Don't you, Varaza?"

"Aye, that we do, Lord Berenicis." To Davin the Huata leader said, "We have much to discuss, also. I would know of your travels. Have you camped with other Huata bands? If so how do they fare in these dark times? And," Varaza said, a twinkle in his eyes, "you have yet to see my second daughter Reanna. Even among such a beautiful race as the Huata, she is an exceptional beauty. And she talks of you. She has heard the stories told around the campfires."

"She knows of Davin?" asked Goran. "And still she wants to meet him in the flesh? Beautiful your daughter might be, Varaza, but it is a pity she is dim-witted."

"Don't mind him," Davin said. He was tempted sorely to accept the Huata leader's generous offer. But Davin would not abandon Lijena so easily. "We cannot linger. For the night, your hospitality is welcomed. But we would burden you if we stayed longer."

The ritual refusal was given, and Varaza sorrowfully accepted it. At least the Huata's reactions were honest. Of Berenicis, he had his doubts; had the Blackheart ever dealt honestly in his miserable life? Still, the man had provided much information to ponder at length.

Felrad lived! That was good. The prince would soon enough spawn an army capable of toppling Zarek Yannis, of that Davin was certain. Felrad was not only the legitimate heir to the Velvet Throne, he possessed a charisma needed in a high king. People instinctively loved and followed him.

That made Berenicis' motives all the murkier to Davin. Felrad was all that Berenicis was not: honest, straight-forward, a good ruler who felt the concerns of the ruled.

"You are needed," said Berenicis.

"What concern is it of mine who sits on the Velvet Throne?" snapped Davin, tired of Berenicis' insistence. "Yannis is distant enough not to bother me. Felrad is a good man, but has hard years ahead to regain his birthright. What do I gain from all this?"

"You speak the words you brand me with—personal gain? Is it not enough to dethrone a tyrant?"

For a fleeting moment Davin almost believed Berenicis' claims. But the instant passed as he considered all that the Blackheart had done to Jyotis, to his family. Such sadism and personal ambition did not vanish overnight, nor in the pursuit of an alleged higher cause of duty to Raemllyn. Berenicis fought for Berenicis and no one else.

"Goran and I ride north with the dawn."

Berenicis appeared indifferent now, and Varaza showed Davin and Goran to a supply wagon, where they spent the night tossing and turning in troubled sleep.

chapter
11

DAVIN RAN A GENTLE HAND along the bay's flank, soothing the horse with whispers as he squatted and worked his palm down the right hind leg to the shin. His fingers gingerly explored a knot half the size of a kelii's egg and the inch-long, red gash atop it half a hand above the animal's ankle.

"Jajhana be damned!" The thief cursed the luck the Goddess of Chance and Fortune had doled out during the night. "The swelling's as hard as a rock."

"It's as I said, Davin." This from Varaza who stood beside his Jyotian friend. "One of the other horses kicked your mount during the night."

Davin stood, frowning at the injury and sucking at his cheeks. He then glanced at the Huata holding the gelding. "Ruggo, let me see him walk a bit."

The lanky man in a flowered blouse nodded and led the bay forward ten feet, then turned and walked back to Davin. The thief's expression darkened with each step the gelding took.

"He favors the injured leg, but the limp is slight," Ruggo offered. "Give him three or four days, and the leg will be as good as new."

"Three or four days," Davin muttered, trying to contain his frustration.

"Ruggo will rub down the leg with liniment, sprinkle sulfur into the cut, and bandage it." Varaza combed fingers through his shaggy black hair as he leaned down and examined the bay's rear leg. "As Ruggo said, the leg should be fine in three or four days."

"But we don't have . . ."

"It seems the gods frown on your mission, brother." Lord Berenicis' voice cut short Davin's lament. "Perhaps it is an omen that you should forsake your quest and join forces with us for the sake of Raemllyn and our homeland."

Davin's gaze shot up to the man mounted on a sleek black steed. A smug smile twisted Berenicis' lips as he brushed wind-blown, sandy hair back from his forehead. "My offer of last eve remains open to you and that one-eyed bear you call a friend, Davin. Felrad has need of seasoned sword arms."

Anger, old hates that had festered over the years, boiled within Davin Anane. The Blackheart's smirk? Was there more to the bay's injured leg than one horse kicking another? Had Berenicis decided other methods might sway his course when words had failed? Davin's right hand crept toward the pommel of his longsword. *Here and now, Berenicis, you shall pay in full for all you have taken from me!*

A viselike hand clamped firmly about Davin's wrist, holding him like steel. Davin's eyes darted to the left. Goran stared at him, the Challing's head moving slowly from side to side.

"The Huata code," the changeling warned. "I'll not let you kill yourself, and probably me along with you. Dying is such a poor way to begin a new day."

Davin jerked his arm away and turned to the Huata leader. "Varaza, you have horses, and we have gold. Name your price for a fresh mount, and I'll pay thrice the sum. Goran, show our friend the pouches you won in Jurka."

The Challing stood motionless. A soft green light shifted across his single eye as he stared at Varaza, then looked up at Berenicis.

"I do not need to see the color of your gold, Davin. Thrice the price?" The Huata chief's enthusiastic voice dissipated Davin's pondering of the witch-fire aplay in the changeling's orb. "Perhaps we can strike a bargain."

Davin smiled. Among the nomadic Huata, Varaza was known for his love of horseflesh, especially that acquired in the still of night while its owner slept. But the small man *was* Huata himself, and there was nothing a Huata loved more than gold.

"Varaza!" Berenicis' stern voice, as cold as Minima's winter breath, called to the band's leader.

Varaza glanced at the deposed Jyotian ruler. The Huata seemed to cringe and shrink beneath the man's scowl. When he turned back to Davin, he shook his head.

"Friend Davin, the price you offer is generous, but I must refuse. The horses I have are all broken to the harness and needed for our long journey to Agda. They are not meant for a saddle."

"Five times a fair price, Varaza, for one horse." Davin upped his bid.

"You heard our Huata host, Davin. He has no horses for sale," Berenicis said. "However, I'm certain Varaza will offer you a place in one of the wagons for the day. We'll reach an inn near the Bay of Pilisi this eve. You might find a horse there."

Davin said nothing.

"Or you and that gorilla in human form can continue on your way, riding double. Then, by night you should have two lame mounts," Berenicis said with an amused smile. "Either way, make up your mind. We have wasted too much time this morn and must be on our way."

Waving Varaza after him, Berenicis reined the black around and rode toward the Huata leader's wagon. Davin stared after the two, wondering what strands the Sitala wove to bind nomad to blackhearted swine.

* * *

"Admit it, Davin," said Goran One-Eye, "this is far better than sitting astraddle a horse and being bounced along and wearing calluses on our backsides!"

Goran lounged back in a deep cushion and supported himself on one elbow while he popped a freshly baked morsel of bread into his mouth. He belched, then washed the bread down with a deep draught of ale.

Davin shook his head in wonder at how the Challing managed to keep from spilling the ale over beard and chest as Varaza's supply wagon lurched over a rock hidden in the shin-high grass.

"And these fine new clothes," Goran added after another swig of ale. "Even though we paid Ruggo twice their value, they are warm . . . and the Huata *do* have exceptional taste when it comes to the blending of colors."

The Challing glanced down, proudly admiring the purple-and-red-striped shirt he wore. Like his black pants, the gaudy blouse was at least a size too small and was hard pressed to contain his bulk.

Davin's own shirt of yellow silk, speckled with large orange polka-dots, brought little relief to the eyes. But the Jyotian did have to admit that the woolen breeches and the fleece-lined coats he and Goran now wore were well-suited for the approaching winter.

"We'll obtain proper clothing when we come upon another town," Davin mumbled as he stared at the featureless prairie from out of the open rear of the supply wagon.

"So glum!" Goran shook his head and guzzled down another healthy portion of ale. "We're warm, we've food and drink, and we still travel northward. Our luck has changed, lad!"

"The only good thing about this is that Berenicis rides at the head of the column like some legion commander," grumbled Davin. "I would slit his throat if he insisted on riding here with us. I can stomach only so much of his arrogance."

"This hatred runs deep within you. Far deeper than I suspected when I heard you mention Berenicis in the past." The Challing studied his friend with his one good eye.

The bloodshot orb began to dance with witch-fire. Davin

turned away from that penetrating gaze.

"Yes," Goran mused aloud, "deeper than I suspected. I sense it."

"You don't have any sense," Davin said.

"Alas, you may be correct in that." Goran nodded and chased his words with ale. "Why else am I out here in the wilderness, getting my arse all rubbed red and raw from a saddle, having my clothes drenched by rains, freezing to death in the most primitive of surroundings, and enduring the companionship of a curmudgeon when I might be enjoying the softer, more intimate pleasures of women in any of Raemllyn's fair cities?"

"You can content yourself at the inn this eve," Davin replied, noting the afternoon shadows grew longer with each passing minute.

Goran downed the last of his ale and tossed the mug over his shoulder into the wagon. It landed against a trunk and rattled around, but the Challing took no notice.

"Do you think Berenicis told the truth when he spoke of the caravansary and the new horses? And what of Varaza's ties to Jyotis' deposed lord?"

"You tell me," Davin said, remembering the witch-fire and the strange look Goran had given Blackheart and the Huata leader that morn. "I saw the magicks adance in your eye this morning. It was as though you saw something beyond the sight of human eyes."

"I did! I had just swallowed the last of Masur-Kell's potion." Goran turned a now fire-sparking eye toward the Jyotian. He said slowly with trancelike steadiness, "Truth has always come from Varaza—but fear Berenicis' corruption. He moves the Huata to other ways."

Davin's brow knitted. "Has the potion transformed you into a seer?"

"Bitter enemies sit in the same room and discuss matters like long-lost brothers. More in common have they than mutual hatred..."

Davin shot Goran a look filled with pure hatred. "Hold your tongue, you ugly lout! Berenicis and I have nothing in common except..."

Goran sat staring into space, his eye unblinking and aglow

with witch-fire. Davin waved a hand before his friend's face; no change came to the Challing's dull expression.

"Ere Minima breathes her sweet breath of spring they shall draw their blades in conflict . . . but no Jyotian blood shall be spilled . . . though the blood of many will flow like a fountain . . . From a sea of red will rise a hero who one day . . . One day shall . . ." Goran's monotone voice droned on.

"Goran?" Davin grasped the changeling by the shoulders and shook him. In all their times together he had never seen the red-haired giant so possessed. "Goran? Goran?"

"What?" Goran blinked, the witch-fire gone from his single eye. "Davin? I admitted my lack of sense, do you now attempt to shake some into my head?"

Davin released those massive shoulders and sank back with a sigh of relief. "What happened to you?"

"Huh?" Perplexed furrows etched across the Challing's forehead. "Nothing happened to me."

"Nothing? Don't you remember what you just said?" Seeing that Goran did not, Davin quickly detailed the return of the witch-fire and the changeling's uttered words. "Has Masur-Kell's potion given you the *sight?* Do you now possess a third eye?"

"Third eye?" Goran lifted thick fingers to explore his forehead. "Oh? You mean can I see the future. I can't remember. I've been locked in human form for too long. I've forgotten what powers I do possess. We Challings are amazing beings, capable of feats beyond human imagination."

Davin turned from his friend in exasperation. Magicks had been astir, of that he was certain. but as to the meaning of Goran's utterances? He shook his head. He had no idea if the Challing had experienced a true vision or if his mind had been simply addled by Masur-Kell's potion.

The hollow sound of galloping hooves drew Davin from his reflections. He looked up to see Ruggo ride by on a buckskin, wheel the horse about, and spur him toward the supply wagon.

"The inn is ahead," the man said grinning widely at

Davin. "Varaza says there are several horses in the stable behind the caravansary. In particular there is a spectacular gray which will delight you."

"A gray?" Davin's attention was fully on the Huata now. "Describe the horse more fully."

"It has four legs, a head and a tail, and feed goes in one end and from the other comes..."

"Qar take you!" shouted Davin. "That's not what I meant."

"Consider his rudeness nothing more than travel fatigue," Goran interrupted, his hand clenching down hard on Davin's shoulder. "He is overly excited at the prospect of again being able to travel. Is that not so, Davin?"

Davin's anger and impatience cooled. For once, Goran showed poise. He nodded and apologized to the man, who returned the nod.

"Varaza said to tell you that the gray appeared to be of the finest bloodlines, bred for the saddle," Ruggo continued. "He also added that if you can not convince the owner to sell, the stable is open and unguarded, and it should be easy for one of your ability to possess such a fine horse by other means."

Davin thanked the man, although he made no mention that it was not the gray that held his interest, but the horse's owner. Since Berenicis traveled with the Huata band, Davin carefully avoided the purpose of his and Goran's northern journey.

"You create enemies when there were none to start with," Goran said as Ruggo reined back to the head of the column of Huata wagons. "You'll need my ability to change form if you continue to be so grumpy!"

"That's Lijena's horse!" Davin burst out. "It has to be. The description..."

"Fits many horses. You yourself said she was at least two days ahead..."

Davin ignored his friend's words of caution. The gray was Lijena's mare Orria, and her owner would not be far away.

* * *

Davin saw her across the inn's main room. Although she sat with her back to him and wore a simple blue dress rather than the clothes she had stolen from Selene, Davin could not mistake the cascading, frosty-blonde hair that tumbled down her back like finely spun gold.

"Remember the wench has tried to kill you twice," Goran said.

The Challing's warning was of no avail. Davin wove his way through the tables scattered about the caravansary, drawing glances from its patrons, and moved to the woman's side. "Lijena."

Lijena's lovely face rose; she looked up at him without a trace of recognition in her aquamarine eyes. Then she blinked and smiled.

"Davin? It is you, Davin." Her voice was soft, betraying little hint of emotion. "So nice to see you again. Come, sit and join me."

"Lijena, are you all right?" He had expected rage and fingernails clawing at his face, not this placid woman who nodded to the chair beside her.

"I am better," she said, her face as expressionless as her voice. "I have learned much since we parted. Yorioma Faine has explained much of my plight."

"Yorioma?"

"The woman who owns the Golden Tricorn. She knows . . . much. She can provide the means to control the demon within my body."

"Then you accept your ensorcellment?" Her calmness as she spoke of the demon completely baffled the Jyotian.

"I know the agent and perhaps how to free myself," Lijena replied, her eyes searching Davin's face. "I truly believe now that you were innocent in all you did, that you spoke the truth."

"Velden would have killed Goran if I had not delivered you to him." Her every word left Davin more perplexed. Could he be certain this was Lijena talking and not the demon? "I am so sorry for that. In hope of making it up to you, I've followed you across half of Raemllyn."

"I understand that now. My desire for revenge has faded.

Yorioma has provided me with the knowledge needed to contain the demon." Lijena smiled as she pressed a hand over her bosom.

Her face held a more tranquil and composed expression than Davin had seen before on any woman. For some reason he felt a cold chill wiggle along his spine.

"But you are not free of Masur-Kell's demon—merely in control of it?" Davin watched her nod. "Then you still have need of me. How can I serve you?"

"If you mean that, then there is hope for me." Lijena's face showed no flare of hope, only acceptance.

"Whatever I can do, I will."

"Sup with Yorioma and me later. I want you to meet her. She will explain, since much is still beyond my understanding." Lijena rose and smiled down at Davin, "In an hour?"

"In an hour," Davin repeated, watching Lijena while she walked from the room, her movements deliberate, as though she balanced on sword blades.

He heaved a sigh, but it held no relief. In spite of Lijena's calm exterior and her assurances she now dominated the demon bound to her, Davin sensed hell raging within her lovely breast.

But she says there is a method to free her from Masur-Kell's binding spell, he thought as he rose to rejoin Goran, who eyed him over a foaming flagon of ale. *And she has requested my aid.*

Yorioma Faine found Davin at the hour he was to sup with her and Lijena. To his surprise the woman was young and beautiful, not at all the matron he had expected. Nor was the rich burgundy gown she wore the usual attire for an innkeeper.

With the rustle of petticoats accompanying her every step, Yorioma, who had once been called Lady Katura Jayn, led the Jyotian and his red-bearded companion to an isolated table in a corner of the caravansary. She glanced about the inn, as though making sure they were beyond the hearing of unwanted ears, then seated herself.

"Your Huata friends are a noisy group, but their voices

will help hide what we have to say." Yorioma's dark brown
eyes shifted between the two men.

"Lijena told Davin you can free her of the demon." Goran
edged aside common courtesies and pressed to the heart of
the matter.

"I can only try. I know personally of the horrors." Her
delicately boned face tightened into a hatred that flickered
only briefly, then fled.

Davin blinked, thinking this some trick of the light. A
quick glance at Goran told the tale. He *had* seen Yorioma
reveal something more—and less—than human within.

"You are similarly possessed?" asked Goran.

"There are few ways to so intimately know of such matters," the dark-haired woman said. She shifted nervously in
her chair, tugging at the high collar of her gown. There was
caution in her voice when she answered Goran. "And few
are those with the sight to notice those plagued as I. Have
you been trained in the ways of magicks? I sense a strength
in you."

"My friend has but a passing knowledge of such matters.
It's difficult not to glean some understanding when one
travels with Huata," Davin replied before Goran's ale-
loosened tongue began to wag. He had no wish for this
stranger to suspect that his friend was more than he appeared. "Where is Lijena?" asked Davin. "She was to join
us for dinner."

"She isn't overly hungry these days. but she promised
to be down in a moment—ah, there she is. Good evening,
my dear." Yorioma held out both hands to welcome the
passive blonde.

Again Davin wondered what turmoil churned beneath
that placid exterior.

"Why don't you join us in a drink?" asked Goran. "Davin
has been terrible company of late."

Davin shot his friend a silencing look, which the Challing
chose to ignore. Goran ordered more ale, passing his to
Lijena, who sipped at it delicately.

"It grows cold." Yorioma leaned to Davin's ear and whispered, "You and I could sit by the fire where it's warmer,
and still be beyond the ears of my other guests."

The smile on Yorioma's lips suggested she wished to discuss more than Lijena's plight. It was an invitation he would have considered exploring were his mind not occupied with Bistonia's fairest daughter.

"Very well." He nodded and ordered another stoneware mug of ale for himself and a mulled wine for Yorioma. A hand on Goran's shoulder forced the Challing back into his seat when he rose to join them. The witch-fire flared anew in the Challing's one good eye, but Davin saw no outward display of the changeling's powers. "Entertain Lijena for a few minutes with tales of your lost eye. We won't be long."

Goran's eye blazed again, but with no hint of magicks. The red-bearded giant turned immediately to Lijena and began spinning a tale that had the young woman first smiling, then laughing. Satisfied that she was in good hands, Davin joined Yorioma by the fireplace.

"This is much more comfortable," Yorioma said, lounging back in a chair near the fire. Again their eyes locked, and Davin felt a special quality about the woman, a depth and a breadth unusual, especially for an innkeeper.

"Why did you come to such an out-of-the-way spot to open your caravansary?" he asked. "You cannot see more than one or two travelers a week."

"Not for profit," Yorioma said sadly. "The demon within me forces me to commit..."

"It drives you. I have seen Lijena when she is under her demon's influence. You cannot be held to account for what it makes you do."

"You understand only the barest part of my—our—agony," she said, staring into the dancing flames within a maw of a fireplace.

Her finely boned face limned by the light gave her an ethereal quality, as though she were some goddess come to earth in human form. Yorioma turned from her pensiveness and smiled gently, almost fragilely, at Davin.

"There are many things for me to do in Raemllyn," Davin said, thinking of Prince Felrad and how his army needed aid. "I would finish with my duty to Lijena and move on. How can I help?"

"First, you must know the nature of the evil. Are you

cognizant of all that has happened?"

Davin nodded, saying, "The powder in the box. Ty-mon—a leader of Huata to the south—confirmed as much."

"Yes, the demon rested in the powder, but it is more complicated. This demon is only a minor one, perhaps not even powerful enough to possess a name."

"Is that important?"

"With a name there is always hope. A deal can be made with more potent forces, but this one is beneath notice of truly powerful spirits." Yorioma reached out and touched Davin's arm. "Without the name, we cannot even determine what sorcerer is responsible for binding the demon to the powder and, through it, to Lijena."

"But the golden box came from Masur-Kell. He must be the one responsible." Davin was uncertain of her meaning.

Yorioma laughed without humor and shook her head, tiny strands of nut-brown hair falling forward to cast shadows across her face. "Sorcerers trade spells and enchantments as farmers barter for spring seed grain. There is no way of determining who actually cast the binding spells. Perhaps Masur-Kell does not even know—or mayhaps it was cast to bind the sorcerer himself?"

"For what purpose?"

"Who can say, save another sorcerer? They are a secretive lot and keep their lore hidden away, jealous of each other's powers."

Davin grimaced. He had no like of sorcerers nor their spells. Conjurations were best kept locked away in some dusty, ancient grimoire rather than used. "You make this sound as if it's hopeless. Lijena held out more hope when I spoke with her earlier."

"She knows what I choose to tell her—not that I have lied, mind you. Rather, I present this matter in the most favorable light so she will have the confidence to continue. It is not easy for her."

"I know," Davin said, his heart going out to the woman. "Is it any easier for you? Can you shed the chains that bind you?"

"No." Yorioma's gaze drifted to the floor.

"Then can Lijena be freed?" he asked, anxious, uncertain.

"There is a possibility," Yorioma answered. "But it requires a devious path, a dangerous one. Perhaps you will not wish to walk such a road. Or your friend yonder."

"I feel responsible for Lijena," Davin said. "I'll do what must be done. And though he will grumble and complain, Goran will be at my side."

"If only I had one such as you to aid *me,*" she sighed. "The task is arduous but not impossible."

"What must be done?"

"You must ride with Lijena, no matter where she chooses to go, until the demon carries her back to the sorcerer casting the binding spells. Then, well, there is no set way of freeing her, but you will know the source of the ensorcellment and something of the mage casting it. From that knowledge, you must use your wits to follow the necessary course."

"What of your demon?"

A tear formed in Yorioma's eye, caught the flickers from the fire, and shed rainbows. "I have traveled widely and endured much. For me, the pain of bearing the demon within is less than the seeking and not finding. While I have learned some small magicks, the greater ones elude me, and so they must always, as long as the demon lurks within me."

"This cannot be a common spell. Perhaps the same mage has conjured both demons, and we can free you, also."

"Would that it were so easy."

"Easy!" blurted Davin. "Do you think it is easy following Lijena? I was almost caught by three of the Faceless Ones who had crossed her trail."

"What? The Faceless Ones again ride?" Yorioma shuddered. "There are magicks aborning in Raemllyn which mean ill for all of us." Her smooth brow furrowed in a frown, and she asked, "You say the Faceless Ones saw her? What did they do? This might be an important clue to freeing her."

"She spoke with them, then they departed, as if they were frightened."

"Impossible," scoffed the woman. "All I know of the

Faceless Ones tells of their unreasoning bravery. They fear nothing. Nothing."

"They ran from Lijena when she mentioned the Blood Fountain."

Davin jumped when Yorioma's hand jerked upward, spilling her wine. One long-fingered hand covered her mouth, and her dark eyes widened in shock. Her complexion had been light; it now turned pasty white.

"No, not that. Not that!"

"What do you know of this Blood Fountain?" demanded Davin. "What has it to do with Lijena?"

"Lorennion," she said in a quaking voice. "She rides to Lorennion."

Davin turned at a scraping sound behind him. He held up his hand and cautioned the woman to silence. From the dark shadows came a flash of light against silver. Davin instantly recognized the sigil thus revealed.

Berenicis the Blackheart sat at the table and within distance to overhear all said. Berenicis had first mentioned the sorcerer's name to Davin, and the Jyotian adventurer had no desire to provide the swine with more information than necessary. While Berenicis claimed a truce, Davin could not forget past vile deeds on the part of the deposed ruler.

"Yorioma, let us find a less public spot to finish our discussion."

She glanced out into the room, scanning slowly until her eyes also rested on Berenicis. She nodded and said, "My room is secluded and the walls thick. None spies on me there. I . . . I go there when the demon seizes control of my body."

Davin's gaze moved to the table where Goran still entertained Lijena with his endless wealth of tall tales. Neither would miss them for a while yet. He motioned for Yorioma to lead the way to her room.

As Davin and Yorioma climbed the stairs to the caravansary's second level, Lijena lowered her mug to the table and turned to Goran. "The damper on the fireplace seems to be stuck. The air inside becomes too smoky for me. I need a breath of fresh air. Order us another round of ale.

I'll return in a moment. Then you can tell me how the God Yehseen himself robbed you of your left eye."

"Aye, and a struggle it was, too!" Goran answered, then turned to the barkeep to roar his order for two fresh mugs.

With his attention thus diverted, he did not see Lijena slip from the inn. Nor did Goran note Berenicis Blackheart rise from his table and follow the young woman. If he had, he would have given it little mind. All Goran cared about was the warmth pooling in his gut from drinking nine mugs of the potent ale.

Lifting one of the foaming flagons the barkeep brought, Goran drank deeply and vowed to make it fifteen before he passed out. It had been ever too long since he'd found such a hospitable place as this!

chapter
12

DAVIN ANANE'S ATTENTION and gaze were captivated by
Yorioma Faine as he ascended the well-worn, highly polished wooden stairs. His eyes were too firmly affixed to the
gently swaying figure of the innkeeper to even glance at the
main room below. The burgundy, silky-thin dress clung with
ecstatic tenacity to her slender figure and allowed the trailing
man to catch delightful glimpses of her every curve.

With such an enticing woman so close, and one who had
hinted that she was not averse to being even closer, Davin
admitted to himself that it was damned difficult to keep his
reason for being in the Golden Tricorn in focus. That reason
being Lijena and the demon possessing her.

*You haven't ridden across half of Raemllyn for a tumble
in the hay with the first attractive wench you meet!* Davin
attempted to edge aside the tempting visions aplay in his
mind. Tymon had said Lijena's and his fates were inter-
locked.

The strands woven by the Sitala to join the thief to the
House of Farleigh's fair daughter did not necessarily mean

142

love. Davin shook his head; he was still uncertain of the strange mixture of emotions Lijena awoke within him. *Could it be love when Yorioma fires such desire?* Yet at the same time, he could not deny the guilt he felt, stemming from the want this lovely innkeeper stirred deep within his core.

Ahead of him, Yorioma stopped at a dark-stained door. Her long fingers tucked beneath the sash of her gown to produce a brass key that she inserted into the door's lock. There was a metallic click as her wrist twisted, and the door opened.

The room beyond that threshold was surprisingly large, clean, and neatly kept. An armoire stood in one corner, a mirror above it. Cushioned chairs sat beside curtained windows, and a small table with colorful vials lined across one end was shoved against a wall, but it was a large four-poster at the center of the room that dominated the chamber. Davin couldn't restrain himself from walking over and testing the softness of the mattress with a hand. The bed felt every bit as luxurious as it looked. He sighed inwardly; it had been so long since he had enjoyed a real bed for an entire night's undisturbed rest.

"Go on, sit, if you like." Yorioma smiled and walked to a crystal decanter and glasses on a small table beside the bed. "Would you care for some sherry? I have nothing stronger here. Or I can order some ale from below if you prefer?"

"Sherry sounds fine," Davin said with a nod as he sat. "I've had enough of the ale. It fogs my brain and makes me sleepy."

"Vice requires practice." Yorioma's smile widened when she saw the satisfaction on her visitor's face as he sank into the feather mattress.

Pouring two glasses of sherry, she handed one to Davin and seated herself beside him on the bed, her thigh brushing his.

"There's little time for vice or anything else when you're chasing a demon-possessed woman through the wilderness." Distractedly he sipped, not even minding that it was far too sweet for his taste.

His gaze continued over the room. Did he avert his eyes to keep from staring at the woman's enchanting beauty? Or did he search for a clue, something that would tell him why a woman like Yorioma Faine would take a total stranger, one to whom magicks had bound a demon, under her wing?

If such a clue existed, Davin did not discover it. The furnishings were simple, elegant, and functional. What few small articles were scattered about for ornamentation appeared quite practical: small boxes, bowls, two fluted, cut-crystal vases filled with softly petaled blue *limna* roses.

All of this did nothing to satisfy the skeptical streak that ran deep in the Jyotian. When one offered aid to another, the surface kindness usually cloaked some private motive. What was Yorioma Faine's? Or for that matter, what was his own?

"The room is secure," Yorioma said, apparently misjudging his searching eyes. "I have had occasion to desire absolute privacy."

A curious choked quality to her words caused Davin to turn and face her. A tear formed in the corner of her eye. Gently, he reached out and brushed it away before the salty droplet ran down her cheek. She glanced away, her face toward the wall.

"Is the need for privacy so evil?" he asked, puzzled at her reaction.

"You and others seek privacy to renew your psychic reserves," the brown-tressed woman replied. "I need it to hide the entity that dwells within me."

"Your demon?" he asked.

"It is hideous. It makes me do *things*—hideous things."

The way she spat out her words chilled Davin. He instantly thought of Lijena's deadly rages, her wild-eyed flights, the way she drove her horse to exhaustion in a headlong flight to the north.

"Would it help to speak of it?"

"Help? You or me?" she said with bitterness thick on her tongue.

"Both of us, perhaps," he replied gently. "I admit my ignorance of your plight . . . cannot conceive of what such possession is like. Yet I have witnessed its effects several times in Lijena."

"Do you love her, Davin Anane?" Yorioma's gaze returned to him, her eyes asparkle with unshed tears.

Davin merely shrugged, unable to explain his jumbled feelings to himself, let alone this woman he had just met.

"Yes, I can see it in your eyes," she finished before Davin could deny the possibility.

"Does it matter what I feel for Lijena?" Davin maneuvered back to the reason for their conversation. "You mentioned Lorennion. How is Lijena linked to the mage? And what is this Blood Fountain?"

"I have sought knowledge in many places throughout all of Raemllyn, and one fact that has never been cloaked with a hint of lie is that Lorennion is cruel, resourceful, and one of the most powerful sorcerers in all the world." Yorioma swallowed and then licked her dry lips, adding, "Perhaps he is *the* most powerful. All accounts mention him as being in control of brutal magicks, spells so diabolical that all fear to challenge his power.

"Some say he commands knowledge equal to the secrets wizards held when magicks ruled our world," she continued. "I cannot confirm that he possesses such great powers. But I do know that Zarek Yannis sought Lorennion's aid. Standing before the Velvet Throne and all of Yannis' bastard court, Lorennion laughed in the usurper's face, named him an impotent maggot, then waved an arm and vanished while all stood with mouths dropping in disbelief. For this Yannis has placed a price of ten thousand gold bists on Lorennion's head, although there is no one in all Raemllyn's realms with the power or the courage to collect that reward!"

"The man sees Yannis for what he is," Davin smiled, wishing he had witnessed the mage's spurning of the usurper. "But the Blood Fountain? What of it?"

Yorioma shrugged shapely shoulders and drank deeply of her sherry. With a hand shaking slightly, she put her wine glass on the bedside table.

"I have no knowledge of the Blood Fountain, but among mystic circles it is spoken of in hushed tones. It is Lorennion's most jealously guarded secret. Stories abound of how he has protected his secrets. You can be certain that whatever it is, its purpose is as dark as Lorennion himself."

Yorioma shuddered, tears welling in her eyes again for no discernible reason. Davin reached out and squeezed her shoulder in comfort. To his surprise, she edged closer, resting her head in the hollow of his shoulder, and sobbed.

"Shhh." Davin's arms cradled her, his right hand lightly stroking the silken strands of her nut-brown hair. Uncertain of the cause of her weeping, he simply whispered. "It will be all right."

The sobbing and Yorioma's trembling eventually subsided, though her head remained pressed to his chest when she spoke again.

"Lorennion is said to have a castle keep in the north, where he has secluded himself away from contact with the world to pursue his arcane knowledge," she said, as though her explanation had never been interrupted by the sudden teary outburst.

"But Yannis has mages of his own, powerful ones." Davin repressed a shudder of his own imagining the power required to conjure forth the Faceless Ones. "Surely he would set them against Lorennion."

"In a duel of magicks, there is no question that Lorennion would triumph. Even Yannis' Payat'Morve would admit that—and more." Yorioma clung to Davin, her body still atremble like some frightened child.

"If I were Yannis, I would seek out Lorennion. Such power would assure the Velvet Throne." Davin's head spun as he conceived of conspiracies churning within conspiracies.

Berenicis Blackheart—who did he truly serve, Yannis or Felrad? Or both? Those days of duplicity in Jyotis were long past him—or so he thought. Now Davin's mind wandered all too familiar paths. Lorennion's power and Kwerin Bloodhawk's sword—with both at his command, Berenicis could conquer Raemllyn and claim the Velvet Throne for himself.

Yorioma laughed harshly. "No, that is the way the mind

of another man might work, but not Yannis. Lorennion spurned him, and now Yannis seeks his head, although there is no one to bring it to him."

Abruptly Yorioma's body tensed, then shuddered violently. She almost shrieked, "You must keep Lijena from falling prey to Lorennion's horrid magicks! He is a monster!"

Again Davin was caught off balance by her startling reaction and the flood of tears that followed. He held her closely, whispering uncertain assurances.

"Velden, Nelek Kahl, Masur-Kell, and now Lorennion," he pondered aloud. "What other horrors await Lijena before she is at last free of this dark force?"

"Kahl?" Yorioma straightened; her eyes narrowed, and her brow knitted in question. "Lijena has been in the hands of Nelek Kahl the slaver? Do you know this for a fact?"

"I do, but that is past. I am surprised Lijena did not mention it to you. Lorennion is of more import now. What purpose would he have for Lijena? She is without magicks, and her family is unknown except in Bistonia."

"That is a story with many turnings, devious and ugly twistings." She shuddered and returned her head to Davin's shoulder. "Finding the proper spot to begin is most difficult . . . In my youth, pleasure was my only goal. Many girls were similarly beset with the need for continual gratification, but few found a lover like Farkarian Ivoni."

A curious sound came deep from Yorioma's throat, an estranged mixing of joy and grief.

"Ivoni was all I could ask in a lover. His prowess was legendary, and never have I found a man to match him." She said more softly, "No man." Then, louder, she continued. "Ivoni charmed me in so many ways. I often wonder if the appeal was totally unbidden on his part."

"Ivoni," said Davin. "The name is familiar."

"It is? Tell me. Where do I find him? I *must* find him."

"The name is familiar, but I cannot tell you. Is Ivoni a sorcerer, like Lorennion?"

"So alike, so dissimilar," she said. "Lorennion is noted for cruelty, Ivoni for his gentleness. But both are implacable in their hatred if they feel someone has crossed them."

"You betrayed Ivoni?" Davin shifted, his arm still circling Yorioma.

"He caught me with another man. Why I strayed from Ivoni's bed I can't say. Call it youthful indiscretion, the need to explore the depths of others, I know not. But he found me. The gentleness he had shown me turned to flaming hatred." She tensed as she spoke now.

"My would-be lover was magically transformed into ... cinders. He suffered greatly as he burned, his flesh first blistering and then charring and finally turning to ash. For me, the punishment was greater."

"Your demon?"

"Ivoni forced me to inhale the white powder he carried in a locket around his neck. Even as I breathed that treacherous dust, *changes* began inside me. I *felt* the demon gaining a hold on my emotions, my very soul!"

"Did Ivoni offer to release you?"

"Ivoni abandoned me. Not since that day ten years ago have I seen him, though I have sought him throughout all of Raemllyn. I ... I believe if I find him and beg piteously enough for mercy, he will release me from this demon gnawing at my guts."

No words passed between the pair for some time. None was needed. Eventually, Yorioma continued her story.

"For a few weeks, only physical discomfort manifested itself, but the demon eventually gained supremacy over my actions. At times I flew into a berserker's rage, killing any close to me, wantonly destroying. The demon then retreated, and I mistakenly thought it had gone.

"But as soon as I grew intimate with a new lover, as soon as I became close to any man, the demon erupted in a frenzy of destruction." Brilliant eyes locked on Davin's. She smiled wanly and said, "Do not worry. I have learned to control the demon, if not to drive it from my soul."

"Your trembling, the tears." Davin understood Yorioma's strange behavior now. "You wrestle with your demon!"

Yorioma nodded, clutching close to him. "Your presence makes it easier. I draw on your strength."

"You can teach these magicks to Lijena?"

"She needs more, just as I do," said Yorioma in a tired voice. "The magicks I've learned rob the demon of its unholy appetite for blood and nothing more. Can you imagine how ghastly it is slaughtering lovers, friends, men, women, even small children? The demon cared little about age or sex or physical infirmity—only death sated its lust."

Davin stared over Yorioma's head at a point on the far wall. A small portrait hung there, but his unfocused eyes saw another scene: Lijena raising her sword and bringing it down with maniac fury. Then another vision replaced that one: Lijena driving off the three Faceless Ones. The demon blazing within her breast carried strengths and hungers surpassing even those of the Faceless.

Gooseflesh rippled up his spine.

Yorioma took no notice of his condition. She lost herself in remembrance.

"My magical powers grew as I sought out witches and mages for advice, for surcease from the demon residing within. All told me the same thing—only Farkarian Ivoni could exorcise the demon. He had released it on me—he must shatter the magic chains he forged. But Ivoni has vanished, and I am left with my pitiful few spells and potions to hold the demon in abeyance."

"Such is a burden of incalculable horror," said Davin. But his thoughts were with Lijena's demon and the horrors it brought to her.

"It is that." Yorioma's fingers strayed to the front of Davin's garish Huata blouse. Cool fingers worked inside and rested against bare flesh, then slowly warmed. "But it turned into more for me."

"How?" For a moment he thought of removing the hand, but it just lay there neither teasing nor taunting.

"I control the demon, even if I cannot drive it from my soul. With use of certain geases, I can employ the demon to enhance my own knowledge."

"I don't understand. You tap this demon's knowledge of Peyneeha?"

"Something like that," Yorioma admitted. "But demons

control vast magicks that no human can hope to use, even
mages of Lorennion's ilk."

For an instant Davin's head spun from the closeness of
this definitely desirable woman and the sweetness of her
perfume. Or was there more?

"Lijena," he said, forcing himself back to the topic. "Can
you show her these spells to bind her own demon?"

"In time, perhaps. She attacked me—her demon forced
her to attack me," Yorioma corrected. "I was able to reach
out and seize control of her demon in much the same way
I control mine. She found herself frozen, unable to move
the smallest of muscles. This seizure passed, but by then I
had forced the demon back into a quiescent state. Other
incantations woven daily keep Lijena's mind in a trancelike
state too placid for the demon to employ."

Davin now understood the lack of emotion in Lijena's
voice, her face.

"It is a stopgap measure, at best." Yorioma's face lifted
to Davin's. "I can teach her no more than to control her
demon. Lorennion is the only one that can shatter the chains
that bind her."

"Yet to control the demon, to keep it under rein is a
beginning," Davin said. "However, seeking out Lorennion..."

The thief's mind turned to Berenicis, who dined below
them in the inn. Goran's words echoed in his mind—that
two bound by more than their hatred would raise their swords
in conflict, but no Jyotian blood would be spilled. Had the
Challing actually glimpsed the future? Would he and Berenicis face Lorennion together?

"And you have not told Lijena all this?" Davin asked,
easing the woman from him.

"No," she shook her head. "For the past three days we
have been too occupied with containing the demon. I had
no wish to add to the burden she already bears."

"Is she strong enough to hear the truth now?"

"Yes, there is no need to keep it from her now," Yorioma
said. "Soon she must ride again—this time seeking Lorennion."

Davin rose from the bed and stepped toward the door. "Then we shall go below and explain everything to her."

"Davin, wait," Yorioma called out to him.

He turned, eyebrow arching when he noticed Yorioma remained on the side of the bed.

"What we have to say can wait until the morning," the lovely innkeeper said. "This night I have need of you . . . of your strength."

Davin's eyebrow arched even higher, though he fully understood Yorioma's invitation. "Is it Yorioma Faine who speaks . . . or Ivoni's demon?"

"Yorioma Faine, the woman," she said softly, smiling when he walked from the door and returned to her bed.

Yorioma lay on her back staring at the ceiling and the shadow play there enacted by the single candle that glowed within her darkened bedroom. Beside her Davin Anane slept on his side, sated and drained by the unexpected passions he had discovered within her body—desires that were not all born of woman. If the Jyotian had suspected the demon had in part controlled her, he had made no protest.

A sad smile passed over Yorioma's red lips. None of the men she had brought to her bed had ever protested the unabandoned lust the demon drove her to. And why should they? Not even the most skilled courtesans in Raemllyn knew the pleasures of the flesh as well as did the creature dwelling in her breast—the same passions that had first attracted Nelek Kahl.

Nelek. Yorioma shivered at the thought of the slaver and the dangerous game she now played. Lijena had to be gone before Kahl arrived at the Golden Tricorn. Had to be! If Yorioma ever hoped to free herself of the demon possessing her.

Yorioma took a deep steadying breath. She had dealt with Kahl on many occasions in the past; she would deal with him again when the time came. He was, after all, only a man.

She glanced at Davin, feeling no guilt for the lies she had told him. They were only minor rearrangings of the facts. Ivoni had been her lover, but he was not responsible for the demon. Ivoni had died in a pillar of flame sparked from the fingers of the mage Lorennion.

She and Ivoni had both been apprentices to the great wizard—and she had been both men's lover. But Lorennion shared his possessions with no man!

The binding spells Lorennion used on his powders were one and the same. Should one be broken, all were broken. And that was Yorioma's hope. If Lijena, with Davin's aid, could find the mage and break his spell on the young woman, Yorioma's own binding spell would shatter, and she would once again be free.

A fragile hope, she realized; but it was a hope, which was more than she had held for years. Davin was strong and willing, and love could often work miracles where magicks failed. Also, there was his companion, the giant of a man called Goran One-Eye. There was more to that one than met the eye. Yorioma had sensed a power in him this night, though she could not define the energies he possessed or their source.

Then there was Lijena. The girl amazed Yorioma. In the course of three days, she had learned to control her demon with the help of only a few chants. Yorioma had struggled for two years to gain the same degree of dominance over her own demon.

Yes, if I've ever had reason to hope, I have it now in this odd trio, she nodded solemnly, *if they can unravel Lorennion's magicks ere he leads them to the Blood Fountain!*

chapter *13*

"ANOTHER ALE, AND THIS TIME don't fill the mug only three-quarters of the way. I want to see froth sloshing over the rim." Goran One-Eye's huge fist slammed down, a hammer of flesh atop the polished wood.

Mugs rattled from one end of the bar to the other, not all jarred by the impact of the Challing's fist. More than one patron of the Golden Tricorn eyed the red-maned giant nervously, fearing the enormous quantity of alcohol Goran had consumed would soon turn the hulking man mean. The man behind the bar cringed, then moved quickly to fill Goran's order and head off any possible trouble.

In fact, those in the caravansary had little to fear from the Challing. It was not anger or a fit of bloodlust that caused the changeling to roar and pound on the bar. Goran simply vented the frustration and self-pity welling in his massive chest.

Here he stood in an inn filled with patrons, and he was alone. Davin had first abandoned him for the brown-haired

wench. Had Goran been given the opportunity to spend the
eve with Yorioma, he would have abandoned even fair Ediena
herself. Raemllyn's Goddess of Love and Pleasure surely
held no more appeal than the sultry Yorioma Faine.

Yet what he would have done given the opportunity was
of little import. He was Goran One-Eye, an ill-mannered
lout, lacking in human social graces, or so his Jyotian companion often told him. For Davin to leave him so rudely
before he had found a suitable partner for the night—that
was inexcusable!

Goran peered around the room and blinked several times.
The blur in his good eye from too much ale only added to
his irritation. There ought to be a dozen serving wenches
hastening about—at least one with that certain gleam in her
eye for the Challing—but the Golden Tricorn was strangely
lacking in women. Yorioma Faine had surrounded herself
with male servants.

*Bah! Even the skinny blonde Davin dotes on so has aban-
doned me.* Goran shook his head, trying to clear his ale-
besotted brain. Hadn't Davin told him to entertain Lijena?
Yes, he was certain that was what his friend had said. If
so, where had Lijena gone? Lacking social graces, he might
be, but he *was* a most entertaining fellow.

Goran shook his head again. A vague memory of Lijena
mentioning air, of going outside, squirmed about in Goran's
brain. He hefted his mug and drained its contents in one
long draught.

Belching, he considered ordering another for a long,
pensive moment. The already spinning room persuaded him
to toss aside the mug and stagger to the caravansary's door.
Fresh, cold air would go a long way to revitalize his muddled
mind and ease the pent-up feelings growing within his breast.

Aye, and I should look for Lijena, Goran nodded to
himself. *Damn Davin! How many other men have so many
wenches that they need a caretaker to see after them?*

Goran smirked as he imagined his friend and Yorioma
upstairs. Such a tasty wench she was. Saucy, well-fleshed,
proportioned perfectly for the Challing's tastes. He belched
and pushed through the door on rubbery legs. From behind

him came a chorus of soft, relieved sighs.

Goran sneered. What did he care about those within? They were men without spines who sipped ale like women nursing sherry. Nor did they appreciate his well-versed repertoire of Raemllyn's finest bawdy songs. They all reminded him of the cold fish Berenicis, who just sat in a corner of the caravansary eyeing everyone.

The cold night air struck Goran like a hammer blow. His giant body shivered, and he flexed cramped muscles, feeling blood begin to flow through alcohol-constricted arteries. He extended his powerful arms, tensed the biceps, and relaxed.

Drawing in a huge lungful of air, he tilted his head back and stared at the stars among broken patches of clouds above. Here and there, the silvered reflections of twin moons peered from behind clouds, then the two guardians of the night slipped out from behind the covering. Bak, the farther of the two, showed only a thin sliver while Kea blazed in almost full glory.

"For spring again," Goran said wistfully. In spring both moons stared down on Raemllyn in fullness; the only other time Bak and Kea revealed their beauty side by side was in late winter.

Goran propped himself against the side of the caravansary and watched the clouds cloak the moons. Kea vanished totally, and only the wafer-thin slice of Bak remained, until it, too, was swallowed by quickly moving wisps.

The chilly night breeze nipped at the Challing's cheeks as it rustled across the grasslands. He sniffed, testing the pungent sweetness of the air, the scent of a northern autumn turning rapidly into winter. Not that he minded the winter months, but he preferred the warmer days, wandering the streets of Raemllyn's cities and ogling the young women in their skimpy summer clothing.

Ah, to be in...Goran's thought evaporated in a shiver that had nothing to do with the weather as full-faced Kea slid from behind the clouds. Goran blinked, stared up. *It can't be!*

High in the sky, among the clouds themselves, with dual tails awrithe and batlike wings spread wide, a *keedehn* glided across Kea, its serpentine head arched as though it spat venom at the silver moon.

Wiping a hand across his eyes in the hope of erasing an ale-spawned nightmare, Goran stared back at the full moon and the silhouette that soared across its face. *A keedehn! It cannot be, but it is!* Goran watched in horror as the creature's flight took it across Kea and into the night's blackness.

Raemllyn had long ago disposed of dragons, if indeed they had ever dwelled in this realm of humankind. Not so in Goran's realm of Gohwohn—and it was there the *keedehn* was native. Twice the size of a horse, the winged reptile was the evil tyrant that ruled Gohwohn's skies, feeding on Challings for which it had developed a particular relish.

Surely, it was the ale that tricked my mind, Goran tried to reassure himself as he strode on suddenly steady legs toward a watering trough near the inn's stable. *That is it! Humans see elephants of various hues when they've upended too many cups. And I see a* keedehn!

Goran wished his thoughts were as steady as his legs. In truth he wasn't certain what he had seen. It was rumored that the delicate fabric that separated the planes of existence had been rent when Zarek Yannis had summoned forth magicks to defeat Bedrich the Fair. If a rent did exist, then the *keedehn* could be as real as the Faceless Ones.

Dipping his hands into the trough, Goran splashed the icy water in his face to wash away the alcohol fog. He shivered loudly and stared down into the water—and shivered again. It was not the face of Goran One-Eye that stared back at him, but the visage of Yorioma Faine!

The Challing thrust a hairy paw out before him–her. In Kea's light the meaty hand flowed like quicksilver, transforming into something more slender, more delicate and petite. Yorioma's hand replaced his!

"'Tis caused by my thoughts lingering on Davin and the wench," Goran muttered aloud in a voice no longer deep and bellowing, but a perfect imitation of the innkeeper's gentle tones. "Glylina returns."

Even as she–he spoke, the metamorphosis coursed through the Challing's body. Magicks worked—magicks

born of the changeling's own powers, but over which she—
he had no control. The muscular battering rams that had
been Goran's arms gave way to Yorioma's slender limbs.

She—for Glylina reigned once again—giggled and
stroked long-fingered hands over her new body, feeling
breasts rising, nipples hardening in the cold night air. Proudly
she reveled in the shapely new form she wore.

"But what a waste!" She pouted. "Davin is already with
Yorioma—or what a night we might spend together!"

The thought that Davin and Yorioma might enjoy a third
companion in their bed was born in her head and died away
almost instantly. Yorioma might become insatiable at the
sight of another self making love to Davin—and what of
the young rogue himself?

*Davin would relish the idea of twins—completely iden-
tical twins* . . . Glylina decided, then shook her head. Yorioma
and Davin's eve had begun. Neither would appreciate an
intruder—no matter how exotic.

Also, there was Davin's odd response when he had first
seen her in Lijena's form—and that strange promise, of
sorts, the Jyotian had extracted from Goran.

*What of the Huata? Their women are unsurpassed lov-
ers—are the men equal?* Glylina turned toward the nomads'
wagons in search of someone suitably male. She had walked
only ten steps, to the front of the stable, when she found
the perfect subject on which to test her new charms.

His name was Heank, Yorioma's groom. Glylina watched
as he pitched the last of the night's hay to the horses and
turned toward his small quarters in the rear of the barn.
Glylina coughed loudly enough to draw the youth's attention. Heank turned, and his eyes widened.

"Is there anything wrong?" the stable boy asked. "I did all
you told me to. Honest. If anything is wrong, it was—"

Glylina silenced the youth with a raised hand, saying,
"Nothing is wrong. In fact, I have come to congratulate
you. The attention you lavish on our guests' steeds pleases
me. You deserve a reward. Yes, definitely a reward suitable
for such a fine . . . stud."

Heank swallowed hard and stepped back from his employer. Yorioma oft flew into rages of impossible dimension and magnitude. It was best to avoid that uncontrollable fury.

"Do you not find me attractive?" the Challing asked, enjoying this seduction more and more. The feel of her new body, the slight swaying of breasts, the empty yearning within her core, all delighted her with their freshness. Sensation! This was the best of being human. How the Challing pitied those humans who were not able to experience more than one sex.

"Lady, you are beautiful," Heank said, his voice cracking.

"And I feel you deserve my personal rewards for your diligence in pursuing a smelly occupation." Glylina's now-straight nose wrinkled slightly, aristocratically, at the odors in the barn.

She crossed to where Heank stood, pale-faced and visibly trembling. One petite hand reached out and stroked the corn-silk stubble on the youth's chin. A surge of arousal passed through Glylina, stronger than any sensation Goran had experienced of late. She would not back down now. The pursuit was as thrilling as the catch ever could be!

"I . . . I like my job here, Lady," said Heank. "I would do nothing to jeopardize it."

"Am I asking such of you? I come only to show my gratitude for all you do in my service." Certainly one as beautiful as she had to be having some effects on one as young and virile as this stable boy.

She was.

"My quarters are not t-the best," Heank started.

"Then let us enjoy the freshness of the straw. Here! Now!" Glylina took the youth's hand and led him to her chosen bed.

Lord Berenicis leaned back in the shadows, watching the innkeeper lead Davin up the stairs. A smug smile moved across his lips. Their night would be pleasurably spent. He himself had considered sampling Yorioma's considerable charms, until he had overheard their guarded whispers. Now his mind moved elsewhere, mulling and digesting what had passed between Yorioma and the sole heir to the House of Anane.

House of Anane. Berenicis weighed the name in his mind. Once the mere sound of it would have driven him into a fevered rage. Now?

He lifted his eyebrows. The House of Anane was as meaningless as was his own title. Davin Anane, however, could be a useful ally for Prince Felrad—for himself. Neither wealth nor promises of title and land would win his former enemy. Yet if one possessed the right bait...

The deposed ruler of Jyotis shifted his attention to the mismatched pair seated at a table across the room. Goran downed mug after mug of ale while Lijena sipped daintily at hers. They were a contrast in character and appearance.

Lijena: lovely, slender, blonde, composed, and not a little tired looking from strain. Goran: hairy and ugly, barrel-chested, red-haired, boisterous, and apparently able to drink until the moons fell from the sky.

And not just Lijena contained a secret within her bosom: Berenicis sensed that Davin's companion Goran One-Eye was more than the uncouth jester he appeared. There were magicks about the flame-bearded oaf, although the exact nature of those magicks eluded Berenicis. He had studied the arcane tomes since Zarek Yannis had driven him from Jyotis, and he had achieved magehood of the fourth level; but Goran and the secrets he possessed remained beyond his abilities.

Nor did he have time to waste trying to uncover the man's magicks. A more important matter now occupied him— Lorennion! And across the room sat his key for locating the mage's castle keep hidden deep within Agda's formidable mountains and forests.

That key now rose to whisper softly in Goran's ear. The hulking man took scant notice of Lijena as she walked from the inn, nor did he note Berenicis' interest in the frosty-haired blonde.

Berenicis considered all that had happened. Davin would not be seen again till dawn or after. Goran's condition was one of intoxication, but the man was unable to tell to what real extent Goran was drunk. Such bulk might consume quantities of ale able to stun a moose with a single blow and still be capable of causing trouble. Yet, without risk there was no reward.

Berenicis pushed himself from the table and left the swaddling shadows as Goran turned to the bar and called for an ale. It was time enough for Berenicis to nod to Varaza, signaling the Huata it was time to leave, and to slip from the caravansary.

Outside, he stood and allowed his eyes to adjust to the light cast by the twin moons. The landscape held a ghostly hue, shadows etched in silver, a terrain lacking contour.

In the soft, rain-soaked ground he saw the impressions of a small foot. He turned and followed Lijena's path into the nearby stand of trees that grew by a small stream. Once under the low-hanging branches, all light vanished and Berenicis relied on other senses.

Ahead, he heard the snap of a twig, the whisper of a foot on wet leaves, the shimmying of a branch pulled out of the path and then released. He hurried forward, confident now of his mission.

The cessation of sounds from ahead caused Berenicis to slow. Cautiously, he advanced. Lijena sat beside the stream, staring listlessly into the water. Other than the soft rustle of wind through particolored leaves waiting for winter's death, there were no sounds.

"Lady," he said softly, "you are distraught. How may I be of assistance?"

Lijena showed no surprise as she turned and stared at him. Berenicis bowed low but never took his eyes off her. The moonbeams glinted from her hair and turned it into a mist of the purest of spun silver; then all color vanished as the moons hid behind a dark cloud. Berenicis took this to be an omen—of good. For him.

"I desire only to be alone. I . . . cannot be responsible for what might happen to you." She sat with hands folded peacefully in her lap.

Although Berenicis recognized the hellion she could be transformed into instantly if the demon seized control, the Lijena he gazed upon seemed worlds distant from the demon-possessed woman he had heard Yorioma and Davin whisper about. Besides, he had no choice but to make his move now.

"We are all responsible for our own actions, lady," he said. "Except when magicks are involved. Being subjugated by another is truly evil. I would help you free yourself of this onerous burden."

"I need no help. My . . . friends already aid me."

"Yorioma?" he asked, manipulating the doubt in his voice. He would have to play this carefully. "She knows much, but she is also . . . bound."

"You know?" Lijena's words were monotone, as if she had no interest whatsoever in this conversation.

"Yorioma Faine and I are old friends," he lied. "She is bound, not only to her own demon, but to this place. She seeks a companion in her misery—not to aid you."

Lijena blinked, and her brow furrowed, but she said nothing.

"And of Davin Anane," he continued, his voice pitched low to force the woman's full attention. "He cannot aid you. He does not *want* to do so. You are little more than an annoyance to him now."

"Oh?" The doubt on her face was now in her voice. "But he has pledged himself to my cause."

"Then why is he with Yorioma now? Do you think they discuss your plight? Throughout a long evening and far into the dawn? Hardly. Long have I known Davin Anane. Be not confused by his promises. He is but a rogue, a scoundrel and adventurer. He will use you for his purposes, then abandon you."

Befuddlement darkened Lijena's face. Berenicis contained a smile that tried to creep to his lips. Whatever spell Yorioma had cast about this girl, it served him well. How easily his words brought confusion—mistrust.

"Consider," Berenicis said, leaning forward, his hand resting on a warm knee. "I also seek out Lorennion. It is to him your demon drives you, is it not? I need the sorcerer's aid for another mission, one given me by none other than Prince Felrad."

Berenicis had expected no overt response on the woman's

part; she gave none. "The prince requires me to find Lorennion and learn certain magicks from the mage."

"Is this of importance to me? Will it exorcise the demon within my breast?" Lijena shifted slightly and tried to dislodge Berenicis' hand from her knee. He moved closer, his hand creeping up her thigh to rest at her waist.

"We can journey together; our missions are linked to Lorennion; together we can petition him for his mercy, and together we might succeed where alone we fail. And there is more. I was once king of Jyotis. A mage is more likely to listen to my petition than to that of a woman accompanied by a self-avowed thief."

Berenicis saw that his line of argument drove a wedge into Lijena's resolve, edging her farther away from Davin Anane. "There is something further. No mage looks kindly on a thief who steals from another mage. You realize, don't you, that Masur-Kell and Lorennion are fast friends."

Berenicis did not laugh aloud when he saw the woman accepting this as truth. In fact he had no idea whether the two sorcerers even knew of one another; the lie came easily to his lips, patterned to give Lijena the motivation needed to leave Davin behind.

"I was sold to Masur-Kell. He will not look favorably upon me, yet I must deal with his good friend Lorennion." Lijena spoke her thoughts aloud.

"Here is where I can aid you!" Berenicis pressed. "A king pleading your case, a king promising all that a mage might desire, those are powerful inducements. Lorennion will be swayed more easily by me than by Davin Anane. I, a king. Davin, a common cutpurse."

"I do not know," she said slowly. Berenicis guessed that whatever ward spell Yorioma had taught the blonde woman not only repressed the demon, but also slowed her mental processes. "These are such complicated matters for me. I am not used to dealing with sorcerers."

"Who is? But together, we can find the right words, the right inducements. Lorennion will grant our mutual wishes. He must!"

"But why do you do this for me?" she asked, again

coming to the crux of the matter.

"My queen is long dead, the victim of Zarek Yannis' torturers. I seek someone of beauty, of intelligence, of regal bearing. You are lovely, dear Lijena." His hand drifted upward from her waist, lightly brushed over her breast, and ended stroking over her cheek. "A king alone on the throne is a sorry sight. The kingdom lacks its heart. But with a queen..." The sentence trailed off.

Berenicis again wanted to laugh at how easily duped this demon-ridden woman was. He would have to thank Yorioma for showing Lijena the binding spell; it held demon and good sense. Such promises he expected to work with serving wenches but not with ladies such as Lijena.

"Come back to the Huata wagons with me. We can partake of some of Varaza's fine wine and consider our course more carefully. I believe our destinies are linked. Together we can free you from your demon and obtain that which Prince Felrad needs to regain the Velvet Throne."

For the first time, Lijena smiled, then emitted a tiny chuckle. She said, "That is such a curious way of putting it. Davin said the same thing, that our destinies, his and mine, are inexorably linked."

"Davin is wrong in one respect. His and your destinies are not the ones intertwined. *Ours* are, however. I feel it. I *know* it!"

Lijena nodded, though hesitantly, and offered her hand to Berenicis. Arm in arm they retraced their steps to the inn, then walked to the Huata wagons beyond. Varaza stood outside his wagon, waiting. Berenicis smiled; the Huata leader's intelligence had never failed him before, nor did it now. He and the members of his band, who now quietly prepared for departure, were perfectly suited to Berenicis' need.

Inside the wagon, Berenicis poured strong wine for the woman, being certain to give her the cup Varaza had specially marked. Lijena accepted it, holding it in both hands, and drank slowly but steadily.

"What do you need of Lorennion?" he asked. "We must make plans on how best to present our cases to the mage."

"The demon is his. Masur-Kell held it in powder for unknown reasons."

"You feel . . . drawn?" Berenicis asked. "You feel that the demon takes you directly to Lorennion?"

"We both go west, then to the north again. You know better than I where to find the sorcerer," Lijena answered.

"Of course, I have a map locating his castle keep," Berenicis assured her, pointing to a chest toward the front of the wagon.

Lijena made no attempt to examine the chest's contents, which was just as well since it contained Berenicis' wardrobe. He sipped at his wine, relishing the warm glow it brought to his belly. How easy this was! This demon-wracked wench would lead him to Lorennion's doorstep and the sheath he sought for the sword of Kwerin Bloodhawk. Then . . .

Berenicis drew a deep breath to slow the dizzy race of his thoughts. Before he could claim the future, he had to possess sheath and sword.

"We move," Lijena said, catching herself as the wagon lurched, tossing her toward the back.

Berenicis opened his arms, caught and held her close. She struggled slightly, then relented to his embrace.

"We travel to Lorennion," he said. "Do you not feel the demon within you rejoicing at traveling again toward its release?"

"The demon grows," she said in a weak voice. "I have a hard time controlling it now. Get Yorioma. Have her come to aid me in keeping it chained within!"

"There, there," Berenicis soothed. "This ordeal will soon enough be over for you. Together *we* will conquer this demon. Those others are behind you now. They care not for you. But I do. I do."

The man's soothing words and the rocking of the wagon worked their spells on Lijena. The blonde woman curled up on Varaza's bunk and soon slept, Berenicis watching over her.

This had been easier than he had thought. Berenicis Blackheart downed the dregs in his goblet, then tossed the wine from Lijena's cup out the rear of the wagon. Varaza's sleeping potion had again worked. By the time it wore off, they would be several days' travel to the west—and the demon lurking within would have worked free of Yorioma's spell.

Lijena would be possessed once again—the perfect guide that Berenicis sought.

chapter 14

A CREAK—the sound of a settling building.

Davin Anane blinked sleepily, rolled to his side, and nestled snuggly against his pillow, letting the cottony mists draw him back toward sleep.

A creak—wooden boards protesting a burden.

This time the thief's eyes opened to narrow slits, adjusting to the night's darkness. Cautiously he repressed the urge to sit erect and flail about until he discovered the source of his uneasy awakening. Surprise had its advantages, but then so did knowledge of a foe one faced—if indeed there was a foe.

Yorioma's bedchamber, he remembered as his eyes alighted on the innkeeper's armoire standing beside an open closet door. The softness beneath him was a feather mattress. The coy sweetness of perfume clung to the sheet tucked beneath his chin; that and the subtle fragrance of recent lovemaking bespoke of intimacies recently shared.

And the mistress of the Golden Tricorn? Davin no longer felt the summery warmth of Yorioma's body pressed to his.

The squeak of wooden boards touched the Jyotian's ears again. Someone walked—crept about—in the room! *Yorioma?*

The whispered hiss of steel sliding from leather sheath made the question irrelevant. Tossing aside sheet and blanket, Davin rolled across the bed and onto the floor, away from the creaking boards, away from that deadly hiss.

He hit the cold floor on hands and knees, then shoved to his feet—to see a glinting dagger plummet downward and sink deeply into the mattress where he had lain but a heartbeat past.

His gaze shot up to stare into the face of the blade's wielder. "Yorioma! What—"

He needed no answer to know what possessed her. It was written in her grotesquely contorted countenance, the way she moved, held her body, tensed, and slashed the sliver of steel at his face as she leaped upon the bed and came bounding at him.

"Worm!" The single word came like the voice of a cobra.

Spittle dotted her lips—those lips that had so recently offered love. Her eyes burned with a feral inner light like watch fires on insanity. Nostrils flaring, her hand trembling with the eagerness of a swift kill, she again lunged at him.

Davin lithely backstepped to avoid the savage thrust meant to open his bare chest. And did so by a hairbreadth!

"Yorioma! The demon! The demon has you! Fight it!" Davin called out.

The possessed woman answered with a wicked upthrusting cut that was intended to gut him like a pig.

Again Davin backstepped. His mouth opened wide to call for help, then closed. His cry would go unnoticed. Surely Yorioma's employees were long accustomed to screams coming from their employer's chamber—the woman's own as she wrestled to control Ivoni's demon.

"Kill you!" A serpent's voice came from Yorioma's twisted lips.

As naked as he, she advanced, the dagger held before her ready to strike.

Davin matched each of her advancing strides with one

of retreat. On the floor behind Yorioma, neatly atop his
hastily discarded clothing, rested his own dagger and sword.
To get to them, he had to reverse...

Davin's back thudded into the cold, hard, unyielding
surface of a wall.

"You will die, worm!" the demon within Yorioma spat.
"I will drive this dagger into your heart, cut it out while it
still beats and then devour it!"

While he couldn't say much for the demon's culinary
habits, he also had no desire to see if it was capable of
carrying out its threat. His left arm snaked out, snared the
covers on the bed, and sent them out in a fluttering net
toward Yorioma.

The woman lightly danced back; the blanket fell to the
floor uselessly.

"Your eyes will be next. Pop them out, eat them!"

Davin edged to the right. Yorioma's knife shifted from
right hand to left. He inched to the left. Again the knife
changed hands. Davin cursed his luck—a demon knowl-
edgeable in the way of knife fighting!

Yorioma—the demon-ridden Yorioma—moved with
lightning speed, the dagger point dipping, dancing, then
moving upward toward Davin's midriff. He shoved out and
down, his arms crossing to catch Yorioma's slender wrist
in a vee. The force of her upward stroke lifted Davin off his
feet, yet he succeeded in gripping that wrist and keeping
the knife from sheathing itself in his flesh.

"Aieee!" shrieked Yorioma, thwarted in killing him.

She twisted in an attempt to free herself, but Davin's
knowledge of barroom fighting came to his aid. Forcing the
idea that this was the woman he had just made love to from
his mind, he fought using every dirty trick he had ever
learned. Even then, he barely avoided a quick switch of
hands and the knife that came at him from a new direction.

Davin dropped to one knee, keeping hold of Yorioma's
right wrist. A circular motion carried her about like a wheel
spinning on an axle. She crashed heavily to the floor. Davin
spun, twisting and pinning her arm in a bar-hold designed
to snap her elbow if she resisted. He kicked out and sent

the knife in her left hand flying—but the demon refused to
relent. For an instant he was certain that the intransigent
demon would force the attack, caring little what damage it
did to Yorioma's beautiful body.

"Cease," Davin snarled. He increased pressure on the
captive joint, and Yorioma cried piteously. "I mean you no
harm, though I would see you freed of Yorioma's body."

"Weakling! Fool!" Spittle dribbled down Yorioma's chin.
Renewed effort accomplished nothing but forming a rabid
froth around her mouth.

"I am stronger," said Davin. Could one reason with a
creature from the nether worlds? Did he have any choice
but to try? "Why kill me?"

"What difference does it make who you are—or who
you pretend to be? It is the sight of flowing blood that I
want, *need!*"

Intelligence and agony flicked alive in those hate-filled
eyes for the merest of moments. Anguish wrenched Davin's
heart. Those were the eyes of Yorioma Faine, not the demon;
she was still partially aware of all that occurred!

In that lay her damnation by Farkarian Ivoni. The demon
did not totally dominate her; that would have been too easy,
too simple—preventing her from experiencing the full depths
of her degradation. Ivoni had allowed her to witness and
despair at all the demon perpetrated using her body.

Was it so with Lijena? Did Masur-Kell's demon taunt
her with its viciousness and wanton killing? Did the woman
know fully all that happened when the demon ruled over
her soul?

Lorennion.

The Blood Fountain.

The Faceless Ones.

Davin's stumbling thoughts were all Yorioma's demon
needed. The woman's body suddenly twisted and broke his
grip. In the next instant, she stood, glaring at him.

"I need no blade for you, worm! I shall dig your heart
from your chest with these hands!"

Naked and empty-handed, they faced each other. Davin
had no doubt that the demon was quite capable of ripping

out his heart, liver, and any other vital organs that it desired. The trick was to make certain it was denied its goal.

My sword! He grimaced. It and his dagger were now behind him. If he turned, Yorioma and her demon-fed strength would be at him. Yet, were he quick enough . . . his thoughts stumbled again . . . could he drive cold steel through her?

The answer was a simple no. It was not Yorioma he wanted to kill, but the demon dwelling within her breast.

Davin dropped, kicked out, hooked a foot behind Yorioma's shapely ankle, and snapped his other foot into her kneecap. Off balance, tumbling, she fell back into the open clothes closet.

Rolling, the thief regained his legs, leaped to the closet door, and slammed it shut. With shoulder to wood, he held the door firmly closed while he reached out and pulled the armoire to him. Seconds later the heavy piece of furniture securely blocked the door and locked the demon-possessed woman inside.

"Yorioma." Davin began to explain his desire to aid the woman.

His words were drowned by a barrage of blows against solid wood and a series of obscene curses that would have made Goran One-Eye blush. With a shrug, Davin stepped toward his clothes. He might not be able to help Yorioma, but at least locked within the closet she could not injure others—mainly one Davin Anane.

"Don't leave me like this, Davin. I love you!" The voice that came from within the closet startled him. Gone was the serpent's angry hiss. Yorioma spoke now, "Together we can, we can . . . oh, please don't leave me!"

He hesitated. Had she regained dominance over the demon so quickly? Dressing hastily, he called to her, "I'll be there in a moment."

"Worm!" came the demon's all too familiar hissing. "Release me! Let me out of here!"

Davin sighed as he strapped on his sword. In another minute he would have opened the door and found his arms filled with a demon seeking his heart, rather than the loving Yorioma.

"I'll let the others know so they can check on you from time to time," he said as he double-checked the armoire's position. "I am truly sorry to leave on this note. I hope you find Ivoni and convince him to remove the demon. I do, Yorioma."

As she answered him in a chorus of curses, Davin left Yorioma's bedchamber and went downstairs. The main room of the inn was deserted at this early morning hour. The dying fire in the hearth revealed tables still strewn with empty mugs and plates from the night before. Taking half a loaf of bread and a wedge of cheese from one of the plates, Davin broke fast as he walked to the inn's main entrance.

Outside, the first pearly fingers of dawn edged away the velvet darkness of night on the eastern horizon. Davin inhaled deeply of the fresh, crisp, cool air. He cocked his head to one side. Upstairs, Yorioma's demon still screamed and pounded on the wooden closet door.

Wishing for wine to wash down the dry cheese and bread, Davin walked around the corner of the caravansary, intent on finding Goran and then Lijena so they could begin their journey westward to Agda and the mage Lorennion.

The thief's heart raced. The Huata wagons were gone! Only deep ruts in the soft ground remained to give testimony that the nomads had ever been there, these and the wheel tracks cutting a course toward the west.

Striding to where the Huata camp had been, Davin's gaze searched the ground. *Yehseen be damned!*

There, mixed in with Huata bootprints, Davin found the impressions of small familiar feet—feet he had come to recognize after chasing them leagues across Raemllyn. *Lijena!*

Why would she have come into the Huata camp? He followed the footprints until they ended at the place where Varaza's wagon had stood the night before. Beside Lijena's tracks were the heavy imprints of a square-toed, Jyotian-styled boot. *Berenicis!*

Lijena and Blackheart? Together? Separately? At different times or together? Davin cursed aloud as coldness that had nothing to do with the morning crept into his chest.

Had Berenicis enticed Lijena to accompany him to Lorennion's keep? He glanced back at the footprints; there was no sign of a struggle. The Jyotian cursed again. Lijena had chosen to go with Berenicis!

And why not? Berenicis could be very persuasive when the tactic suited his ends. Davin shivered at the idea of Berenicis commanding Kwerin Bloodhawk's magical, famed blade. Another shudder wracked his frame when he considered how Berenicis would regain the blade's sheath—at Lijena's expense.

No! Not while I live!

"Goran?" he bellowed. "Where are you, Goran?"

There was no answer. Davin snorted, his breath turning to mist in the morning's chill. Had Berenicis also convinced the Challing to travel west with the Huata band? After all, he had left Goran with Lijena last night. Davin called again; still no answer came.

Racing toward the stable, Davin could not edge away the black thoughts that wedged into his mind. Goran would never leave with Berenicis, nor would he allow the Blackheart to take Lijena—that is, not while he lived!

Davin came to a dead stop as he entered the stable. The stalls—all the stalls—were empty! The horses were gone!

"May Black Qar take you Bereni—"

Snoring as loud as the grunting of a rooting pig snapped Davin's head around. There atop a pile of straw lay Goran One-Eye—nestled on the arm of the stable boy Heank. Both were as naked as newborn babes.

"Goran! Damn your arse!" Davin strode to the straw and planted a well-placed boot on the Challing's exposed backside.

"Wha—Nyuria be cursed!" Goran sputtered as he bolted upright and rubbed a hand over his haunch. "Davin! What's got into you?"

"By the gods!" Heank was awake also. There was horror in his wide eyes and voice as he scurried away from Goran's naked body. "No, by all the gods, I couldn't. I didn't!"

"You did," Davin said without a trace of sympathy.

"No," Heank's voice cracked. "Not the fat one. It . . . it

was Yorioma who came to . . . I . . . no! I had naught to drink.
Not for days! How could such a thing happen? No! Nooo!"

Like a man beset by Peyneeha's demons, Heank snatched
up his clothes and ran screaming from the stable.

"Um? The boy made no such protests when Glylina came
to him last night. He claimed she was a goddess come to
earth!" Goran stared after the fleeing Heank, the Challing's
expression one of total innocence. Then he roared with
laughter. "What an experience! Words can hardly describe,
Davin. When women speak of the earth moving for them,
it only begins to . . ."

Davin cut off his friend's description with another ap-
plication of boot to bottom. "You disgusting lout! You se-
duce stable boys while Berenicis makes off with Lijena and
our horses! From under your huge, snoring nose!"

"Ummm, yes, so it seems," Goran said, peering at the
empty stalls. "I always credited Varaza with being the best
horse thief in all Raemllyn. To commit such a deed while
Goran One-Eye—or Glylina as the case was—slept so close
is the mark of a master."

"You were so sated that the gods themselves might have
held an orgy here, and you wouldn't have noticed."

"Ah, there you are wrong, Davin. I would have turned
into Yehseen himself. Or perhaps Ediena. Yes, I would have
shape-shifted into gorgeous Ediena herself and, as Goddess
of Love and Pleasure, satisfied both male and female deities!" Goran grined broadly. *"That* would be an event worthy
of many a folk tale!"

"Get your arse moving," Davin growled, lifting a threatening boot. "We are afoot again and you sit there amusing
yourself with erotic fantasies! Don't you understand? The
Blackheart has taken Lijena!"

"Is it Lijena you want?" Goran said mischievously. "Then
I shall give you Lijena!"

Witch-fire blazed in the Challing's good eye as he stared
up at his companion. Slowly, his massive arms began chang-
ing into ones whiter, more slender. Goran's form liquefied
and in the blink of an eye solidified as Lijena.

"Not too bad, eh? I am regaining some small control

over my changes. Not much, mind you, but enough to keep us both happy. If only you weren't such a prude in these matters." It was Glylina who spoke now.

"Swine! None of that! Not that I like you one whit at the moment, but I prefer you as I have come to know you. You are *not* Lijena or Yorioma. You are Goran One-Eye, and be cursed for it!"

"You are in a surly mood, Davin." Glylina's voice faded to Goran's as the Challing once more became the red-haired giant. "Was Yorioma more than a match for you?"

"Dress, you bastard!" Davin's boot descended for a third time, putting the changeling into motion.

While Goran tugged on his clothing, Davin hastily explained Yorioma's demonic possession and how he had locked her in the clothes closet after fighting off her attacks.

"Murderous lovers," sighed Goran. "Aren't they all like that? Each and every one of them? That is one reason I take so much delight in assuming the feminine form. For once, I desire seeing what it is like being treacherous and..."

Davin paid the Challing no heed. He stalked about like a caged tiger, searching each stall, hoping to find something that would aid them in their pursuit of Berenicis. Even a plowhorse would be helpful, but Varaza had been thorough.

Cursing, angry, Davin Anane motioned to the Challing, then walked from the stable and headed west, following the ruts left by the Huata wagons.

"Davin, you take this much too seriously," said Goran, trooping along to one side. "Before she changed into the demon, surely she wove untold pleasures. For once you picked one with fire, with flesh on her bones. I envied you that misspent night."

"Your own night was pretty well dissipated," said Davin. "I had thought better of you and your tastes. At least Yorioma has an excuse. The demon Ivoni cursed her with escaped when she lowered her guard."

"And your prowess is what caused it, eh?"

Davin ignored the jibe.

"What is your excuse for seducing that poor boy?"

"Excuse?" said Goran, surprised. "I have no excuse, nor

do I need one. The change came upon me unbidden. I had been thinking of you and Yorioma, envious of the delights you found in her arms when the change took me. Heank, his name was, stumbled upon me and professed his undying love for his mistress. Could I turn him away, spurn him, make him feel lower than the manure he scrapes daily off the stable floors?"

Davin lifted a doubting eyebrow. Goran's recounting of the seduction rang similar to his tales of the loss of his left eye.

"At least you kept your word and did not try to present yourself to me as Yorioma. I don't know what I would have done had I been faced with two Yoriomas."

Davin turned in time to see the guilty expression pass like an errant shadow across Goran's face. This confirmed what he had suspected; the Challing *had* intended such an impersonation, but the stable boy had come along first and distracted him.

Davin heaved a disgusted sigh and picked up the pace. There was no telling how much of a headstart Berenicis had on them. Walking helped him burn off energy that otherwise would have gone into anger directed at the Challing.

"The night was well and happily spent," Goran said, somewhat subdued.

"That it was, even if the morning brought much sorrow with it." Davin thought of Lijena, of Yorioma, of their demons and the sorcerers controlling their destinies. "At least there is not much more that can go wrong."

The rumbling of nearing thunder and the dark clouds on the western horizon told the two adventurers just how wrong Davin could be.

chapter
15

THE SEA OF BUA stretched from horizon to horizon. Gem green, the water rolled easily, stirred by a soft, summer breeze. Sunlight played across the ocean's surface, fracturing into myriad diamonds that sparkled and glittered as they leaped from wave to wave.

Lijena sighed contentedly as she stretched lazily beneath Raemllyn's equatorial sun on the deck of *Nalren's Song*. Those in Kavindra had complained of the muggy weather all week. Yet here at sea, with the breeze stirring about her, it was as though Raemllyn's God of the Oceans did sing, his pleasure beaming down upon her.

Another purrlike sigh slipped from her throat as the pleasure yacht knifed through the waves, rocking gently, water lapping at its hull. She closed her eyes, only too willing to let the ocean rock her to sleep.

"Lijena!" her father called to her. "Lijena, hurry! The storm!"

"Storm?" Lijena pushed to her elbows, shielded her eyes with a hand, and turned to her father. "No . . . No!"

Chesmu Farleigh stood scowling down at his daughter. Then, in the next instant, her father was no longer her father, but the slaver Nelek Kahl, gray eyes glaring as he stroked his moustache. "On your feet, bitch. A storm is upon us and I've no wish to lose valuable merchandise to the sharks!"

"Nelek Kahl! No!" Lijena shook her head in disbelief. "I won't..."

"I said, on your feet!" Kahl reached down to ensnare her wrist in his viselike hand.

Lightning seared across the sky and thunder rolled.

"NO!" Lijena bolted upright, her eyes wide with fear.

She blinked as she caught her breath and tried to quell the racing of her heart. This was not the deck of some pleasure yacht sailing the Sea of Bua, but a narrow bunk that bucked and pitched with each turn of the wagon's wheels.

Wagon?

Lightning flashed. The rumble of thunder reverberated through the small wagon.

The smell of rain filled Lijena's nostrils. Through a tiny window in the rear of the wagon, she saw glistening sheets of water rolling down in torrents. Even as she listened, the rainstorm pelted the roof so hard the interior of the wagon rang like a wooden bell.

The demon!

"No." Her head moved from side to side with uncertainty as wisps of memory returned.

The demon had not brought her here. She had left the inn, seeking solitude to control the demon's rage as Yorioma had taught her. Then there had been a man. He had brought her to the wagon—*a Huata wagon!*—and given her wine.

"The wine!" Her head still spun from it. And the man? "Lord Berenicis!"

"Good morn, my dear." Almost as if he had listened for his entry cue, Berenicis edged aside an intricately woven curtain at the front of the wagon.

Smiling over a shoulder at her, the man sidled backward into the wagon, carrying a tray laden with fragrant, steaming-hot oat cakes, several kinds of cheeses, and another glass of the wine.

"Did you sleep well?" he asked, as he mulled over the name he had heard her call to in her sleep—Nelek Kahl. Did this wench fear Kahl? There had been panic in her voice when she cried out. "I did not have the heart to wake you any earlier."

"Why am I here?" Her head was still fogged.

"The Huata agreed to carry us northward to Lorennion, of course. But you remember that," Berenicis said. Then, seeing her puzzled expression, he frowned and shook his head. "You *do* remember, don't you?"

"The wine," Lijena began. The taste had been strong, almost bitter. Memories of Ansisian's Breath, the sleeping potion Amrik Tohon had disguised in wine the night he sold her to Nelek Kahl, flickered through her head. Had Berenicis drugged her? The fuzzy feeling, the way her tongue felt as if fur grew on it, the strange lethargy were all terrifyingly similar.

"The wine is quite good, isn't it?" said Berenicis. "Try some more with your breakfast." He poured the golden liquor into a goblet and handed it to her. "Drink up."

"I . . . I'm so hungry. May I have one of the cakes?" She accepted the wine, but put it aside, unwilling to risk the chance that her suspicions were correct.

She ate slowly, relishing the taste of the food as it crossed her tongue. Berenicis watched her carefully, not speaking.

"Is anything wrong?" she finally asked. "You look at me so strangely."

"Strangely? No, it is nothing. Or more. I . . . I have trouble putting this into words. You inspire me with your courage. Truly, you do."

"Courage?"

"You bear up so well to all that has befallen you." Berenicis moved the goblet of wine closer to her hand. Lijena ignored it.

"The demon is held in check by Yorioma's spells," she said. "This is nothing she has not coped with—and for many years more than I have."

"Yorioma is part of what I refer to," said Berenicis. Then one eyebrow arched, and he shook his head in wonder. "You don't remember, do you? Nothing of Yorioma or that scoundrel Davin Anane . . ."—his pulse doubled its tempo as he said the name that had so disturbed her rest—". . . or Nelek Kahl?"

"What? Kahl? What of him?" Lijena placed a hand to her brow. She remembered nothing of this—only that Kahl was the slaver who had sold her to Masur-Kell. "Why do you mention *him* in the same breath as Yorioma and Davin?"

Berenicis performed an eloquent shrug, carefully repressing the smile that sought to uplift his lips. She *was* frightened of the slaver. To play on that fear, he conjured a twisted tale as he spoke:

"I thought you knew—remembered. The three are in league."

"No, that is not possible!" Lijena knew Berenicis lied to her now. He had to be lying. Nothing else made any sense.

"The distance to Lorennion's keep is great," Berenicis said. "These are empty reaches we traverse. Only the Huata know them, and sometimes I think they only rely on certain signs, the position of the stars and nothing more."

"What are you getting at?"

"We must pass the time as we can," he said, slipping over to sit beside her on the narrow bunk. His hand strayed and impudently touched her breast. Lijena jerked back, as if prodded with a branding iron.

"Do not touch me in that way," she said coldly.

"Oh? You would have me touch you like this?" He grinned and reached out again.

She slapped him. Dark anger blossomed on his face, accentuating the red imprint of her hand on his cheek. He rose as if to return the blow, then sank back. The grim visage chilled her more than any blow could have.

"You need friends out in this wilderness, Lijena, and you run short of them quickly. Think not that Varaza will aid you over me. He knows his mission. He knows how Prince Felrad relies on my success."

"Leave me—now!" she snapped.

"You've changed your song since last night," Berenicis lied. "You were more than eager to spend a pleasurable hour with me as we bounced along."

"You lie!"

"Do I?" he asked in a low voice that almost convinced her. But he shoved her back and dropped onto her body, crushing her under his weight.

With arms and legs Lijena fought, pushing, kicking, succeeding in toppling Berenicis to the floor of the wagon. "I would never lie with a swine like you!"

Yet how could she know for certain? When the demon seized control, she remembered so little. And the fuzziness of her memory hinted strongly that she had been drugged. The woman knew there would be no limit to what Berenicis might have done to her in such a state. She studied the man with wary eyes, knowing that she was at his mercy. And hadn't Davin called this man "Blackheart"?

"You need me," he said. "We need one another if we are to succeed. Lorennion cannot deny you—you have the demon driving you back to him. And my petition, well . . ." Berenicis smiled wickedly.

Lijena cowered against the wall of the bunk as he rose.

"There"s no need to fear me . . . you have made clear your reluctance. But the journey ahead of us is long, and you will come to change your mind. I am your *only* ally, your only hope in the dismal fate awaiting you." Neither his expression nor voice betrayed the anger seething in his breast. She *would* be his, in time.

"Davin," the name trembled weakly from her lips. "He will follow me."

"Davin, yes, Davin," he said bitterly. "The man deals with Nelek Kahl, the same as Yorioma! They would sell you into slavery, you realize."

"No." Lijena could never believe this of Yorioma. The woman aided her, at great risk to herself.

"Yorioma and Kahl are lovers." Berenicis had no idea of how closely his words struck to the truth, only that he spun a tale designed to thrust a wedge of doubt into Lijena's mind. "They have been for many years. The slaver requires fresh young blood for his patrons, and Yorioma seeks to exorcise her demon. Kahl gives her information in return for . . . human flesh."

"No, she wouldn't. Why tell me of the binding spells if she meant to give me to Kahl?"

"Give? Hardly would Yorioma give anyone anything. The spells merely kept you in one place long enough for Kahl to arrive, nothing more. She couldn't have your demon forcing you to the west and Lorennion's protection. Lorennion is the most powerful mage in all of Raemllyn. No, Yorioma wanted you docile and content until Nelek Kahl put in an appearance." Berenicis shook his head sadly.

Lijena simply stared. She detected no hint of deceit in his voice, and his words did hang together. But she *knew* Yorioma. To believe ill of such a person required an enormous leap of faith in Berenicis she simply did not have.

"Yorioma would gladly slay entire cities, entire kingdoms to be rid of the demon plaguing her. Do you think she values you above release from her demon?" Berenicis snorted and turned away, as if offended by her lack of trust in him.

Lijena felt the foundations of her faith in Yorioma crumbling. Berenicis could be correct. For surcease from the demon that drove her, Yorioma might betray her. Lijena knew that she would do anything—*anything*—to be free of Masur-Kell's curse.

"Even if this is true, Davin is steadfast in wanting to aid me. He has followed all the way from Leticia to . . ."

"Rescue you?" Berenicis finished her sentence with contempt in his voice. "Is that what you call it? Who kidnapped you from your uncle's estate?"

"But he ransomed off his friend Goran."

Berenicis simply shook his head, as if saying she was demented for believing such a tall tale.

"But Davin and Kahl," she muttered. "It can't be. Davin rescued me from Masur-Kell after Kahl had sold me to the mage. Why would he do that if he were in league with Kahl? It makes no sense to rescue me after his ally has just sold me."

"Good business," Berenicis said instantly. "You are a desirable woman. Kahl sells you, Davin kidnaps you again, and then they resell you. This might continue for a dozen times!"

Lijena sat dumbfounded, her mind numbed by all this deposed lord of Jyotis said.

"Then, maybe you are one of those women who revel

in being passed from man to man," Berenicis said with a smirk.

"How dare you!" Lijena flared angrily. Berenicis deflected her blow and looked at her with a sad expression.

"No, how dare Davin Anane? How dare Nelek Kahl? How dare Yorioma Faine? These are the people who are using you for their own ends. The demon was Masur-Kell's way of binding you to him, but Davin kidnapped you!"

Lijena sat, stunned. The facts were all as she knew them, but the way Berenicis put them together differed so from what Yorioma and Davin had told her. Could she have been so wrong about them?

Lijena had never truly trusted Davin Anane. He *had* kidnapped her and given her over to the Emperor of Bistonia's thieves. No amount of rationalizing erased that fact. Yet his actions afterward had seemed honorable—until Berenicis revealed the obvious link between Davin and the slaver Nelek Kahl. Lijena shuddered.

"There, there," said Berenicis, moving closer, his arm circling her shaking body and pulling her in to his shoulder. "I will let nothing happen to you. With me, you are safe."

Lijena's mind railed at the idea of Yorioma betraying her; yet this, too, made sense. She of all people knew the lengths to which Yorioma might go to be free of the demon crouching within. Lijena had been possessed by a supernatural being for only a short time. What would she do if she had to endure it for the long, torturous years that Yorioma had? Friends? Sell them into slavery for release from an even worse imprisonment.

"Let us seal our friendship," said Berenicis, easing back her head, his lips lightly touching hers.

Lijena never felt the transition. One moment she worried over the entangling webs that spun about her, the next, her lips curled back to bare her teeth. The demon shrieked with maniacal fury as it launched her body, fully intent on ripping Berenicis' jugular from his throat.

Berenicis had not survived repeated assassination attempts without constant vigilance. As the demon forced aside Lijena's conscious mind and seized control, as the first high-pitched note yowled rasping from her throat, Berenicis shoved the blonde away and pushed to his feet.

Lijena's was a preternatural strength that flowed from the same dark well that set her eyes ablaze with hellish fire. Growling, she leaped from the bunk, lunging at Berenicis with fingernails and teeth and fury.

Another man might have hesitated, his mind ajumble with the fact that he faced a woman. Not so with Lord Berenicis, who was called Blackheart. Sidestepping Lijena's flailing claws, he swung out his right fist and connected solidly with the demon-possessed woman's jaw.

The effects were immediate: Lijena's head jerked back under the impact, and she crumpled to the floor—unconscious.

Berenicis stared down at her still body, his chest aheave and his temples apound. A wicked smile moved over his thin lips. She had refused, but now . . .

He thrust the thought from his mind. Lord Berenicis of Jyotis did not sate his lusts on helpless women—or at least unconscious women. She would be his ere they reached Agda, of that he was certain, even if he had to have her while bound in chains.

Chains, the thought repeated in his mind. Perhaps it would be best if she *were* in chains when she woke. It wasn't his pleasures he considered now, but his life. There was no guarantee he would be so lucky when the demon presented itself next time, and he intended to take no further risks with his own neck.

Turning to the front of the wagon, Berenicis went to summon Varaza to bring manacles for his guest.

chapter 16

DAVIN ANANE SQUINTED westward into the misty drizzle, thinking that his first glance was only a trick of mind and eyes rebelling against the monotony of the grasslands. A smile uplifted the corners of his mouth—it remained.

"Goran, look ahead. What do you see?" The Jyotian thief turned to his Challing companion.

"Davin, you've no need of a seer to view what lies ahead for us. There are snowflakes mixed in this rain," the shivering giant replied dourly. "Ere our eyes see civilization again, our mortal forms shall be frozen in solid ice . . . while our souls roast in Nyuria's fiery pits."

"Damn your hairy hide, look to the west!" Davin's patience was thin; Goran's complaints had been constant for the past week.

"There is nothing but grass—a house! By the gods, it's a house! And, if my eye does not deceive me, those are two trees beside the house!" Gone was the Challing's sour face, replaced by a wide grin. "A lowly abode to be certain, a mere sod house, but I do detect smoke coming from its chimney, and that means a fire to melt the ice from my toes and fingers and—"

"The horses, damnit man! Are those not horses in the pen beside the house?" Davin cut off his friend's windy comments.

"Horses?" Goran squinted his one good eye. "Aye! Those are horses." The Challing's expression abruptly sobered. "But what is a house doing out here in the middle of nowhere? And those horses, there must be at least twenty. Why so many?"

"A way station for caravans that travel this prairie," Davin said. "There can be no other explanation for a house being located here. Does it matter who or why? In another hour we'll have mounts."

"And a fire to cut the chill from our bones," Goran replied, hugging himself and shivering. "I swear, it's as cold as the mountains of Norgg."

"Norgg?" Davin frowned at his companion as they started toward the sod house. "I never knew you had journeyed to the far northlands of Norgg."

"To be certain. 'Twas shortly after Roan-Jafer stole me from Gohwohn. I traveled there in search of the wizard Ri-Roit who was rumored to have the powers to physically shift between the planes of existence. It was in Norgg that I lost my eye."

"No," Davin groaned with the realization he had once more been neatly maneuvered into one of the Challing's yarns.

"Aye," Goran said with hearty enthusiasm. "I had been without food for a week, on the verge of starvation, a mere skeleton. 'Twas then I stumbled on the cave of a dreaded ice-lizard—the grandfather of all . . ."

Davin's attention purposely turned from the tale to the horses ahead. The way station was truly unexpected luck! With the Jurkian gold still bulging Goran's money pouches, purchase of two suitable mounts would be easy. And should the horses' owner prove to be reluctant to sell, that would be but a minor delay—Goran and he were thieves, after all.

* * *

Nelek Kahl's gray eyes lifted to the face of Yorioma Faine. For a woman born of royal blood, she was not a good liar. The tension at the corners of her lovely eyes, the tightness of her full, red lips, and the exaggerated gestures of her hands belied the certainty of her words and her unquavering voice. She lied, of that he had no doubt—but her motive?

"Jyotians, you say? Lord Berenicis himself and a rogue named Davin Anane?" he asked softly and sipped from a flagon of mulled wine.

"Yes," Yorioma nodded. "While I slept, they stole her away. They travel westward with a Huata called Varaza and his band. Five wagons in all. Most of the Huata were men. I saw only four women among their wagons."

Kahl knew Berenicis, and that the deposed ruler of Jyotis now served Prince Felrad's cause. But this Davin Anane was an unknown factor. Why did he want the woman Lijena Farleigh?

"Nelek, did you realize you and Davin could be brothers? There is an age difference, and your moustache and your manner of dress is that of a gentleman, but the similarity is striking," Yorioma said, a smile moving across her lips.

"You say they seek the mage Lorennion?" Kahl ignored her attempt to shift the subject. "To Agda?"

Yorioma drew a breath. "Lijena to free herself of a demon, Davin Anane to aid her, and Berenicis . . . I know not Lord Berenicis' purpose. Although he looked to be a man of—"

"Thank you, Yorioma." Kahl cut off the woman's words. The Lady Katura Jayn had changed little since her days in Kavindra. She still placed too much weight on a man's appearance and ignored what he carried in heart and head. "'Tis a pity you could not have delayed their departure."

"It was beyond my power, Nelek."

"Yes, I understand." He downed the remainder of his wine, then pushed from the table. "I have tarried here longer than I had planned and still have many leagues to travel ere nightfall. Please excuse my rudeness, but I must be on my way."

"Are you certain? It's not often I have visitors who remember Kavindra . . . the way it used to be." Yorioma could not disguise her sadness.

"If I could, I would stay longer," Kahl replied, "but I have much that must be done."

Leaning forward, he lightly kissed the woman's cheek, a brotherly peck that gave no hint of the passionate kisses they had once shared. But that had been, as Yorioma had said, in "Kavindra, the way it used to be."

Kahl drew his black *sartha* fur coat about him, then tugged on gloves of that same fine fur before he turned and walked from the caravansary. Outside, Sentan Briss and the girl Eirene waited in the saddle for him.

"North, Sentan," Kahl said as he mounted. "We must find a ferry across the Bay of Pilisi before night."

"And the Lady Yorioma?" the slaver's servant asked as they reined their horses from the Golden Tricorn.

Kahl rode silently for several long moments. "She was told to retain the girl until I arrived. She failed me. In these times that cannot be tolerated, especially by a member of the royal family."

Glancing back over his shoulder at the caravansary, Kahl looked at Briss. "Tonight I want you to pay Yorioma Faine a visit. I want no harm to befall her, but she must understand that failure will not be endured. Burn her stable. She'll know who has sent the message."

"Yes, my lord," Briss said with a smile that contained more than a touch of relish.

Payat'Morve sank back into the overstuffed cushions of his couch. A dark grimace shadowed his face, and his jowls were aquiver with frustration. *To come this far, to reach out and be fingertip close . . . and then fail! The gods themselves are turned against me!*

The three Faceless Ones Zarek Yannis had lent him had proven ineffective, impotent—or perhaps they were too effective in their mission? Their task had been simple, to find Lorennion's keep and destroy the mage so that Payat'Morve might possess the Blood Fountain.

Instead, the hell riders found me a demon-ridden woman!

Payat's corpulent form trembled as he sought to contain the seething rage that churned within him. Lorennion's powers should have been his now.

"It was Lorennion's demon, of that there is no question," he spoke to his little pet, a horned lizard he held and gently stroked in an attempt to calm the frustration and fury.

A forked tongue hissed out and shook itself at the wizard. The lizard was unappreciative of the pudgy fingers that played across its multihued scales.

What the creature liked or disliked were of no concern to Payat'Morve. "How is this woman linked to him? Is she some instrument through which Lorennion focuses the energies of the Blood Fountain? Damn their failure!" Payat'-Morve raged.

The Faceless Ones rode Raemllyn, invincible and unquestioned, but that did not mean they approached a mage of Lorennion's power without fear. He had ordered them to bring him Lorennion's head, and they delivered a myriad of questions for which he had no answers.

"Fear," scoffed Payat'Morve. "Who would have thought the Faceless Ones feared anything, much less Lorennion?"

He turned onto his side, the lizard's leash still wrapped about the little finger of his left hand. With his right, he reached to a tray of food atop a table beside the couch. One pickled delicacy after another vanished into Payat's mouth as he considered the course open to him.

Without more knowledge of Lorennion's most potent magicks, he dared not openly attack the other mage. And Zarek Yannis had returned the Faceless Ones to the company of their comrades, robbing him of a mobile source of information, such as it was. Payat'Morve considered his next move.

"Not against Lorennion, will it be, my little one?" He chucked the lizard under its wattles until its head turned away from him. "Lorennion is too strong, and we lack the lever to use against him. If only I could have cut him off from that damned Fountain, all of Raemllyn would now be mine!"

In his anger, Payat jerked too hard on the leash. His lizard let out a death hiss and died as its neck snapped. The sorcerer stared at the lifeless body and shook his head sadly. Another pet lost to him for all eternity.

"If I controlled the Blood Fountain, it would be otherwise," he said, visions of resurrection and even more drastic magicks dancing in his brain.

Payat cast off the leash and rose, walking to a nearby table where his grimoires were opened, passages marked in human blood. The ability to cast most of the spells lay far back in history, in the halcyon days of Edan and Kwerin Bloodhawk, but a few of the more useful minor enchantments remained to him. He searched through the books of magic until he found the spell he used most often.

Not for the first time he wished he could utter the spells without the book in front of him, but this, too, was an ability long lost. No mage—except perhaps Lorennion—worked without his grimoire open. Magicks fouled the brain, confused thought, made speech difficult and memory impossible. Although he had uttered this spell a thousand times, Payat'Morve still had to read it line by line from this ancient tome.

He did so now.

If he had failed to gain what he wanted from Lorennion, there still remained Zarek Yannis. Spying on him had proven easy in the past—and immensely profitable.

The scrying spell caused the air to shimmer, then take on a translucence that slowly cleared to reveal Yannis in his private chambers. Gathered before him were four of his generals. Payat's heart raced at the sight. There had been palace rumors that an offensive against Prince Felrad would soon be mounted. Perhaps the wench in the torture chamber had actually known the prince's campsite. Payat leaned forward, as if this would place him any closer to the generals.

"... attack at dawn. We must be quick about this, for Lorennion supports Felrad now," Zarek Yannis was telling his generals.

"He never told me of this!" Payat cried aloud. "He opposes Lorennion and without my aid? The fool!"

"No," came an icy voice from behind the sorcerer, "it is not I who am the fool. You, Payat'Morve, have betrayed my confidence by spying on me in this fashion."

Payat spun and saw Yannis in the doorway. Behind him in the hall was arrayed a squad of soldiers, all armed and with swords drawn. Startled, confused, Payat turned back to his magical scrying window and saw Yannis unfurling a map to show the terrain over which the soldiers would attack Felrad's camp. Payat snapped back to the man in the doorway.

That was Zarek Yannis. But who was the man revealed by the scrying spell?

"Such a confused expression. You are a sorcerer, Payat. A man of magicks. Can you not figure it out for yourself?" said Yannis, motioning the soldiers forward.

"Stop!" commanded Payat. "These are my private quarters. None enters without my permission."

"You forget much, Payat. I am ruler of all Raemllyn. You are in my service, not the other way around. I go where I please, and I bring along any I want with me."

"Stop!" cried Payat, allowing the scrying spell to collapse. He fumbled in the book for the proper page, the appropriate spell to paralyze the soldiers. Finding it, he hastily muttered the incantation.

Nothing happened.

Again, he cast the spell. And again no effect. The soldiers seized him, pinning his arms, forcing him back over his worktable.

"That spell should have frozen them. But what . . . ?"

It all became obvious to him. His apprentice, the lovely— and cunning—Valora, entered. Tucked beneath an arm was *her* book of magicks.

"You muddled my scrying spell," Payat accused. "You sent a false vision."

"Quite nicely, too," cut in Zarek Yannis. "Valora has a quality that makes her immensely useful to me. She values me as a king and leader." Yannis turned to the raven-haired woman and lightly touched her cheek. Valora took his hand in hers and kissed it. Yannis laughed, saying, "No, make that *two* qualities I find interesting in her."

"You sold me out, you slut!" cired Payat.

A hard fist in his belly abruptly ended the sorcerer's words. He groaned, spittle drooling from the corner of his mouth. The soldiers pulled the sorcerer erect again to face his king and accuser.

"There had to be something to sell out, Payat," said Yannis. "You sought out Lorennion's magicks, not for my use but for your own personal ends. That is a crime. You spied upon me during secret meetings. That is a crime. But worst of all, you thought to unseat me and assume the Velvet Throne for your own. That is more than a crime. That is treason!"

"No, lord, it is not like that. I . . . aieee!"

Strong hands forced open Payat'Morve's mouth. The mage's eyes widened in horror as the guard captain pulled forth a shiny silver dagger. One soldier held the end of his tongue while the captain crudely sliced the organ from the wizard's mouth.

"He will bleed to death, my lord," said Valora in a voice that bespoke of little real interest in her former master's welfare.

"Do something about it," said Yannis.

Valora opened her spell book and found the proper magic. A bright flash filled the room, and the nose-twitching odor of burned flesh permeated the air. A gurgling sound came from Payat'Morve's throat, and he crumpled to the floor, his severed tongue now cauterized magically.

"You do that well." Yannis smiled, obviously enjoying the mage's pain.

"I do it for you, my lord," Valora said, bowing deeply.

"You lie as well as my former master mage." Yannis hid a yawn of boredom behind his hand.

"Former, lord?"

"Former," he said, glancing at Payat'Morve's sagging bulk. "The position is now open. Do you have any recommendations for a mage to fill such a responsible post?"

"Seawight might be amenable, lord, but he is far distant. Simply informing him might take weeks."

"A long time to be without the services of a wizard."

"Aye, it is, lord. Or the sorceress Fionella might be convinced. There was never any love lost between her and Payat'Morve."

"Fionella, eh?" said Yannis, as if actually considering her. "No, I think not. Her allegiances tend more toward Felrad than me."

"Lord, those are my best suggestions," Valora said, boldly staring him in the eye.

Her midnight eyes blazed with—what? Yannis decided it was desire for power as his mage rather than simply desire. "Let us retire to my quarters for a private discussion. I feel that it is possible to find Payat's replacement closer at hand. Perhaps the one responsible for informing me of Payat's perfidy might be persuaded to assume the post."

"Lord, I would be most honored."

"My quarters. In one hour. And do not be in a hurry to depart once you arrive." Yannis spun and walked out, flanked by two bodyguards. The remaining soldiers would dispose of Payat. And Yannis did not have to be a mage to know that Valora and his guard captain would quietly discuss her windfall. Yannis would have to consider how best to use the carnal relationship between the captain and his new master mage to the fullest.

Until then, he and Valora would . . . explore.

"Your blood, Berenicis! I will drink your blood!" Lijena threw herself against the chains as the demon voice within her head demanded the Blackheart's death. "And yours Varaza! Your life's blood will fill my belly!"

"We play a dangerous game with this one, my lord." The Huata leader's eyes shifted from the possessed woman chained to the bunk to Berenicis. "The demon grows stronger with each westward turn of the wagon's wheels. Perhaps we should release her and travel to Agda without such an evil guide."

"No, Varaza," Berenicis said, shaking his head. "One does not set a good hunting hound free because it snaps at its master. One simply trains it to obedience. I will train this bitch. By the time we reach Agda's mountains she will lead us straight to Lorennion's door."

"Your bones! I will suck the marrow from your bones!" the demon growled as it threw itself against the chains again, spittle flying from the lips of the woman it controlled.

"Come, Varaza, we'll leave her alone for a while. Our presence only gives strength to the monster dwelling within her." Berenicis nodded to the wagon's forward exit. "When this fit passes, I will begin my training with a simple spell— one that will teach the demon respect—fear."

"Are you certain such a creature can be taught..."

The Huata's voice was lost as the two men left her alone. The demon within her head slowly retreated, abandoning its control for the time being.

Chains rattled, unyielding links of steel bruising her flesh, as Lijena moaned and rolled to her side, trying to find a more comfortable position. It was not possible. Varaza had chained her to the bunk in such a fashion that she could barely move.

For long minutes Lijena lay there, her mind clouded. As her memories returned, so did shame. The demon had crept up on her and seized control. All the while she had been its unwitting collaborator. He fear and confusion over what Berenicis had told her allowed the demon to slip its spell and enter her mind once more.

Lijena didn't know which feeling caused her the most shame. Was it the demon and all it forced her to do, or being little more than a slave to Berenicis? A hound he had called her, a bitch that would sniff her way to Lorennion's castle keep.

Tears misted her eyes as she tried to slip her wrists from the manacles binding them. All she succeeded in doing was cutting her flesh; blood trickled in rivulets over her wrists and onto her palms and fingers.

Sobbing in frustration, she shifted again. There was no relief from the chains that bit into her body. But she might be able to once more restrain the demon now that it had crept back into the dark corridors of her mind.

Drawing a deep breath, she clamped her eyes tightly

closed to stem the flow of her tears. Then as Yorioma had
taught her, she inhaled slowly and steadily through her nostrils, imagining a mist drifting into a cavern. When she
exhaled, it was through her mouth, and the mist retreated
from the cave's mouth.

The rhythm of that simple breathing exercise offered a
focal point around which she gathered her strength and
cleared her mind. Silently she began to chant the incantation
Yorioma had made her memorize: *Ataria kiilam shan
yeladi . . .*

A brand glowing white hot sizzled deep inside her brain.
She screamed as the agony radiated outward, suffusing
through every cell of her bound body. Spasmodically, like
a woman beset by the falling sickness, she writhed and
twitched and jerked.

And when the pain at last subsided, the voice within her
head spoke:

—I will not be chained again. Not by you, bitch. You
will serve me, and only me!

Then it was gone, and Lijena lay sobbing on the bunk.
she wasn't strong enough to contain the demon by herself.
She still needed Yorioma beside her to chant the spells, to
guide her.

Yorioma, her silent plea went out to the caravansary's
owner. Only to be drowned in a fresh flood of tears. Yorioma
would never help her—only return her to the slaver Nelek
Kahl.

"Why have the Sitala done this to me?" she cried aloud.
"How have I offended the gods? What have I done to deserve
such cruel punishment?"

Yet it was not the gods who had destroyed the life that
had once been Lijena Farleigh's. She had not felt the hands
of a deity locking these chains about her body. They had
been the hands of men—and one woman!

Burning tears of self-pity flowed down her cheeks. She
was alone in the world with no one she could trust. *No one!*

Her eyes opened, and she stared to the window in the
wagon's rear door. Outside snow fell. How beautiful she
had once thought winter's whiteness to be. Now the flakes
only served to remind her of the icy emptiness in her breast.

Yorioma Faine had tried to sell her to a slaver. And at her side was the scoundrel Davin Anane—how many times had he betrayed her? The cold filling her melted as her anger awoke, burning brighter and brighter: a fire that provided strength when none should exist.

Her body tensed and pulled futilely at the chains on her wrists and ankles. She shook her head and told herself, *No, save your energy. In time the opportunity to escape will present itself. Until then rest and prepare yourself.*

Lijena Farleigh's self-pity faded and blended with the rage to form something even more potent. Determination grew like a spring wildflower. Vengeance would be hers. Vengeance against Davin Anane for kidnapping her, for starting the chain of events that led to her demon-possession and her captivity in this Huata wagon.

Davin Anane.

The name blazed in her heart. Revenge for all he had done to her. Only that kept her sane. And the others who had betrayed her so.

The list etched in her brain became longer and longer with each passing day.

Yorioma. Varaza. Berenicis. Her lover Amrik Tohon for his betrayals. Nelek Kahl for selling her into slavery. The sorcerer Masur-Kell for being the instrument of her demonic possession. Jun for the abuse he had heaped upon her while she was a captive in Velden's underground empire.

But most of all, Davin Anane. One day he would feel the full force of her revenge. How, Lijena did not know. But he would. He would!

The End

Book Two: *A Yoke of Magic*
in the *Swords of Raemllyn* series

MURDER, MAYHEM, SKULDUGGERY...
AND A CAST OF CHARACTERS
YOU'LL NEVER FORGET!

THIEVES' WORLD ™

EDITED BY
ROBERT LYNN ASPRIN and LYNN ABBEY

. . . .

FANTASTICAL ADVENTURES

One Thumb, the crooked bartender at the Vulgar Unicorn...*Enas Yorl,* magician and shape changer ...*Jubal,* ex-gladiator and crime lord...*Lythande the Star-browed,* master swordsman and would-be wizard...these are just a few of the players you will meet in a mystical place called Sanctuary. This is *Thieves' World.* Enter with care.

__80583-3	THIEVES' WORLD	$2.95
__79580-3	TALES FROM THE	$2.95
	VULGAR UNICORN	
__76031-7	SHADOWS OF SANCTUARY	$2.95
__78712-6	STORM SEASON	$2.95
__22550-0	THE FACE OF CHAOS	$2.95
__80594-9	WINGS OF OMEN	$2.95

Prices may be slightly higher in Canada.
